I0557845

GATESOF DEMONS

KEEPERS OF THE GRAIL 1

TAMAR SLOAN

KEEPER
CHRONICLES

Cover by Laercio Messias
https://laerciomessias.com.br

CONTENTS

CHAPTER 1

REIGN

There's a certain freedom that comes with driving a car that's not your own.

Reign lets the heady abandon sweep through his veins, no matter how temporary it is. Darnell spills his cherry soda on the leather seats? The three of them laugh it off. Rico sticks his ass out the window at a parking inspector eating a burrito? They laugh even harder because the number plates aren't theirs and they'll never be traced. Reign leaves a layer of adrenaline-soaked rubber on the road each time he takes off at a set of lights... His two partners in crime whoop and holler, spilling even more cherry soda.

Not their tires.

Not their car.

Not their problem.

Except, as the Audi idles outside some backwater tech store, Reign's adrenaline high quickly dissolves. Darnell and Rico are inside, leaving him alone, hyper-conscious of every set of eyes that wanders past. If someone glances for more than a millisecond, he glares at them, projecting all the ugliness he has inside until they turn away.

Reign thrums his fingers on the steering wheel as he guns the gas, frustrated that the engine is practically silent. The tension filling his body needs a voice. It wants a fully loaded V8 monster to roar his frustration.

Darnell and Rico are taking too long.

Reign's restless hand shifts to the gear stick, the need to get the hell out of here pulsing through his veins. He doesn't like sitting still. Staying in one place too long. Each time he does, thoughts and memories crowd in, demanding an audience.

Plus, the longer he sits here, the more chances there are of getting caught.

Slipping the stick into first, Reign feels the gears grip. Darnell and Rico would do the same thing if they were sitting here, stuck with being the getaway driver in a stolen vehicle, without any sign of his fellow law breakers. Reign doubts they'd give this as much thought as he is.

Except, running would make him even more of a slime-ball than he already is. Jamming the car back into neutral, Reign returns his hands to the steering wheel, clenching it hard. Where else was his life going to end up, anyway? His trajectory was mapped out for him when his parents died and even his first set of foster parents couldn't handle him longer than a year.

The door to the tech store crashes open, and Darnell and Rico fly out. Hoodies flapping wildly, they streak for the Audi. Behind them is a short, stocky man, huffing and red-faced as he chases them.

Jumping in and slamming the door, Darnell punches the dash as Rico throws himself into the back seat. "Go, go, go!"

Tires squealing, Reign swings the Audi away from the curb, his pulse feeling like it's spiking along with the revs. He glances in the rear-view mirror and sees the store owner standing in a haze of blue-white smoke, waving a furious fist.

Accelerating away, Reign takes the next corner, glad the street ahead seems mostly clear. Darnell is beside him, staring out the back window while Rico holds up two laptops.

"They're not top of the range, but I got two!" He leans forward, nudging Darnell. "What about you?"

Darnell slips his own haul out from under his oversized sweater. "Just one. That guy was watching us too closely."

Reign focuses on the road as Rico lights a celebratory cigarette in the back seat. Is he really putting everything on the line for three freaking computers? Accelerating, he reminds himself they have to pay for food somehow. And this way, they won't have to do another haul for at least a week.

The end of the street brings them to a set of lights. Reign grinds his teeth when he sees they're red. They need to put as much distance between themselves and the store as possible, then dump the Audi.

The lights turn green, and Reign takes a right. He'll use the back roads to make their way to the hangout. Darnell flops back in the passenger seat, letting out a relieved breath. Rico offers him a drag of the cigarette, and Darnell takes a deep draw. He holds it up for Reign, but he shakes his head.

He's never seen the point of drawing toxic smoke into his lungs if it's not going to help him forget the crap-cluster that is his life.

Rico stretches his arms out like some gangster in a limo. "Now, that's what I call a success."

"We need to get back first," Darnell mutters, glancing over his shoulder. He pauses, then glances again. "Shit. It's the pigs."

As if on cue, blue and red lights flash in Reign's rear view mirror. His pulse spikes as he jams his foot on the gas. "Hold on."

The Audi surges forward, the engine far more than a gentle purr for the first time. Reign jerks the wheel as he swerves around a truck, quickly slipping back into his lane. Glancing in the mirror, he sees the police car do the same, closing the distance between them.

Crap.

"Gun it, will ya?" shouts Rico. "We need to lose these douches. That asshole store owner must've called them."

Pressing his foot down harder, Reign ignores the climbing needle on the odometer. He already knows he's going fast. Too fast. They zoom forward, slipping between traffic and through another set of lights. Reign allows himself a brief second to thank fate that they were green.

But the cop car steadily gains, the wailing siren starting to grate on his nerves. Darting around a blue sedan, he sees a straight stretch of road in the largely industrial area they're in. A handful of people are walking along the pavement, heads shooting up when the speeding car flashes past them. One man gives them the bird, waving his one-fingered fist in fury, but Reign ignores it. As long as others stay out of his way, they can get as angry as they want.

Rico leans forward between the front seats. "We need to get into the 'burbs, dude." He points left. "Turn up here."

"Not happening," Reign states flatly. The suburbs mean more people. Moms out for a jog. Kids on bikes. Dogs off lead thanks to their clueless owners.

Adding a little more pressure to the gas pedal, he tries to think through the adrenaline. If they get caught, they're all on their way to big boy prison now that they're almost eighteen. Reign's clocked up a few too many misdemeanors, while Darnell and Rico only just got out of juvie.

Which means losing the cop on their tail...without anyone getting hurt.

"I'll get us to the River District," he says through gritted teeth. "Then we'll dump the car and run."

"That's where the hangout is!" Rico says incredulously.

"Which means we know the area better than they do."

Darnell shakes his head. "Darnell doesn't like this."

He mustn't, because Darnell only refers to himself in third person when he's stressed. Hunkering down in the leather seat, Reign sets his gaze on the road. "We're almost there."

In fact, one set of lights and they'll be in familiar territory. The route they'll take is already mapping out in Reign's mind. The cops won't stand a chance among the narrow twists and turns of the city's poorest area.

His chest gripped by the cold hand of fear, he accelerates again, the cop car falling a few more feet behind. Their surroundings zip past, people and faces no longer distinguishable. The traffic lights appear ahead, a glorious green waiting for them to pass through. Impossibly, Reign speeds up again. The needle of the odometer trembles in the red, as if even it knows this is too much. A quick glance shows Darnell's charcoal skin has taken on an ashen tinge. Rico is whooping like he's having the time of his life.

Suddenly, the green orb of go disappears, an amber circle of light appearing beneath it. Reign curses under his breath. The sirens still piercing his ears, he does some quick calculations. Going any faster is guaranteed suicide.

The cop isn't backing off.

And they're not going to make it before it turns red.

Reign eases his foot on the gas as his hands tighten around the steering wheel. He needs a plan B.

"What are you doing?" Darnell asks in a high-pitched panic. "You're slowing down! Darnell doesn't want to slow down!"

"It's a red light!" Reign shouts back.

Rico thumps the back of the driver's seat. "So what? Run it!"

But Reign has no intention of doing that. He learned years ago that Lady Luck turned her back on him. It's inevitable that someone will be crossing. That the Audi will plough straight into them.

And he doesn't need another life on his conscience.

The police car pulls out into the other lane and speeds up.

"He's going to be next to us!" Darnell screeches.

Which is exactly where the cop is. The sirens wail over Reign's eardrums as the flashing red and blue feel like strobe lights puncturing his eyeballs. The police car inches forward, and Reign's foot twitches. If he jammed on the gas, this wouldn't be happening.

A frantic glance at the lights show they're now red. He grips the steering wheel, everything feeling totally out of control. And for three freaking computers...

The police car appears alongside them. "Pull over!" comes a male voice.

"Go suck yourself!" shouts Rico.

Reign affords himself one glance. His gaze darts left, seeing it's a single cop driving the vehicle. That look is all it takes for his blood to freeze.

Two, glowing red pricks of light gaze at him from sunken, black sockets. The thing smiles, its gray-colored skin stretching around rows of pointed teeth. It flexes its hands on the steering wheel, yellowed claws glinting dully in the light.

Terrified, Reign wants to scream, but the sound is trapped in his constricted throat. The Hell-face in the police car is monstrous, impossible...and he can't tear his gaze away from the nauseating sight.

"Turn right!" shouts Darnell. "Now!"

His fear-saturated brain responding instinctively, Reign yanks down the steering wheel, jamming his foot on the brake. He sees the side street that Darnell's talking about, and the Audi's rear end fishtails wildly as they take the corner wide, slamming into a dumpster. Hands scrambling to right the vehicle, Reign drops down a gear, then returns his foot on the gas.

Tires squeal as they leap forward once more. Behind them, the cop car zips straight past the turnoff.

"We lost them!" whoops Darnell.

But Reign's eyes widen as he discovers where he just turned down.

Shops line each side of the road. People who were peacefully shopping a moment ago leap out of the way, faces painted with shock and fear.

Reign slams on the brakes, pulling back on the steering wheel as if that will make a difference. The tires screech as they lock, but the car continues its trajectory.

A few feet ahead, a girl steps off the pavement, trying to brush a strand of blonde hair from her face despite the shopping bags in each hand.

"Move!" Reign shouts, even though she wouldn't be able to hear him.

Her head snaps at the sounds of the car, and all he can see are wide, terrified eyes in a pale, beautiful face. Her mouth pops open in a silent scream

Reign yanks down hard on the steering wheel and the Audi swerves, slamming into a trash can. The contents explode over the windshield and onto the street as the car jerks to a halt several feet away. He twists to look over his shoulder, bile hitting the back of his throat when he can't see the girl.

No! He was so sure he missed her!

His frantic gaze finds her a second later, back on the pavement. She must've leaped back just as he swerved. Lightheaded with relief, Reign flops back into the seat. She's alive. He's not responsible for another death.

Rico shoves him. "She's fine! We need to get the hell out of here!"

Surprised to find his hands aren't shaking, Reign does as he's told. It's only a matter of time before the cop car is back on their tail. Ignoring Rico's demands to go faster, he makes his way down the busy street like any other person out on a sunny afternoon. A few turns and they're at the River District.

They dump the car a few blocks away from the hangout, then jog the rest of the way.

They're around the corner when Darnell doubles over, breathing hard. "Reign! We don't all climb the city buildings like we're possessed or something."

"Shut up," growls Reign, the reference to evil spirits far too fresh after what he saw. "Have you thought of eating less takeout?"

Sweat glistening on his ebony skin, Darnell rolls his eyes at him. "As opposed to all those home cooked meals waiting for me?" he spits sarcastically.

Reign falls into step beside him, mentally acknowledging that Darnell has a point. In their world, home cooked meals are as scarce as love and affection.

Stepping around a pile of trash, the three of them fall silent as they approach the abandoned pile of bricks they call the hangout. Decrepit and decayed, the only color splashed across its drab façade is graffiti, it's no doubt on the list to be destroyed—which is just what they were looking for. A place where no one cares who's in it, and where all evidence of their inhabitance will be gone when it's demolished.

They climb up the porch steps, all avoiding the rotting middle one, and slip through the door hanging drunkenly on one hinge. Inside, there's a kitchen to the left. With no electricity or running water, they couldn't cook even if they knew how.

The room they jokingly call the games room is to the right. It would've once been a living room, probably with a couple of couches and a TV. Now, the carpet is the color and texture of dirt, with a few strewn milk crates for seats and a couple of saggy mattresses to crash on.

Rico flops onto the nearest one, spreading out the laptops. "We're gonna celebrate hard when we cash these in."

Darnell picks one up and holds it out like a tray. "Would you like three or four buckets of chicken wing dings with that, sir?"

Rico rolls his eyes haughtily. "Just get me a wheelbarrow, will you?"

The two of them laugh as they outline what they'll buy. Clothes. Food. Headphones.

All the things so many kids their age have, because there's someone in their life to buy it for them.

Darnell passes the computer he's holding to Reign. "Let's see if there's any games on them."

But Reign doesn't find their excitement infectious. Shaking his head, he makes his way to the stairs. He takes them two at a time even though the bannister was smashed long before they arrived—some fellow lowlife shoved another too hard, either in fun or in fury. A part of him has always dared fate to have him slip.

In the room he's claimed as his own, he pauses, wiping his hand down his face. There's less furniture here than downstairs —a musty couch that doubles as a bed and a scarred wooden table—with even less to do. Why isn't he celebrating with the guys, riding the rush of adrenaline after losing the cop? The sort of rush he's always seeking. Always needing to help him feel...alive.

Because he can't shake the Hell-face that he saw in the cop car. The glowing eyes. The too-long, lethally pointed teeth. Those gruesome, yellow claws.

Long-buried guilt crawls through Reign's mind, and he

starts to panic. He needs to make the memories, the awful loathing, go away.

Something on the table catches his gaze. A bowl is sitting on it, a tendril of smoke climbing up from its contents.

"You've got to be kidding me," Reign mutters.

He grabs it angrily and storms back out, relieved he has something tangible to do.

Anger is preferable.

Anger is familiar.

Anger is the only way he can make that awful image of the Hell-face go away.

It's what worked every other time he's seen it.

CHAPTER 2

ARIELLE

"Oh god no," Arielle gasps as she stares down at herself. "No, no, no."

Panic climbs up her throat with each denial, hiking her voice.

She heard the sound of glass smashing when she dropped the shopping bags, but she'd been too busy trying to stay alive as that car came at her. Now, with her heart still hammering hard against her ribs, she can't tear her gaze from the thick red lines trickling down her legs.

She moans, feeling lightheaded. "This can't be happening."

"Are you okay, darlin'?" An elderly woman with pink hair totters over and peers at Arielle, the soft lines of her face crinkled with concern. "That was a close call."

Arielle looks down, her eyes stinging with tears. "No, I'm not."

The woman gasps, drawing back in horror. "Sweet Lord, you've been hurt."

Arielle's hands flutter down, only to come back up, hovering as she figures out what in the world to do with them. It's too late. The damage has been done.

The elderly woman glances around frantically. "Help! This girl needs help! She's bleeding!"

One or two people pause, but when they hear the final words, they quickly resume walking past as if a near-death experience never happened.

The woman huffs, asking under her breath whether anyone's heard of the story of the Good Samaritan. She comes around to look more fully at Arielle's injuries.

Arielle's lip trembles. Nothing can make this right.

The woman shuffles closer only to reel back. She takes in the broken glass and red spatters. "It's ketchup!" she says incredulously. "You're covered in ketchup!"

"I know!" Arielle wails. "My boots have been destroyed!"

The woman's gaze flies to hers. "You're acting like this because of shoes?"

"Not just any shoes! These boots are practically an extension of my soul!"

The woman retreats, now looking at Arielle as if she's grown horns. She shakes her head, muttering as she walks away. "The Good Samaritan never had to worry about a drug-screwed generation."

Arielle ignores her, too distraught to point out she's never taken anything harder than Tylenol. Not when her boots have ketchup splattered all over them.

"Jerk!" she shouts down the street, even though the silver car is long gone.

The douche who was zooming down the market street is the one responsible for this. Arielle doesn't care how big his eyes were as he desperately swerved around her, looking horrified. Her knee-high Converse will never be the same again.

Pulling her leather backpack from her shoulders, she carefully withdraws the packet of tissues she always keeps in the front pocket. Bending over, she dabs at the pale canvas on her calf, wincing as the blood-colored blotch only expands.

"I've had these boots for over a year, and I've kept them immaculate," she mutters to herself. "When some guy fails to kill me, he decides to ruin my one treasured possession, instead."

Her heart aches as she catches a trickle of sauce before it treks any further down. The ketchup on her laces is the hardest to get off seeing as it's already started to absorb.

"If this stains, so help me..."

A few feet away on the pavement, a woman tugs her child closer as she hurries past, looking at Arielle strangely.

Arielle returns to her job. "And now I'm getting weird looks again," she mutters darkly. "That asshat is lucky he drove away."

The piercing wail of a police car has her straightening. It turns into the street in the same way the silver sedan did, slowing when it sees pedestrians everywhere.

"Which is exactly what jerk-dude should've done," she says to herself.

Arielle considers waving the cop car down so they can understand the trauma she's endured, and what direction the no-doubt stolen vehicle went, but the car's gone before she can lift her hand. Sighing, she goes back to mopping up the gore on her beloved boots.

"They'll never be the same again," she whispers dismally.

When her phone rings, Arielle fishes it out of her pocket, not surprised to see Aunt Shell's name on the screen. That woman has a sixth sense when something's happening to her niece.

And today has been disastrous.

She presses the connect button. "Aunt Shell, the worst thing has happened!"

There's a pause. "You've heard?"

It's Arielle's turn to hesitate. "Heard what?"

"So, you don't know?"

There's something in Aunt Shell's tone that has Arielle frowning. "I'm confused. What are you talking about?"

"Ari..."

Aunt Shell seems to lose momentum, and Arielle's confusion morphs to fear. Her gregarious aunt could talk the legs off a millipede.

"What's going on?"

Even to herself, Arielle's voice sounds small. Like she's suddenly eight and not eighteen.

"You need to come home. Something's happened."

Arielle freezes, her throat too constricted to talk.

"It's your mother," Aunt Shell chokes. "She's missing."

THE TAXI PULLS AWAY from the curb, but Arielle barely notices it. Her panicked mind tries to process what she's seeing. The door to their townhouse is wide open, ready to welcome her.

She blinks. Her mother is almost obsessive about security. She'd never leave the door open.

Rushing up the stairs, she takes one step inside and comes to a halt. The antique hall table is where it always is, the Persian vase her mother brought back from the Middle East after a conference still sitting on it. Everything is where it should be. Like nothing's changed.

Arielle finds herself creeping down the hall, as if she doesn't want to fracture the normalcy. She pushes away the sense of surrealness. Like she's stepped onto a movie set. Or some sick practical joke.

"Mom?" she calls out instinctively, only for Aunt Shell's words to start their nauseating parade through her mind again.

It's your mother. She's missing.

How could her mother be missing?

Inside, the living room is like the hallway—exactly the same. Her mother's favorite reading chair, the one all the way from Iran, faces the fireplace she tiled over. The lounge has several sheets of paper—the journal articles her mother never seems to stop reading—scattered on it. The rugs, the tapestries on the wall, the hookah she never used, are all where they were this morning.

It's as if her mother could walk in at any moment.

"There you are." Although the voice is familiar, it's not the one she needs to hear right now.

Aunt Shell rushes in from the kitchen, engulfing Arielle in a thick hug.

Arielle clings to her, sinking into her familiar softness. "What happened?"

"That's what we're here to find out," says a male voice from behind them.

Pulling back, Arielle finds a suited man standing in the kitchen doorway. His friendly, smooth features lift into a smile. "Good afternoon, I'm Detective Kane."

"Ah, hi," she says guardedly.

He's a cop, which means Arielle instantly doesn't trust him.

Brown haired with intelligent dark eyes, he schools his smooth features into a wider smile, the motion probably meant to put her at ease. "We're going to do everything we can to find your mom," he assures her.

Arielle has no doubt her mother was told the same thing when her father went missing before she was born; if law enforcement had come through with their promises, then Arielle would know what he looks like.

Aunt Shell slips an arm around Arielle's shoulder, squeezing a little as she addresses the detective. She tucks a stray blonde hair back into the bun it never stays in. "Thank you, your help is most appreciated."

Detective Kane pulls out his notepad. "So, Arielle—"

"Why do you think my mom's missing?" she interrupts. "Just because no one can contact her, doesn't mean she's been taken."

The detective's face softens with sympathy. "Your mother didn't arrive at work today." He tucks his hand into his pocket and pulls something out. "A woman fitting her description was snatched from Argyle Street earlier today." Arielle opens her mouth to ask, but he seems to expect that. He holds out the item—a watch. "My guess is this belonged to your mother."

Arielle's knees go weak. The glass of the watch is cracked and the face barely legible, but Arielle recognizes it. It's most definitely her mother's.

"We already have officers asking people in the area if they saw or heard anything," the detective quickly assures. "And we've done a thorough forensic sweep. If the perpetrator left behind any evidence, we'll find it."

Aunt Shell nods and Arielle follows her lead mutely. Words she's never heard outside a TV screen have now become her reality.

Forensics.

Evidence.

Perpetrator.

Her head aches as she struggles to assimilate it all.

Detective Kane clears his throat. "Arielle, can you tell me what happened this morning, before you left the house?"

"The usual. We had breakfast. I went to college."

Her mother was supposed to arrive at work.

He raises his eyebrows a little. "Was there anything unusual? Was your mother acting strangely in any way?"

"No."

Aunt Shell squeezes Arielle's shoulder again, but Arielle ignores the subtle nudge. Her throat is too tight to say more than a few words right now.

Plus, she doesn't believe for a second that this smooth smiling detective will be able to help them.

Aunt Shell smiles apologetically. "Sierra has never bothered to follow rules and norms. She's always been a bit...unusual."

Detective Kane scrawls a few lines in his notepad. "Can you think of anyone who would want to cause your mother harm?"

"No," Arielle says again, this time with more force.

Her mom is an academic. She spends more time exploring the written word than real life. Who would want to hurt her?

Aunt Shell shakes her head. "Sierra lectures at the university, in the history faculty. She's highly esteemed by other academics in the area."

"So, no jealous coworker? Maybe a possessive boyfriend?"

Anger flashes through Arielle, straightening her spine. Aunt Shell quickly jumps in before Arielle can point out that her mother has never even glanced at another guy after her father.

Arielle has always wondered if her mother harbors the same secret wish—that one day he'll walk through the door, smiling, maybe a bit teary, proving that the death certificate tucked away in their filing cabinet is false.

"Sierra is single," says Aunt Shell. "And I doubt few people have the level of expertise she does in Middle-Eastern history. She has no competition."

"And you were at work, Michelle?" he asks her.

"Yes. I came by when I finished my shift at the hospital to chat over a cup of tea. It's a routine we have."

Sierra and Shell aren't just sisters, they're best friends. If Aunt Shell has a tough shift in the ER, she debriefs with Sierra. If Sierra wants to share her latest discovery amongst her dusty tomes, then Shell is the first to hear about it. In fact,

Aunt Shell has been a second mother to Arielle as she grew up.

Detective Kane turns to Arielle. "And where were you after university?"

Arielle's hands clench. "We're your best suspects? A missing woman's sister and her daughter?"

Aunt Shell is about to jump in with another peace offering, but Detective Kane simply nods in understanding. "This has all been a terrible shock. But I promise, finding your mother is my number one priority."

Arielle clamps her mouth shut, not wanting to point out that's highly unlikely. She may know her mother is a wonderful, caring, kooky woman, but to Detective Kane, she's little more than a case number in a long list of case numbers.

She sighs. She's not normally this rude and obnoxious. It's just that she's never had so much taken from her in such a short period of time.

"I went to the market after school to pick up the ingredients for dinner." It was Arielle's turn to cook, and she planned on preparing pumpkin ravioli. "I was—" she stops herself from relaying the near miss with the speeding car. Aunt Shell has enough to worry about right now. "I'd just accidentally dropped the bags when Aunt Shell rang."

Detective Kane pauses in his scribbles. "We had an incident with a speeding vehicle on market street. Do you know anything about that?"

"I heard some commotion, but I didn't really see anything," Arielle hedges, conscious she's not a great liar.

Detective Kane waits to see if Arielle will say anything else, but she gazes at him blankly. She doesn't want the jerk on market street to be any more of a priority in the detective's caseload.

His mouth thins. "Well, if you remember anything, let me know."

He passes Arielle his card and she takes it, nodding. So much for her mother being his number one priority.

A few more scribbled notes and Detective Kane snaps his notebook shut. "Our next step is to see if anyone saw or heard anything, and to get the forensics report. I'll be in contact with you tomorrow morning, either way."

Arielle waits as Aunt Shell sees the detective out. The room is disturbingly silent. The emptiness is a suffocating weight.

Aunt Shell returns and stops on the other side of the room. She swallows, her gaze roaming over the room before it settles on Arielle. She scans her from head to toe as she approaches, as if making sure she's unhurt.

Arielle's lip trembles. Then her heart shudders in her chest. She's most definitely hurting.

Her legs give out and she sinks to the floor. She runs a shaky finger over the splotches on her boots, now the color of dried blood.

"Oh, Ari," Aunt Shell chokes as she sinks beside her, pulling her into her arms.

Arielle clasps her back, hating the grief that's crowding around them.

"Where is she, Aunt Shell?" she whispers.

Her father disappeared and was never found. Assumed dead.

And now, her mother is gone, too.

CHAPTER 3
REIGN

Reign stomps out of his room and into the adjacent one. Just like his own, it no longer has a door, but he and Mac are long past the need to knock. Reign strides past her as he sits on the bed and shoves open the window, only getting more irate when it's more difficult than he would like it to be.

Once it's creaked and groaned a few inches open, he pushes the bowl through and holds it out over the street. "Someone left their bowl of weed in my room, still burning," he growls angrily.

Mac is reading a newspaper, and she doesn't bother to lower it as she answers, "That's annoying."

"Dammit, Mackenzie! It's your bowl!"

She lowers the newspaper, arching a dark eyebrow. "I'm not using it anymore. Thought you might want it."

Reign jerks his arm in, holding the bowl toward Mac. "So, you thought you'd leave your dope in there, too? Still lit? What if I hadn't come back today?"

Because he'd been caught by the cops. Arrested. And was sitting in a cell, waiting for his one-way pass to jail.

The newspaper crinkles as Mac folds it in half. "Ah, the bowl's empty, Reign. Just like it was when I dropped it off in your room."

Reign's mouth opens to correct her, only for the words to be wiped away. She's right. The bowl's no longer smoking.

Because it's empty.

Reign yanks it closer, peering at the smooth interior. "What the..." He scowls, looking back up. "Is this another one of your practical jokes? Because I ain't laughing."

Mac shakes her head. "Not this time. Although a part of me is wishing it was..."

He blinks, his stomach contracting painfully. He's seeing things again? First the Hell-face, and now imaginary smoke?

With a flick of his wrist, he throws the bowl across the room. It hits the wall with a thud, leaving a dent beside a faded drawing of a skull with roses for eye sockets.

"Maybe it's time you lay off the happy herbs yourself," Mac suggests.

Reign clenches his teeth. "So now you're all kale smoothies and downward facing dog, huh?"

Mac shrugs. "I didn't want it to ruin my complexion."

Reign snorts. "You don't want all those face creams to go to waste?"

Although Mac is a power punch of beauty with her caramel skin, thick black curls and dark eyes flashing with intelligence, she never acknowledges it. In fact, she spends more time pointing out she's short and her hair needs to be permanently tamed into a bun. Even if they had the money for face creams, she wouldn't use them.

Picking up the newspaper again, Mac narrows her eyes. "What's with you today?"

Reign's hands clench, wishing he had the bowl so he could throw it again. Harder. Maybe through the window this time.

He committed larceny.

He almost ploughed through a terrified girl.

He's seeing things.

"Crap day," he states flatly.

"Why don't you go suck on a dead dog's nose and see if that helps?" Mac arches a brow. "I think there might be one in Rico's room."

An unwilling smile hovers over Reign's lips. "I think he's under the impression it's still alive."

Mac angles her head. "I'm pretty sure it's just an old sweater of his."

They both chuckle, and Reign flops onto a milk crate, the closest thing they have to a chair. Although they haven't been friends for long, they both recognized a kindred spirit the first day Reign arrived at his seventh foster home.

A run-down house a suburb away, Reign had barely paid attention as he was taken through the usual tour and welcome smiles, counting the number of bedrooms in the house—five— and quickly reaching the conclusion about the sort of people Avril and George Blackwell are.

Avril had shown him his room, the one beside Mackenzie's, before waddling her bulk away, saying dinner was in half an hour.

Mac had been sitting on the bottom bed of a triple bunk. She hadn't looked up from her book as she'd spoken. "She only cooks when a new kid arrives."

Reign had looked around the messy, drab room. "So, most Fridays?"

He had no doubt the Blackwell house was a revolving door of foster kids, one that ensured Avril's porcelain doll collection would continue growing. He'd already decided there was no point unpacking his duffel bag. He didn't plan on staying long.

Mac had looked up. "And some Tuesdays." She'd pulled her book back to her face. "Don't touch my books."

Which meant Mac had already broken the first rule of foster care—don't get attached to belongings. Reign had glanced around the room, seeing a stack of paperbacks in the corner of the cluttered space. It seemed there was nowhere safe to store them. "That sounds like an issue, not an—"

"As opposed to an ish-me?" she'd retorted.

Reign had snorted a laugh before he could stop himself, surprised she got the reference to ish-you. Mac had lowered her book again, and their gazes had connected. They'd been fast friends since.

The rustle of a newspaper brings Reign back to the present. He cocks his head. "What's with the newspaper? Have you finally run out of books?"

Mac rolls her eyes. "I like to keep up with current events, and the TV's not working."

"Have you tried turning it on and off?"

Mac shakes her head, smiling a little. No TV is going to work without electricity. She points to the page she was reading. "There's been a series of abductions across the city. Apart from them all being middle-aged women, there's no clear link between the victims."

Reign's mind starts to wonder about how many of them are mothers, possibly the same age his mother would've been if she'd lived, but he shakes his head before he starts down that dark path. "Sounds like an ish-them."

Mac stills as she looks at Reign a little more closely. "Something has definitely climbed up your nose. What's going on?"

Reign shoots to his feet. "You know what? If I'm just going to get the third degree—with no happy herbs in sight, I might add—then I'm outta here."

He strides to the door, conscious that Mac is sitting there, watching him. He's just reached the door when his friend's words reach him.

"Yep. Definitely an ish-you of some sort."

Reign pretends he didn't hear her as he goes back into his room and flops onto the mattress. He throws his arm over his eyes, pretending the rumpled, gray sheets don't smell gross.

He closes his eyes, wanting today over with. For a brief second, he considers going back to Darnell and Rico and finding oblivion in a joint, but the thought of getting back up suddenly feels like too much.

He's exhausted, hitting a low that's directly proportional to the highs he enjoyed in the stolen car. Before everything turned to shit. He feels sleep start to steal over him as his body sinks into the lumpy mattress, and he cautiously welcomes it.

If the Hell-face is going to appear in his nightmares, he'd prefer to stay awake. He'll see if Rico has any uppers if he needs to.

But the fog that blankets his mind is nothing but seamless black. Reign gives in with relief, chasing the promise of oblivion. Some days, nonexistence is the only way he can stop feeling...

He doesn't realize the dream is happening at first. There's no Hell-face to warn him, the glowing eyes always a signal to get the freak out of there. Instead, he finds himself in some sort of cave. It's not a big one, jagged gray walls curving only a few feet above his head, and quite dark.

It means he sees the young bearded man at the other end, hears the metal rattle as he desperately shakes the prison cell he's trapped in. Three men, all in brown robes, stand on the other side, staring at him.

The young man shakes the locked door again. "You already hung the son of God on the cross, you fools! Your wickedness only multiplies by sealing me away like this!"

The men shift uneasily, glancing at each other. They start to retreat, moving away from the darkness of the cell, toward the opening of the cave.

"The Son of God whom you hanged upon the cross, will deliver me out of your hands." the young man shouts after them. "All your wickedness will return upon you."

The men's shoulders hunch as they leave, but they never glance back. The young man slides to his knees, his forehead pressed against the prison bars. There's a grinding sound and the pool of light in the center of the cave begins to shrink. Reign realizes the men are rolling a stone across the mouth of the cave. They're entombing this poor guy.

This guy definitely has an ish-him.

Questioning where in the world such a weird dream came from—probably Avril's love of bible passages—Reign glances around, noting the impermeable walls around him, wondering when his consciousness is going to get him the heck out of here. He frowns. Since when did he have so much clarity in dreams? Since when did he know he was in a dream?

He takes a step back, wondering if he's tripping. It's like he's *here*, in the cave.

The young man's head snaps up. "Who's there?"

Reign freezes, even holding his breath. The stone at the mouth of the cave *thumps* into place, plunging the room into darkness.

There's a scratching sound and a small flame flares to life. The young man holds up a stubby candle, waving it around as he scans the room frantically. Reign doesn't twitch a muscle. For some reason, he doesn't want to be seen.

The man's gaze falls on him, his eyes widening. "It's you..."

Reign shakes his head so hard the room spins. Whoever this guy thinks he is, he's not.

The man throws himself against the bars. "They're coming!" he screams. "You need to stop them!"

Another step back and the rough, cold wall of the cave slams into his back. Reign lifts his hands as if he can ward away the man's words.

"The Gates are opening!" The man reaches an arm through the bars. "Save them! Save them all!"

Reign sits up with a gasp, glancing wildly around the room. It takes long, heart-thumping seconds for him to register the graffiti on the walls. The light from the street filtering through the cracked window. The bare, dead globe dangling from the roof.

He lets out a shuddering breath as he realizes where he is— the closest version of home he'll ever have. Not in some cave with a crazy, desperate dude who's about to die a slow death.

How could a dream feel so real? He could practically taste the dust and desperation. Smell the cold hard stone walls. There's only one way that could occur.

He draws his knees up, his head sinking into his hands. It's happening.

He's following in his brother's footsteps.

The inevitable decline has begun.

Arielle glances around. "What if she can't?" she asks in a small voice.

"Oh, Ari." Aunt Shell rushes over as Arielle's knees give out and she collapses onto the lounge. "She's strong."

But Arielle is struggling to find any optimism. "Mom's an intellectual. A vegetarian. She's Buddhist. She doesn't know how to fight."

Aunt Shell snorts as she sits on the arm of the sofa, making Arielle look up in surprise. "Your mother used to sneak out all the time. She told me she gave a cop a mouthful when he tried to arrest someone at a frat party once."

"She never told me that..."

Aunt Shell nudges Arielle. "Most kids are surprised to hear their parents had a life before they had children."

Arielle leans against her aunt, her soft curves so different from her mother's lean lines, but familiar and comforting all the same. "I'm so scared, Aunt Shell."

"Don't lose faith, Ari," she says as she squeezes Arielle's shoulder. "You heard Detective Kane. The police are going to do everything they can to find her."

Arielle shoots to her feet, any sense of hope now shattered. "Like the police found my father?"

Aunt Shell flinches, and Arielle is instantly contrite.

"I'm sorry. I shouldn't have said that."

"I understand, love," Aunt Shell says quietly. "We're all worried out of our minds right now."

Arielle's arms clamp around her middle, the brief flash of anger already gone. Now she just feels sick. And scared.

Aunt Shell's gaze softens with compassion. "Why don't you go to bed? It's late, and hopefully Detective Kane will have some news for us tomorrow morning."

Arielle nods, even though she knows she won't be sleeping anytime soon.

In her room, she looks around. She had no idea how everything would change today when she got ready this morning. Sitting heavily on the bed, she blinks. Then blinks again. Where is her mother right now? What's happening to her? Has she been hurt?

Biting back a sob, Arielle quickly leans down to undo her shoes, needing to keep herself occupied. But untying her shoelaces is the worst thing she could've done.

Her mother bought her these boots. The day after Arielle had broken down crying as they'd been trying to choose her first year subjects. She had no idea what she wanted to do for a career. She still doesn't.

Her mother had comforted her, murmuring that it doesn't matter. That she'd find her path.

When Arielle had come home the following day, her mother had been waiting in the kitchen. The deep blue eyes Arielle had inherited had glowed as she'd passed the large box. "Every journey starts with a single step, Ari." She loves all the clichéd sayings. "These will carry you. Be a witness to it."

Arielle had taken the box, excited but nervous. Her mother was just as likely to give her a dream catcher as a textbook on career planning.

But the boots—the cream Converse that reach all the way up to her knees—had been perfect. She'd worn them every day since, letting them become everything her mother said they'd be.

But now they're stained, a red-brown record of the most devastating day of her life. The day her mother was violently taken from her.

Arielle carefully slips them off, moving slowly as if she's going to shatter any second. Clutching the boots like they're a teddy bear, she curves around them.

"Please be okay, Mom," she whispers brokenly.

Arielle holds herself there, no longer feeling the need to move. What's the point? There's nowhere to go, nothing to do. Her life has been cut adrift.

She's not sure how long she sits there, but she waits until she hears Aunt Shell walk to the guest bedroom. Then she waits another half an hour. When she's sure the coast is clear, Arielle sneaks back to the living room.

There, she curls up on the sofa. Tucking her knees up to her chin, Arielle wraps her arms around her legs. Her eyes feel gritty, her mind filled with a thick, black fog, but she doesn't intend on sleeping.

If her mother comes through the door, she wants to be the first person to greet her.

The silence of the house envelops her, no longer comforting like it used to be, and Arielle's eyelids become heavier with each blink.

She doesn't even know she's fallen asleep until the dream starts, and she's standing in a dark place. She tries to jerk herself awake, but she's in too deep.

"There has to be an exit," she says as she spins around. "What if Mom gets back?"

But she's in a field of some sort, gently undulating hills blotting out the indigo horizon.

Continuing to turn, she stops. She's not alone in this field.

A thick stone column punches through the soil several yards away. An obelisk. The sizable chips missing from the corners along with the cracks spreading through it like veins suggest it's old. "An ancient obelisk," Arielle says quietly.

The color of granite, the pale monolith seems to throb with energy. For some reason, it's wondrously new and achingly familiar all at once.

Arielle's about to take a step when she realizes there are others already there. Seven others. Her eyes widen.

"With wings," she whispers in awe, then ducks her head when she realizes she said it out loud.

But the figures don't seem to have heard her talking to herself. All dressed in white robes, they stand in a circle around the obelisk, facing it with their arms interlinked. Seven sets of magnificent wings arch out behind them, proud and massive.

Almost like she doesn't have a choice, Arielle moves toward them.

"Hello?" she calls out softly, almost reverently. "Where am I?"

But no one turns around.

"Of course they can't hear you, Arielle. This is a dream," she admonishes herself.

"A dream I shouldn't be having," she points out as if she's having a conversation. "I want to wake up."

But as she waits, the obelisk glows, the seven figures maintain their ring around it, and Arielle remains where she is. Starting to grow a little impatient, she starts walking. Maybe she can try to get one of these people's attention. Get this dream over and done with.

But she's barely moved when the obelisk flares with light. It grows brighter and brighter, forcing Arielle to stop and shield her eyes. There's a guttural groaning sound and the ground beneath her starts to tremble. Arielle stumbles back, confused and frightened, but the shaking is everywhere her feet land.

"What's going on?"

But the white figures have disappeared and it's just Arielle and the brilliant obelisk. The ground groans again as it splits open, fissures snaking along the surface. She leaps back, terror clogging her lungs, making it hard to breathe.

Screams rip through the air, so loud and piercing that Arielle slams her hands over her ears. She watches in horror as long, black fingers claw up from the bowels of the Earth, reaching for the obelisk.

"Leave it alone!" Arielle shouts, fierce protectiveness flooding her. "Get away!"

She tries to run, only to find the same black wrapped around her ankles. The fingers surrounding the obelisk reach higher, becoming clawed, obsidian hands. Impossibly, the obelisk blazes brighter, the veined cracks illuminated like lightning.

Desperately, Arielle tugs at her icy bonds. Instinctively, she knows what's going to happen next.

The black hands grasp at the obelisk greedily, the clawed nails snagging on the glittering cracks. And then they're scraping and lacerating, ravaging and destroying.

"No!" Arielle screams, feeling the destruction deep in her bones.

More hands clutch at her but she tries to push them away. She has to stop this!

"Ari, wake up!"

Arielle sits up in a rush. "Mom?" she gasps.

But although the hands holding her arms are familiar, they're not her mother's. Arielle blinks the strange, scary dream away. "Gabby?"

Her cousin shifts back a little. "Sorry. I didn't mean to scare you."

Arielle blinks in the half-light, trying to shake the sensation that the claws weren't just ripping apart the obelisk. They were ripping apart her soul.

"No need to apologize. I must've been having a bad dream."

In fact, a nightmare is a perfect way to finish such an awful day.

"I came as soon as I heard," Gabby says quietly.

Arielle throws her arms around her cousin, squeezing her

tightly, her bouncy blonde hair tickling her nose. Gabby clasps her back, her hug full of compassion and understanding.

Although they've only seen each other during school breaks as Gabby's always been away at boarding school, their bond is a close one. Not only are they cousins, born of two sisters who are also best friends, they're both only children of single mothers. Plus, they're both always a little... different.

Gabby was the one Arielle spent each summer with. Gabby is the only one who knows about Trinity, Arielle's childhood imaginary friend.

Arielle yanks back with a start. "I thought you were going away?"

Gabby's just graduated school. She was going to celebrate with a trip.

Gabby tucks a frizzy curl of blonde hair behind her ear, her gaze averting. "I wanted to check in on you."

Tears sting Arielle's eyes, and she quickly blinks them away. "I'm so sorry." Gabby really sounded like she was looking forward to it, but Arielle knows she won't be leaving now.

"It's fine, Ari. Sierra's my aunt. I want to be here," she says quietly. "Plus, I have Colt. That's all I need."

Arielle's left mute by the conviction in her cousin's voice. They used to whisper about a love like that. They knew it existed—they'd both watched their mothers choose to live alone rather than with the men who had their hearts—but they'd always wondered if they'd find something like that themselves.

It seems Gabby has.

She clasps her hands. "But enough about me. Tell me what's happened."

Arielle's situation crashes back down on her shoulders, dragging at her heart. "Mom's been abducted. She was snatched right off the street," she says simply, as if they're not the worst tasting words she's ever said.

"Oh, Ari. I'm so sorry," Gabby whispers thickly. "What have the police said?"

Arielle pushes herself up so she's tucked into the corner of the sofa, glancing down at her hands as they twist together. "They've done a forensics sweep, and they've asked around whether anyone saw or heard anything. We'll find out more in the morning."

"That's good. They're taking it seriously, then."

Arielle frowns, wondering why they wouldn't. Then again, people go missing all the time... She straightens in alarm. "Do you think they'll just give up? That they won't find her?"

Gabby's eyes widen. "Of course not! That's most definitely not what I meant." She clasps Arielle's hands again. "I'm sure your mom is fine, and you'll see her again soon."

But Arielle's known Gabby long enough to hear the lack of conviction in her tone. She nods, withdrawing her hands. "Of course, they will."

"What are you thinking, Ari?" Gabby leans forward, peering at her.

It seems her cousin has the same ability to detect a lack of sincerity.

"Dad disappeared and they never found him, Gabby. I'm not going to sit around and have that happen again."

"This is exactly why I came. The police have got this. You need to stay out of it."

There's a thread of steel in her cousin's voice that Arielle's never heard. "But—"

"No buts, Ari. This could be dangerous."

Arielle looks down at her hands, focusing on the only truth she can say right now. "I'm so scared for her, Gabby."

Her cousin engulfs her in a hug. "I know. But she's strong. And the police know what to do."

Nodding, Arielle clasps Gabby back, glad she's able to hide her face. If Gabby can sense a lie just from her voice, then she certainly doesn't want her seeing her expression as she says the next words. "You're right. I'll wait and see what the police come up with."

Relief loosens Gabby's arms, and she pulls back. "Good." She glances over her shoulder as if she's worried someone is watching. Or about to appear out of the shadows. "I have to go. I just came to make sure you're not going to do anything stupid."

Arielle pulls up a weak smile. "Like the time I tried to prove Trinity is real?"

Gabby grins. "Yes, exactly like that."

Arielle walks her to the door, and with a last, quick hug, Gabby silently steps onto the front porch. Arielle's about to close the door when she sees a movement. A shadow separates from the others—a guy—and Gabby sinks into his arms. They hold each other for long seconds, almost seeming to become one, before slipping away.

Back in the living room, Arielle settles in to wait for the dawn. She'll keep her word. She'll listen to what Detective Kane has discovered.

And after that, just like her cousin is following her heart, it's time for her to do the same.

No matter what.

CHAPTER 5
REIGN

The moment Reign wakes up, he craves oblivion again. The Hell-face. The nightmare. His ever-growing list of wrong moves, still waiting to be acknowledged.

Lying on the musty mattress, he opens his eyes, shuts them, then opens them again. There's no guarantee chasing sleep is going to do that for him, but then again, reality isn't something he likes to spend too much time in.

Rolling over with a groan, he acknowledges sleep won't be happening, anyway. His brain is awake and is going to be fast looking for some self-flagellation to start the day.

Shoving himself up, he staggers to the door, jamming his hands through his hair. His mouth feels like sandpaper, and he's hungry, but he's used to hunger and thirst. There's something more important he needs right now.

He thumps down the stairs, figuring there will be something somewhere in this house to fix his predicament.

The sounds of chuckles and guffaws reach him as he enters the front room. Darnell and Rico are too busy tussling to notice him. Rico runs at Darnell, head low and aimed for his gut. The moment they connect, Darnell clamps his powerful arms around Rico's lanky frame and lifts him. Rico whoops like he's on a rollercoaster as Darnell flips him over and drops him on the mattress. There's a crunch as his foot goes through the wall.

Reign leans against the door jamb. "I think you two have redecorated enough, don't you?"

Rico scrambles to his feet, shoving his thick brown bangs out of his eyes. "Oh, it's sleeping beauty."

Darnell plants his hands on his hips as he scans Reign from head to toe. "If you went on a bender and you didn't share, Darnell ain't gonna be happy."

Reign wipes his hand down his face. "I didn't go on a bender. I just slept in, okay?"

Mac enters from the kitchen, eating cereal out of a box. "You never sleep in."

"You know me," Reign mutters. "I'm always up for trying new things."

Rico hikes up his pants. "About time, dude. We need to go cash in our haul."

He walks to the other corner of the room and picks up a garbage bag full of clothes. Beneath sit the three laptops.

He holds them up. "It's payday!"

Mac slams the cereal box down on a decrepit set of shelves. "Ah, Reign. Could we talk?"

Sighing, Reign nods. He should've known this would be coming.

"Uh oh!" Darnell says in a stage whisper. "Lovers' tiff."

"My money's on Mac," Rico responds.

Both Reign and Mac ignore them. They've told both Darnell and Rico a thousand times they're nothing more than friends. Best of friends. Friends you know have your back. They've lived on the streets long enough to know how precious that is.

Pushing off the doorjamb, Reign leads Mac into the hall. "Look, I know—"

"You stole laptops?" Mac explodes.

Reign jams his hands in his pockets. "Well, *I* didn't."

Mac raises a brow, waiting.

"I just drove the getaway car."

Mac's fingers jam into her thick curls. "Of all the dumbass things to do, Reign! We steal food because we need to eat. Stealing luxury items from a store is only going to invite heat!"

Shame trickles down Reign's spine. "Yeah, I know. If it counts for much, the cop chase wasn't the most fun I've ever had."

Not to mention he saw the Hell-face again.

Mac's eyes widen at the mention of a police chase. "I should never have invited Darnell and Rico here."

"As opposed to leaving them next to the dumpster in the rain?"

Mac may spend a lot of time cultivating her tough exterior, but as much as she doesn't want it, she has a heart. It's probably all those books she reads.

Reign shakes his head. "I chose to go." His lips twist into a smile. "And it was a rush."

Mac jams her hands on her hips. "You get caught doing this stuff, and I'll kill you."

Reign grins. "Noted."

"You get killed, and I'll resurrect you, just so I can personally do the job."

The grin multiplies. "I'm smart enough to know you're probably capable of doing that."

Her hands slip off and her shoulders sag. "Maybe just don't do it? Don't, you know, leave me to make this shitty journey called life on my own?"

Remorse is like a sucker punch to Reign's gut. "We both know my trajectory is inevitable."

Mac leaps forward, shoving Reign hard. "If you think that, then you've had too many knocks to the head, dumbass."

He absorbs the hit, just like he's done most of his life with everything else that fate's thrown at him. "But if it's any consolation, I won't do it again."

If being that scared is going to mean seeing what he did on the cop's face, then no amount of chicken wing ding filled wheelbarrows are worth it.

Mac unwinds a fraction. "It's a start." She angles her head. "What are you up to today? You should head back to Avril's at some stage. Have a shower. Get some clean clothes."

Avril started doing laundry more regularly after the last check by child services questioned her ability to care for so many kids. Of course, the next time the social workers visit and see nice stacks of clean clothes around the place, then it'll stop. And those well-meaning saps will go on their way, telling themselves these foster kids have it better than if they were on the streets.

"Yeah, maybe later." First, Reign needs to check out for a few hours. Days. Maybe lifetimes.

She grins. "Why don't you see what Lizzie's up to."

He rolls his eyes. "I haven't spoken to Lizzie in weeks. That was over a long time ago."

"Does Lizzie agree with that?" Mac asks, her eyebrow arched.

"Shut up," Reign growls good naturedly. "I'm sure she's found someone else by now."

"Well, I might go check out what's happening at the campus library."

Reign heads back to the main room. "Now there's time well spent. Didn't the librarian ask for a student card last time?"

Mac shrugs. "I like annoying her. She almost pops a gasket each time I tell her I must've left it at a different frat house."

And Mackenzie likes the library. There are few things that are free in life, but one of Mac's few joys is that books are one of those things.

Reign waves goodbye as he joins Darnell and Rico. Both boys are slouching over their phones as he enters.

"Can we go now?" Darnell whines. "We're out of cherry cola."

Reign leans against the wall, crossing his arms. "You guys sell them."

"It means you'll get less of the cut," Rico says sharply.

Reign nods. He knows the rules—less risk, less reward. "I'm cool with that."

Darnell and Rico glance at each other. A second later, they're gone, not waiting around to see if Reign's going to change his mind.

The moment he's alone in the house, Reign starts to search for a reality-wiping fix. He checks the underside of the shelves, only to find nothing. Frowning, he opens the bag of clothes and checks every pocket. Nothing.

Tension winding through him, he squats in the corner of the room and lifts the threadbare carpet. Beneath, he slips his hand underneath the loose floorboard. His fingers brush over air and dust.

"Assholes."

Reign can have a pretty good guess where Darnell and Rico are going after they get their cherry cola. But that doesn't help him now.

Not when he's feeling like this.

Leaving the house, Reign breaks into a stride. He doesn't have any money, which means he needs to find someone who's willing to do him a solid. Unfortunately, people like that aren't easy to find in the River District. Trust is about as common as bake sales around here.

Picking up the pace to a jog, he heads for the central shops. Surely, he'll find someone there.

As his feet hit the pavement in a steady rhythm, Reign tries to keep his mind blank. He counts light poles as he jogs past, but when he discovers there's an eight second space between them—long enough for images of red glowing eyes to climb into his consciousness—he decides to count trees as well.

Fifty-five.

Fifty-six.

Gray skin. Sunken sockets.

Fifty-seven.

Fifty-eight.

And then it's Lance's face before him. His foster brother has his mouth open in a scream, exposing rows of pointed teeth, but there's no sound.

Like he knows there's no point asking for help.

Pain slices through Reign's torso, making him gasp. He stops, bending over as he breathes hard and he grits his teeth. He feels like he's bleeding from the inside out, but he knows there's no blood to be seen. This pain can't be healed.

He needs a fix. Now.

He needs to escape... himself.

The main drag of Mercy City is only a block away, so Reign straightens and sets his sights on a cafe on the corner. He's going to get there as quickly as he can. He's about to break into a sprint when a panicked voice reaches him from across the street.

"No, this can't be happening."

A middle-aged woman is standing beside her car, her hands clutching her hair. She walks one way then the other. "Not today, of all days."

A closer look and Reign sees she has a flat tire. She bends over, inspecting it, as if she can will it to re-inflate.

Looking away, one word floats through his mind. *Ish-her*. He has a dealer willing to take an I-owe-you to find.

"I can't do this today."

The words, said on a broken sob, have Reign stopping. They echo the struggle that he faces every day.

"Dammit," he mutters under his breath. "Dammit. Dammit. Dammit."

He's crossing the street before he thinks this through too much. He stops a few feet away. "I can help you with that if you like."

The woman jumps back, her hands flying to her chest. Her eyes widen even further as she takes Reign in.

Resisting the urge to cross his arms, he waits, having a pretty good idea of what she's seeing.

Messy hair. Rumpled clothing. A face that doesn't smile very often.

A street rat.

He almost dares her to take an involuntary step back. To stammer out a "no, thank you" as she quickly slides into her car and locks the doors. It would save him a whole lot of trouble.

But she lets out a breath on a huff, her loose bun wobbling. "I would love a hand, young man."

Great.

"You'll need to open your boot."

The woman blinks. "Of course."

She presses the button on her car key and it pops open. Reaching in, Reign removes the tools he'll need followed by the spare tire. Wordlessly, he sets about jacking the car up.

The woman hovers behind him. "Is there any way I can help?"

"No point getting yourself dirty." Reign doesn't look up from where he's undoing the lug nuts.

She shifts so she's to his left. "I can't say how much I appreciate this."

"No need," Reign grunts as he slips off the flat tire.

"I need to get back to my niece. She's had some...terrible news." She points to a brown paper bag sitting on the passenger seat. "I just slipped out to pick up her favorite bagels."

Reign glances at the woman's round curves. She looks like she's a feeder. He's heard about women like that—they equate nurturing with nourishing. He hopes this niece appreciates having people and words like that in her life.

Rolling the spare over, he slots it on. Making quick work of screwing the lug nuts back on, he tightens them one by one.

He pushes to his feet, dusting his hands off on his jeans. "All done."

The woman clasps her hands to her chest. "Oh my, you've done a wonderful job."

"It's just a tire change," Reign points out.

"Oh goodness no, it's far more than that. I can't thank you enough." Her eyes shine with sincerity. Reign tries to put a stop to the gratitude, but she steps forward. "You're my knight in shining armor. My savior."

He leaps back like she just tried to slap him. Savior? Too far. "Seriously, it's no big deal." Another retreating step and he's back on the street. "I hope your niece gets some good news soon."

The woman scrabbles for her purse, yanking out a twenty-dollar bill. "Here, at least take this. My way of saying thanks."

Reign holds his hands up as he shakes his head. "It's fine, really."

He'd like to think that he could help a lady out and not take payment for it. That maybe there's some shred of decency within him.

His gaze flickers to the bill in her hand. Even if it means he could pay for his weed...

"Please, take it."

Turning away, Reign breaks into a jog. The woman doesn't call out again as he quickly crosses the road and streaks away, and he's relieved. Now, he can forget about his momentary lapse of judgment and find someone who's going to help him disappear for a few hours.

He reaches the cafe and rounds the bend. It's not a street he's been down often, but it's a busy one, which is just what he wants. The more people, the more shady deals can be made. Large, old buildings line either side of the road as Reign slows down, scanning faces. His body coils in anticipation. Not long now.

He finds what he's looking for several yards down the street. A slouched figure wearing oversized clothes. One he knows. Candy is one of the better known dealers around this area. He's also known to be a little lenient in desperate times.

And these are desperate times.

Keeping his gaze on the one person who can give him relief right now, Reign puts his head down and strikes forward. He can almost taste the acrid smoke, feel the thick nothingness that'll fill his mind.

There's a blur of movement and a body slams into him. His arms automatically reach out to steady the person he just walked into.

"Sorr—"

Reign reels back in shock.

Shit.

It's the girl he almost hit with the car.

"You're sorry?" Arielle has to modulate her tone, suddenly remembering that she's standing in the middle of the street. "You could've killed me!"

He shifts uncomfortably. "I know. I took the corner too fast. It was stupid."

But for some reason, the apology doesn't make a difference to her simmering anger. The nightmare she's currently living started when he came barreling toward her.

"You're damn right it was stupid!"

His lips thin as something shifts in the jungle depths of his green eyes, but he doesn't say anything.

Which just makes Arielle madder.

"Sorry isn't going to cut it!"

His gaze slips away, focusing on his worn sneakers. "It never does," he mutters quietly.

Arielle's heart is thundering. He ruined her boots. Her mother disappeared. The association isn't logical, but then again, nothing is making sense in her world right now. And this drop-kick doesn't seem to understand exactly how much everything is falling apart around her.

Well, she's going to educate him.

"You, you ruined my shoes!" Frustration has Arielle's voice spiking again. "There are stains everywhere!"

The guy blinks as the words hit him. His gaze travels to her feet and up her calves. "But..." he looks back up, confused. "There are marks all over them."

Arielle flushes, annoyed that it's the truth. Just like her mother wanted, Arielle's boots have become the witness to all the moments in her life. The pivotal ones. The funny ones. The ones she didn't want to forget.

Each time, she took a felt tip pen and scrawled a word or two in a random spot. Over time, the cream canvas has been decorated with a multitude of scribbles.

And now with red, splotchy stains.

"That's beside the point! They'll never be the same again."

His eyes narrow so slightly, if Arielle wasn't so hyper-aware of the black-lashed green, she wouldn't have noticed it. "I'll buy a new pair and replace them, okay?"

"No, it's really not! You could never replace them!"

"Look, I said I'm sorry, okay? I did everything I could to miss you. What else do you want from me?"

Arielle clenches her hands as heat flushes through her. Some small, sane part of her brain knows she's overreacting. She needs to get herself under control.

He jams his hands in his pockets. "I mean, you weren't hurt. And they're just a pair of shoes."

And the anger is back, hotter and more virulent. Arielle steps in close, glad when she sees his beautiful eyes widen. "What's your name?"

"There's no way I'm giving you my name."

Practically shoving her face in his, she repeats the question through gritted teeth. "What's your name? You asked what else I wanted from you—I want your name."

"No."

"Right now, it's Asshole."

"That'll do," he snaps back. "It's familiar enough."

"Why doesn't that surprise me?"

When the guy shoves his face back, bringing them only inches apart, Arielle's own eyes widen.

"Because you're a judgy, self-righteous, beauty-is-apparently-only-skin-deep girl who's already made her mind up about me!"

They stand there, faces close, breaths mingling. Arielle doesn't think she's ever felt so wired in her whole life. She wants to shake this guy. To kick him with the very same boots he's forever marked.

For some reason, she *needs* to know his name.

"Lovers' tiff," someone mutters as they walk past.

The two words are enough to snap them out of their strange state of suspended animation. Arielle steps back at the same time he does. People she hadn't been aware of rush past, the bustling noise of cars and city return.

Unsure why she's breathing as if she just jogged around the block a few times, Arielle opens her mouth to demand his name again, but before she can, he retreats a step.

"Some things you can't change, no matter how much you want to."

Spinning on his heel he strides away, only to hesitate. He glances around, seeming to focus on something down the street. His hands ball into fists as he takes a sharp left and jogs up the stairs of the library. A moment later, his lithe, tall body is gone.

For a long second, Arielle has to resist stomping her foot, no matter how childish the urge is. Of course he would go into the one place she came to visit. But there's no way she's going in there now. Not after the most infuriating encounter she's ever had.

"What a jerk!" She takes a step toward the library. "And what a jerk apology!" Another one, and her foot hits the first stair. "And I was supposed to do some research!"

She'd told Gabby all about her dream when she woke up. For some reason, the visions didn't dissolve once morning arrived like every other dream she's ever had. The looming obelisk. The winged forms. The evil that had torn it all apart. I had felt so real that the words had tumbled out of her before she could stop them.

Aunt Shell hadn't had a chance to respond because her cell rang. It was Detective Kane, essentially saying they didn't have any leads. Forensics hadn't found any fingerprints or fibers or any shred of evidence. The witness who saw the abduction didn't get the number plate. No one else had heard or seen anything. He said they were going to widen their search, whatever that meant.

Afterward, Arielle had crossed her arms, looking at her aunt with raised brows.

Gabby had frowned. "Why don't you go to the library and see if you can find out anything about your dream?"

Arielle's arms had fallen to her sides. "What? I don't—"

"Call it a hunch," Gabby had said, her frown still in place.

Aunt Shell had glanced at her cell as if it were withholding information. "I really don't think that's a great idea."

But Gabby had pulled up a smile. "While you do that, Ari, Mom can go get us some bagels."

"I'm not hungry—"

But Aunt Shell had interrupted Arielle again. "Actually, maybe that's a good idea. Bagels are just what we need."

Gabby had nodded. "And I'll be here if anyone comes by." She'd clasped Arielle's shoulders, speaking under her breath. "Imagine how tickled your mom will be when she gets back to hear you've been researching."

Arielle's mouth had snapped shut. In a crisis, the first thing her mom did was hit the books. She always said that's where she'd find the answer.

Arielle had decided to humor Gabby. Her dream was a product of the heart-tearing situation she's found herself in, and no raisin cinnamon bagel is going to fix it. But the thought of telling her mother that she'd done exactly what she'd do in such a situation had given Arielle something to cling to. Something to *do*.

But as she stands outside the library—the very same building that the unnecessarily hot asshole just disappeared into—Arielle knows she won't be going in there. In fact, she now has something else she intends on doing.

She may not have his name, but she knows exactly where he is. In fact, Detective Kane may focus on her mother's case more if she hands over the information she's now holding.

In the backpack she never leaves home without, Arielle fishes out her cell phone out of the side pocket and the detective's card out of her purse. She quickly dials the number, throwing heated glares at the library door every few digits.

It's him.

Arielle jolts as the words flash through her mind, this time with far more urgency. She ignores it as she presses the final number with force.

It's him!

Gritting her teeth, Arielle's finger hovers over the small green phone icon. "Shut up," she mutters. "I don't care who he is."

No! You can't do this!

"Shut up, Trinity!"

Arielle doesn't realize she's shouted the words until several people stop and glance. One elderly man side-steps around her as he continues on, taking a wide berth. She spins and looks around, even though she knows there's no one beside her, saying those words.

Cheeks hot with embarrassment, she tries to tell herself she's used to the weird glances. In fact, they'd stopped bothering her long ago. Arielle no longer cares what people think of her talking to herself.

Except she just shouted. Like, really loud.

And at Trinity.

Jamming her cell phone into her pocket, Arielle hunches her shoulders as she turns so abruptly she almost crashes into someone. Muttering an apology, she ducks her head to hide her flaming face as she quickly walks away.

She's going home to wait for her mother. And pretend that none of this—the dream and the guy and that moment—just happened.

Her eyes sting as she covers her mouth with her hand. Trinity used to be a comfort. A companion. A friend to fill the empty spaces of her only-child existence.

But that's when Trinity had been left behind in her child-hood. Imaginary friends were acceptable then.

Now, hearing voices just makes her crazy.

CHAPTER 7
REIGN

What the hell does he do now?

Reign watches the girl pull out her phone and start dialing. She's calling the cops on him.

Of course, she is. That's what girls like her do.

She was so righteous. So indignant. Completely unwilling to consider that there are reasons people make stupid choices. In fact, she was more worked up about her darned boots than anything. Sure they were cute, maybe even a little sexy, but that just makes her shallow.

He doesn't care that he's never seen a face like that—flawless, timeless, faultless. Or eyes that defy the word blue. They're deep as oceans, clear as skies, and as mesmerizing as the hottest part of a flame.

None of that matters. She's calling him in. He doesn't know why, but that feels like a betrayal.

"Excuse me, can I help you?"

Reign spins around, almost knocking over the rotating bookstand he was tucked behind as he spied through the library window. A primly dressed woman is standing a few feet away, hands clasped in front of her brown knit top.

Reign smiles, his gaze catching hers as he notes the way her cheeks flush a little. "Hello"—he glances at her name badge—"Dorothy. I was just reflecting that there are so many books in this world, and yet so little time."

She stiffens, arching a brow. "Is there anything in particular you were looking for?"

How to get snarky blondes off your back. "I'm fine, but thank you for checking," he says warmly.

Her gaze flickers to the doors. "A library is a place for learning and quiet contemplation. Maybe it's not the right place for you right now?"

Reign keeps his smile in place even though his gut contracts. Another person who's just made a whole bunch of judgments based on how he's dressed. But this time, Reign can't afford to get her offside.

Unlike Dorothy's suggestion, the library is just where he needs to be right now. The cops will assume he'll run. They'll probably scan the whole block—which means Candy is going to hightail it, taking Reign's fix with him. All Reign needs to do is blend in, in the one place no adult is going to assume he'll stay in.

And if his good looks aren't going to sway Dorothy the Judgy Librarian, then it's time to take a different tact.

He glances down at his worn shoes, scuffing one against the other. "I need to research some...stuff. I was going to book a computer, but I wasn't sure how."

"Oh." The librarian's posture softens. "We did just introduce an online system."

Reign rubs the back of his head. "Yeah. It's kinda complicated."

Dorothy jolts into action, going full maternal-librarian on him. "Come this way. It's really quite simple." She smiles. "We designed it to be as user friendly as possible."

He smiles gratefully. "Much appreciated, ma'am."

She leads him to the bank of computers Reign has already made a note of, and talks him through the booking system. Reign nods, keeping his interested face on, but his focus is on his surroundings. There are at least thirty computers stretched out over two rows. Most of them are taken, which is just what he needs—people to blend in with.

"See? It's simple," Dorothy says warmly. "We just choose an available computer and click this blue button here."

"Can I have the one down the end there?" Reign drops his gaze. "I'd just like a little privacy. We don't have computers at my place."

The woman's face melts with compassion, just as he suspected it would. Reign learned long ago that the poor kid angle can open doors and hearts. Despite that, he hates using it. Pity always leaves a bitter taste in his mouth.

"Of course. This is why libraries exist. Knowledge should always be free and easily accessible."

"Thank you, Dorothy," says Reign, injecting some honesty into his words.

She means well, and that counts for something.

Flushing, she bustles away. Reign makes his way to the end of the row and takes a seat. He hunches a little, glad to see a large guy is at the computer on his left. If cops do a quick sweep of the library, looking for a dark-haired delinquent, they won't expect the half-obscured guy tapping away at a computer to be him.

Flicking the mouse, he brings the screen to life, then blinks. What exactly is he going to research? He glances over his shoulder to find Dorothy back at her desk, watching him. She smiles encouragingly.

With a sigh, Reign turns back to the computer. He's pretty sure Dorothy has a program that will send this place into lockdown if he types in anything drug related, which means the whole reason he's ended up here is going to remain unresolved for a little longer. He rests his fingers on the keyboard, wondering what to type. What to do when you're exited out of the foster care system at eighteen? How to get a job when you've dropped out of high school? Where to get a free mattress that doesn't smell?

Reign's fingers start to type of their own volition.

All your wickedness will return upon you.

He startles when he realizes he just typed what the man in the cave shouted to the others in his dream. Frowning, Reign deletes it. There's no need to Google his life story. But then he's typing again.

The Son of God whom you hanged upon the cross, will deliver me out of your hands.

Reign grits his teeth. Avril's warnings of fire and brimstone have finally gotten to him. Just what he needs.

The big guy next to him jerks with silent laughter as he stares at his screen and Reign instinctively ducks, his hovering fingers pressing the enter key. In a split second, he watches with wide eyes as the first hit finds an exact match.

An uncomfortable feeling tightens around Reign's spine. He clicks on the blue headline, quickly scanning the information as words jump out at him.

Gospel of Nicodemus. Joseph of Arimathea. Holy Grail.

Avril tends to stick to words like sin and repent and eternal damnation. He's never heard her mention any of these.

Then how the hell did they end up in his dream?

Suddenly not okay with the thick walls surrounding him, Reign shoots to his feet. The guy next to him doesn't even notice as Reign strides past, desperate to get out. Dorothy opens her mouth as he shoots past, but he doesn't hear what she says. It's probably a good thing. Reign would just point out that sometimes knowledge isn't the panacea she believes it is.

He doesn't need the realization that his too-real dream was already written about in some ancient text. A text he didn't even know existed.

In fact, Reign has wished a thousand times he was never told his father dumped him at children's services.

And he sure as hell would love to wipe the knowledge that he was the one who killed his Lance.

Outside, he draws in great gulps of air. Bright sunshine pierces his eyes, snapping him out of his panic. Crap. He's supposed to be lying low in case Ms. Boots called the cops.

Turning sharply on his heel, Reign tucks his shoulders up and pulls his hood over his head. He strides away from the library, his gaze focused on the edge of the building. There's an alleyway on the left. He'll duck down there and find a short cut. Then, he's going back to the hangout. If Darnell and Rico haven't picked up some reality-numbing goodness, then he's going to sleep.

For about a month.

Relieved to find the alley deserted, Reign walks halfway down before leaning against the brick wall. He lets his head flop back, welcoming the sharp pain that ricochets through his skull. A quick glance from side to side reveals no law enforcement on his tail. If the girl called them, surely they'd be here by now.

Maybe she had better things to do. Like brush all that glossy blonde hair of hers. Or eat a meal her equally-beautiful mother made her. Or clean those freaking boots, wiping away the stains of his existence in her world.

The first shred of relief is contemplating taking hold when Reign glances down. He frowns. Smoke is creeping over the ground in the alley, tendrils coiling through milk crates and around trash cans. A quick glance around shows he's alone. With no clear origin for the smoke.

"Mac, if this is your idea of funny, then you're way off," he calls out into the empty alley. "As in, I doubt this would be humorous in the next several thousand galaxies or so."

But there's no answer. And the silvery smoke continues to accumulate.

Reign kicks at it, his stomach lurching when it fractures only to come back together like it's made of millions of magnetic particles. It coalesces and consolidates, multiplying and thickening. Pooling into one spot in front of him.

He swears it starts to form into an outline of a man.

"Shit," Reign breathes. "It's happening."

After years of being shoved from one foster home to the next followed by semi-homelessness, after losing every family member he's ever had, after choosing the oblivion of drugs one too many times, he's finally snapped his biscuit. Lost his mind.

Followed in his foster brother's legacy.

The thought is terrifying. And if there's one thing Reign hates, it's being scared.

He clenches his fists and coils his muscles. He'll fight that feeling with everything he has.

The mist continues to swirl into a man-shaped column, defying gravity as it climbs upward. Reign swings at it, his fist slicing through the hallucination he wishes he wasn't experiencing. The mist divides as his wild punch cleaves the vapor in two. But as soon as his arm has cleared, the smoke fuses back together, as if Reign just missed. It starts to create a vortex, spinning faster and faster as the mist sparkles with dots of color.

"Oh no you don't," Reign mutters.

He swings again, this time harder and faster, as if he can

win this by sheer force of will. His fist collides with a male chest, the impact reverberating up Reign's arm.

"Oomph," grunts the man.

Reign stumbles back. "What the—"

A man stands in front of him, old and gray, and exuding calm strength. Pale brown robes hang on his wiry body in regal layers, a thick beard brushing his chest. Reign instantly recognizes him as an older version of the man in his dream.

The guy straightens, recovering from the strike to his torso. "Your surprise is understandable, and your defense of yourself is commendable." He bows. "Grail Keeper, it is an honor to meet you."

Reign blinks. Then blinks again. Then slams his eyes shut and opens them again, just for good measure. The man in robes is still standing in front of him. Reign takes a step back only to hit the wall behind him.

"Fuck off."

His plan was to practically shout the word, but it comes out as little more than a whisper. Reign swallows, desperately hoping this is another dream.

The man straightens, looking perplexed. "I do not understand your use of words." He glances around. "What year of the Lord is this?"

"It means get the hell out of my space, you freak. And take your magic tricks and shove them up your—"

"Ah," the man says knowingly. "I assure you; I am no apparition. I am Joseph of Arimathea, the first of the Keepers of the Grail."

Joseph. Of. Arimathea.

The Grail.

Since when did snaps from reality become so intricate and interconnected? His dream. The library. Then this.

Reign's head is thumping so hard it hurts. It feels like it

wants to shatter under the pressure of everything that's unfolding in front of him, but he knows if that happens, his thin hold on sanity will be destroyed along with it.

The weirdo who just stepped out of his dream smiles. "And your name?"

"Outta here."

Reign uses the flash of confusion across the man's face to try and sidestep him. But the man's mind and reflexes are quicker than he expected, and the dude—Reign refuses to give his hallucination a name—quickly mirrors the movement to block him.

"You cannot."

"Watch me," Reign growls like he was just issued a challenge.

"But, the Innocents," the man says, his voice full of concern. "They must be saved or the Gates of Hell will be opened. Death and destruction will be inevitable."

"Oh, goodness me!" Reign exclaims, his hand flying to his chest. "I hadn't realized it was that serious."

The man unwinds a fraction. "I'm glad you understand the urgency of the situation. We must find the Grail at once."

Reign shoves past him, grimacing as his shoulder collides with what should be a figment of his cracked mind. "You'd better go get yourself a Grail Keeper, then."

He strides away, not looking back. The last thing he wants to see right now is the place his mind finally snapped. The place he broke.

Just like all the other craptastic moments in his life, he's going to pretend this one never happened.

CHAPTER 8
ARIELLE

Gabby meets Arielle at the door, almost as if she'd been waiting for her. She searches Arielle's face with an intensity that's almost unsettling.

"So, did you find anything about your dream?"

Arielle frowns. "No. I ran into a jerk."

With too-green eyes and too much attitude.

Gabby's face scrunches with frustration. Arielle's about to ask what the big deal is when Aunt Shell's voice rings down the hallway. "Is that Ari? Is she back?"

"Yes, Mom," Gabby calls over her shoulder. "We'll be there in a sec."

She turns back to Arielle, but Aunt Shell appears in the kitchen doorway. "But I have bagels." She holds up a paper bag. "Raisin cinnamon bagels."

Gabby turns to her mother and stares at her for long seconds. Aunt Shell simply smiles, shaking the bag so the contents rattle inside. With a huff, Gabby takes Arielle's hand and leads her to the kitchen. Arielle allows herself to be pulled along, feeling like she's missing something.

Why is her cousin so interested in her dream?

In the kitchen, Aunt Shell already has three plates set out at the bench. She serves the bagels as Gabby brings over the coffee.

Aunt Shell sits down, already looking tired even though it's only midmorning. She breaks off a chunk of bagel. "I almost didn't get back in time. I had a flat tire, and if it wasn't for a lovely young man, you'd be having toast."

Gabby looks like she's clenching her jaw as she cups her mug. "I'm sure we would've coped."

Arielle glances at her in surprise. Gabby and Aunt Shell have always been close. They rarely disagree, and Arielle doesn't think she's ever seen them argue. But there are definitely some undercurrents shifting around the table right now.

Aunt Shell winks at her daughter. "But isn't this better?" Before Gabby can respond, Aunt Shell turns to Arielle. "We thought we'd move in for a while your mom is...isn't here? We can keep you company."

Arielle blinks in surprise. "That would be great. Thank you."

Aunt Shell smiles fondly at her. "Of course. You and Sierra are family." She glances pointedly at Gabby. "And family sticks together."

At the realization that their family unit is now down to three, Arielle's gaze drops. Her grandmother died before she could remember her. Her grandfather left before she was born. She's never known anything about her father's family. Her mother's absence is like a quarter of this table has just been torn away. She stares at the speckled bagel, smelling its warm cinnamon scent, and knows she can't eat it. Her stomach is little more than a bunch of knots.

She looks up at her aunt and cousin. "Has there been any more news?"

Aunt Shell's gaze flickers, but it's Gabby who answers. "No, nothing."

"That's what I suspected." Arielle straightens her shoulders. "I'm not going to sit around and wait for the police to fail my family again. I'm going to find Mom myself."

Aunt Shell sits up like she just received an electric shock. "What? I don't think that's a very good idea at all."

Gabby pops a piece of bagel in her mouth and doesn't say anything. In fact, she picks up the newspaper sitting on the table beside her and idly flicks through it.

Her mother leans forward. "Ari, we don't know who took your mother. Sierra would want me to keep you safe."

"I'm not talking about storming into warehouses full of gun toting mafia, Aunt Shell. I'm just going to do my own...research. It's what Mom would've done if I were missing."

Aunt Shell frowns, possibly not liking the logical argument.

Arielle turns to her cousin, noting her unusual quietness. Gabby usually has an opinion on most things. "What do you think, Gabby?"

Gabby folds the newspaper and picks up her bagel. Aunt Shell seems to be holding her breath.

"I think if it were me, I'd do whatever I can to get my mother back."

Aunt Shell gasps. "Gabby! I don't think you realize what you're suggesting."

Gabby turns her steady gaze to her mother. "I know exactly what I'm suggesting. Ari has a right to know."

Arielle glances between the two of them. "A right to know what?" Do they know something about her mom? Surely, they wouldn't keep something like that from her...

"If anything comes to light," Aunt Shell rushes to assure. "You know how much Gabby values honesty."

Gabby has gone back to breaking chunks off her bagel, avoiding both their gazes. "I most certainly do," she says quietly.

Aunt Shell pushes Arielle's bagel a little closer to her with an encouraging look. "Remember when the two of you tried to keep the mouse you caught as a pet?"

Arielle almost smiles at the memory. "When you caught Gabby sneaking cheese from the fridge, she just up and confessed."

Gabby frowns. "I couldn't think of any legit reason I had a pocketful of cheese, okay?"

"Like that you were hungry?" Arielle teases.

Aunt Shell raises her mug of coffee to her lips, smiling indulgently. "No mouse could've eaten that amount of cheese."

Gabby picks up the newspaper again, rolling her eyes. She shakes it like a disgruntled old man as she disappears behind it. "We were going to have a cheese party."

The tangled mess in Arielle's gut loosens a little and she wonders if maybe she could fit in a little bagel. Except Gabby lifts the newspaper a little higher as she reads something. The headline facing Arielle grabs her attention and doesn't let go.

Serial abductions of Mercy City moms have cops baffled.

Arielle's heart jolts. "Gabby, can I see that newspaper?"

Gabby appears over the top of the pages. "Sure. Were you after the sports section or the crossword?"

"Just the back page, thanks," says Arielle, finding it a little hard to breathe.

"No probs, bestie-cousin."

Aunt Shell's mug clatters back onto the table. "What is it, Ari?"

Gabby passes Arielle the page, shrugging nonchalantly at her mother. "Maybe there's a recipe for raisin cinnamon bagels."

Arielle takes it, eyes rapidly scanning the small black print. "Several women have been abducted across the city," she reads beneath her breath. "There are no apparent links between the victims, apart from age. Each woman was thirty-eight years old."

The same age as Arielle's mother.

"Ari, I don't think you should—"

But Arielle cuts off her aunt and continues. "Despite most of the brazen abductions occurring during daylight hours, very little forensic evidence has been found. Police are assuring the community they're doing everything they can to identify the perpetrator and bring him or her to justice." Arielle carefully places the newspaper back onto the table. She wants to read it over and over, glean every shred of information from it. She has to stop her hands from clenching and crushing it as she looks up at Gabby and Aunt Shell.

"Detective Kane didn't mention this."

"He most likely didn't want to worry you unnecessarily," Aunt Shell says soothingly. "Your mom is probably nothing more than a coincidence."

Arielle lifts her left foot and points to a single, tiny, scribbled word on the side of her boot. "Hitsuzen," she tells her aunt. "It means inevitably. Destiny. Fate as the driving force in this world." Arielle puts her foot back down and looks at Gabby. "There's no such thing as a coincidence."

Something flares in her cousin's hazel eyes. But before she can talk, Aunt Shell leans forward and places an imploring hand on the paper.

"Please Ari, don't do anything rash."

Before Arielle can answer, the doorbell rings. They all startle, looking at each other in question. When no one seems to know who it could be, Aunt Shell turns to Gabby. "Could you—"

But Gabby shakes her head as she holds up her hands. "Crumby fingers, sorry."

Aunt Shell sighs and pushes up. "If it's those girls selling cookies again, I'm most definitely saying no this time."

The moment she's gone, Gabby puts down her bagel. "So, what's the plan?"

Arielle chews on her lip, wishing it was that simple. "First, there was the dream." Arielle swallows, knowing she's going to sound as crazy as she feels. "Then today, Trinity spoke to me."

Gabby's eyes widen. "Trinity's back?"

Arielle fiddles with the edge of her paper napkin. Gabby is the only one who knows about Trinity. "It's probably the stress of everything." Her mouth twists. "Or I'm going crazy."

Gabby's hand reaches out and covers hers. "You're not crazy, Ari." She squeezes her hand. "Promise me you'll follow your gut on this."

But isn't that what Trinity is? Her instinct? Her conscience?

Except Trinity told her not to call the cops on hot-angry guy. "Sometimes that seems to be two different things."

Aunt Shell appears in the doorway, eyebrows raised. "We have a visitor."

Arielle shoots to her feet. Maybe Detective Kane finally has some information. Something more than terrifying crime sprees across the city and dreams and voices in her head.

But the guy who steps from behind Aunt Shell isn't the detective.

"Colt," Gabby says in that breathless way she always uses for her boyfriend's name.

He flicks his rich auburn hair out of his dark brooding eyes, the harsh edges of his face softening as his gaze devours her. "Hey." He glances around the kitchen. "I thought I'd stop in and check if you needed anything."

Arielle sits heavily back on the chair. She doesn't answer, although one word flashes painfully through her.

Mom.

Gabby walks over to Colt, slipping her arms around his waist in the way she always seems to do when he's near. "The police have been useless so far."

"Gabby," her mother admonishes. "They're doing everything they can."

Arielle glances at the newspaper. *Are they?*

Colt presses a kiss to Gabby's blonde hair. "I'll ask around."

Gabby nods gratefully although Arielle isn't sure how that's going to help. Admittedly, reserved, quiet Colt is still a mystery to her. He appeared in Gabby's life several months ago and has been a fixture since. Knowing she doesn't have the headspace to figure it out, Arielle smiles her thanks.

Colt takes Gabby's hand. "Can we talk for a sec?"

Gabby glances at Arielle then her mother. "Sure.

Aunt Shell watches them leave, her lips pursed. But when she turns back to Arielle, her soft smile is back. She sets about clearing the table, removing the half-eaten bagels, unfinished cups of coffee, and the newspaper.

Arielle's hand shoots out to grab it back, but Aunt Shell is too quick. She tucks it under her arm. "Reading things like that is only going to worry you more," she says gently.

"Gabby seems to think that there's something I could do. Something I *should* be doing."

Aunt Shell shakes her head. "Gabrielle also believes that no matter what, everything will work out okay."

She's right. Gabby has a deep-seated belief that good will prevail. That dawn will always follow the night, no matter how dark it is.

"It's just that—"

Aunt Shell's face tightens with intensity. "Do you really think your mother would want you getting involved in...whatever this is? Or would she want to know you're safe? That you'll be here when she returns?"

The final question is like a slap. Arielle doesn't want to make this worse.

"What do I do, Aunt Shell?" she whispers. "What if..."

Arielle can't finish the sentence, but the words hiss through her mind, nonetheless. *What if it's too late?*

Her aunt places a comforting hand on her shoulder. "I had a look around earlier today. The attic could use a clean."

"You think I should clean the attic?" Arielle asks incredulously.

"I think you should keep busy. And this way, you'll have a nice surprise for your mother when she returns."

Arielle glances at the newspaper tucked under Aunt Shell's arm. "I suppose so..."

For some reason, her next smile is almost relieved. "I know so." She bustles over to the kitchen drawers and pulls out a few cloths. "Here, start with the dusting."

Arielle takes them, feeling torn. She has no idea what the best thing to do is, and the two people whose opinions she trusts are giving her very different advice.

Aunt Shell's eyes moisten. "A lot of your baby stuff is up there. It'll make you feel closer to her."

The promise that her mom won't feel so far away has Arielle moving. With a quick kiss on Aunt Shell's cheek, she rushes to the hallway. On the way, she passes Gabby and Colt in the living room. They're holding hands, their voices lowered and their faces intense.

Gabby pulls away as she sees Arielle rush past. She calls out from the doorway. "Hey, I'll be there in ten to help with the research, if you like."

Arielle waves a hand over her shoulder, not bothering to stop. "I'm off to tidy the attic."

"You're what?"

But Gabby's stomping footsteps don't follow her. Instead,

they sound like they're heading to the kitchen. Arielle turns into the laundry, deciding her cousin and aunt can sort out whatever weird difference of opinion they seem to have going on. The thought of some peace and quiet in the attic is suddenly very appealing.

Inside, Arielle flicks the switch and the attic fills with pale light. She's instantly assaulted by second thoughts. The air is musty and stale, and everything is covered in an aged layer of dead dirt. Boxes are stacked haphazardly in wonky rows, while sheets have been thrown over who-knows-what, creating strange, ghostly shapes.

Yes.

Arielle stills, but then rolls her eyes. "Glad you approve, Trinity."

Taking a step into the mote-riddled attic, she realizes why her childhood friend is back. Trinity returned because her mother's gone. And to be honest, Arielle's glad. Trinity is a comfort of sorts as her world falls apart. Just like the attic.

The cloths Aunt Shell gave her aren't going to cut it—Arielle needs a bulldozer for the amount of dust in here. But it doesn't matter. Arielle doesn't plan on cleaning. It's obvious no one has been up here for a very long time.

Arielle slips through the disorderly piles of boxes. Each one is carefully labeled—*Nichomancus.*

"The father of mathematics," Arielle murmurs.

Apostolic age.

"The onset of Christianity."

The Library of Alexandria.

"Destroyed 642 AD." Arielle brushes a finger over the label. "Mom never stopped mourning the loss of so much knowledge."

Tears prick along her eyelids. Each label ignites a memory of her mother talking too fast and scribbling even faster, Arielle listening in wonder as she tried to absorb it all. This attic is like her mother's mind—full of history, the reams of information carefully collated, yet stored with chaotic abandon. It's probably why Arielle feels closer to her here.

She ventures further in, tracing labels and peeking under sheets. She finds a cane bassinet, a metal trike, and a stack of board games. Her eyes light up as she recognizes a familiar timber square-shaped box.

Carefully, she slides it out from underneath Monopoly and Mousetrap. The game pieces rattle inside the drawer built into the base. Arielle's legs crumple and she plops cross legged onto the dusty floor, a bittersweet memory assailing her.

Her mother's face had been so animated when the parcel arrived. She'd opened it with such care. "It's a replica of one of the oldest board games ever discovered," her mom said excitedly. Her eyes had flashed with humor. "No one knows how to play it."

"Then how will we?" Arielle had asked, gazing at it. Little more than a flattened box with a grid of squares carved into the top, the mahogany had been buffed to a shine.

Her mother's dazzling smile had flashed. "We'll make our own rules."

And so they had.

The pieces had been tiny carved pigs and dogs and smooth oval eggs. Her mother had giggled as she placed the first one down in the top corner.

"Uncle Moses had a farm, ei-ei-oh."

A flush of happiness sweeps through Arielle, so poignant it hurts. "Mom," Arielle whispers brokenly.

As if on autopilot, she removes the pieces and places them around the board. The pigs in the top left, the dogs in the bottom right, one egg in the center. The aim of the game was to get four of your animals in a formation around it.

Arielle takes the pigs—they'd been both their favorites—and gently sits them around the egg in the middle. "North, south, east, west," she sings softly. "Ei-ei-oh."

Before the grief clogging her throat can erupt in a sob, there's a *click* and the central square drops away. Arielle gasps, leaning closer. "What the—"

There's another, louder *click* and a drawer pops open beneath the board. Except it's not the drawer that holds the pieces. It's on the other side.

Arielle holds still for long seconds, not sure what just happened. "A secret compartment?" she asks in amazement.

With a quick glance over her shoulder to confirm she's still alone, she pulls the drawer open the rest of the way. Her breath halts when she realizes there's something inside.

A small, leather-bound journal.

She lifts it out with trembling fingers.

Yes, Trinity whispers, but Arielle ignores her. She doesn't need her imaginary friend to tell her she just found something important. Something from her mother.

Something only she was meant to find.

Barely breathing, Arielle opens the journal. The air whooshes out of her lungs as she recognizes her mother's looped handwriting. Her awe dulls as she frowns.

The first page has a name. A name she's never heard her mother mention.

Joseph of Arimathea.

CHAPTER 9

REIGN

R eign's just reached the end of the alley when he has to stop himself from crashing into someone who just turned into it.

"There you are," Mac says in exasperation. "I've been looking for you everywhere."

Reign's about to respond when he notices Darnell and Rico standing behind her.

Darnell looks over Reign's shoulder. "Who were you talking to?"

A heavy feeling plunges through Reign's gut as he slowly spins to look down the alley, too.

The mist is gone.

The guy has disappeared.

The world is normal again.

Great. His descent into madness was witnessed.

"No one," he snaps.

Darnell raises a black eyebrow. "You most definitely were. We heard you."

Wanting to be as far away from the alley as possible, Reign

starts to walk away. "You need to get your hearing checked," he growls over his shoulder.

Mac quickly catches up, falling into step beside him. A quick sideways glance reveals she's frowning, but Reign pretends he doesn't notice. From behind him he hears Rico loudly whisper.

"Do you think it's happening again?"

Reign spins around and Rico finds himself pinned against the wall of the library, Reign's hand at his throat. He shoves his face close to Rico's wide-eyed gaze. "What's happening again?"

Rico grins. "Don't they say history likes to repeat itself?"

Fury flashes through Reign, burning away the images of what just happened in the alley. He welcomes it. In fact, he stokes the furious flames. His hand tightens around Rico's throat. "They also say there's a first time for everything."

He may never have hit Rico, but today seems a good day to right that wrong. But the threat only has Rico's pale eyes flaring in anticipation. It seems he's wanting this fight as much as Reign does.

Darnell moves in close, blocking the view to any bystanders. He clears his throat, his eyes darting nervously from side to side. "Darnell doesn't want any trouble, guys. And he's pretty sure you two don't either."

Because it was only yesterday that they were being chased by a cop in a stolen car...carrying three hot laptops.

Reign releases Rico. He glares at him, his hand still wanting to pin him to the wall. "Keep your mouth shut. You don't want this history to repeat itself," he warns, indicating toward the red marks on Rico's neck.

Rico shrugs as he straightens his shirt. "Looking forward to the fun and games."

Mac's cool hand slips over Reign's forearm as the need to pummel Rico flares again. "He's a douche, but not a next-level douche," she says quietly.

Reign huffs. They decided long ago that only asshat douches are worth the bruised knuckles.

Darnell's body unwinds. He shoves his hand in the pocket of his jacket and wiggles it around. "We just saw Candy," he sing-songs. "You coming back to the hideout?"

Despite that being the exact reason that he came here, Reign shakes his head. Looking for an escape is what had him running into that girl, reading up on his dream, and then punching a far too solid hallucination. "Maybe later."

Darnell's about to speak when Rico grabs his arm. "You heard the guy. He'll be by later." With a sideways glance at Reign, he tugs Rico away. "Maybe there will be some left."

Mac stands beside Reign as they watch them walk away. "To be honest, he was edging towards next level douche. Possibly super douche."

"Now you tell me," Reign mutters.

Mac shrugs. "Still not worth damaging your soft white hands."

Reign shoves her lightly. "A guy needs to harden them up somehow."

Mac rolls her eyes, jamming her shoulder into him in retaliation. "You have enough armor, my friend." Her face falls serious as she indicates to a nearby bench seat. "Although it doesn't fool me."

Uneasiness slides up Reign's spine and for a moment, he considers refusing the offer to sit down and chat. Mac must see his reticence because she juts a hip and raises an eyebrow. "I can outrun you."

Which is true. Mac is faster than anyone he's ever seen. With a resigned sigh, Reign walks over and flops down. He feels like a teen who's about to get the third degree.

Mac sits next to him, staring straight ahead as cars drive

past, unaware of her heavy gaze. "Who were you talking to in the alley?"

"I told Darnell. No—"

"Cut the crap, Reign. You were whiter than white." She glances at him then back out to the bustling street. "Like you'd seen a ghost."

"It wasn't Lance," he says quietly.

Although Rico and Darnell have heard the rumors about Lance, only Mac knows Reign's fear that he'll follow in his foster brother's footsteps. Reign keeps no secrets from her.

Apart from one.

Mac lets out a sigh. "That's something. He's a ghost you should've laid to rest a long time ago." She lifts a knee, picking at hole in her jeans, seeming to understand Reign couldn't cope with her perceptive gaze right now. "Then what? Or who?"

Reign leans forward, his head falling into his hands. "I think I'm losing it, Mac."

"What did you see?"

This is one of the reasons he loves Mackenzie. His best friend isn't interested in giving him platitudes or lip service. She's willing to meet him wherever he is.

No matter how dark it could be.

"I saw a whole bunch of smoke. Then a guy wearing robes appeared." Reign sighs. "Then he spoke to me."

There's a pause and Reign wonders if Mac's considering running and never looking back.

"And?" she coaxes. "What did he say?"

Of course Mac couldn't leave it at that. She has to know every weird-ass detail.

"He said his name is Joseph of Arimathea," Reign blurts. "He told me I'm some Grail Keeper."

Mac whistles softly. "Cool."

"It's really not." Reign turns her. That wasn't the response he was expecting. "You don't get to jump on the crazy train."

Mac shuffles closer, her eyes alight with something that doesn't make sense. She looks...excited. "Hear me out. About a year ago I was hanging around the university library—"

"Even back then? You hadn't even graduated."

She wrinkles her nose. "I was bored, okay?"

Reign snorts. "I'm pretty sure I'm not the one who needs an intervention here..."

"Don't knock it till you try it," she says playfully. "Anyway, I was reading up on Arthurian legend when I bumped into a woman in the medieval history section. She had a massive stack of books, so I helped her bring them back to her table." She turns to look more fully at Reign. "She invited me to join her."

Reign rolls his eyes. "And of course you said yes, so you could nerd out with some woman you'd only just met."

Mac shoves him with her shoulder. "Who wouldn't?" She sobers. "The books were on Joseph of Arimathea."

Reign freezes. "Bullshit."

"No bovine feces, I swear." Mac lifts her hands as if to prove her point. "This historian, the Professor, told me this Joseph guy was pretty darned interesting." Mac's eyes glaze and soften, as if reminiscing over a fond memory. "She was so passionate. I reckon she could've told me about this stuff for hours."

As much as Mac would never admit it, she would've loved that. Her brain is a sponge for information, and the tap of knowledge never seems to run fast enough.

"She said he was tasked with a great responsibility, and to do that he created some secret organization to help him with it," she continues. "The woman didn't really know what the task was, or who the organization was, which is why she was there."

"I'm not sure what freaky-assed link that brain of yours is

making right now, Mac, but I'm thinking you need to stop. Like you said yesterday, I need to cut back on the happy weed."

Right now, Reign's not sure he'll ever smoke it again.

But Mac is practically bouncing on the seat. "It makes total sense. This is why the woman was so sure. Because it's real!"

Reign shakes his head, wishing he'd never brought this up. He doesn't need anyone joining in his hallucinations. "Is this why we're friends? Because you've lost more marbles than I have?"

"I'm thinking our guy Joseph established these Keepers of the Grail he told you about." Mac grins. "He seems to think you're one of them."

Grail Keeper, it is an honor to meet you.

"No, I'm really not."

Mac ignores him. "And y'all need to keep the Holy Grail safe."

We must find the Grail at once.

"Don't care." Reign pushes to his feet. This conversation is over.

Mac joins him, eyes alight in a way that only makes him more uneasy. "And I know just where to go to find out."

CHAPTER 10

ARIELLE

"What the…"

Arielle leafs through the journal, stopping a few pages in when the dark lines of a drawing catches her eye. It's a face, but no human face. The eyes are sunken and shadowed, the mouth a black hole. The face is so tortured and angry, she's not sure what the thing wants more—to kill her or die.

If she didn't know better, she'd say her mother had drawn a demon.

"Except there's no such thing," she tells herself.

No wonder her mother had this book hidden. When they'd finished laughing, her academic colleagues would've sent her packing.

Returning to the front, Arielle focuses on the scrawled text. It seems the elders weren't happy that Joseph of Arimathea removed Jesus's body down from the cross and entombed him. In retaliation, they trapped him in a cave to die.

Except Joseph miraculously escaped. Arielle leans closer. He left Bethlehem for England, and went on to establish a secret organization.

"For what?" Arielle muses.

"I don't know," comes a voice behind her. "You tell me."

Arielle spins around, her hand flying to her chest. "Gabby! I didn't hear you come in."

Gabby smiles. "That's because you were reading that book like it was going to give you all the answers you're looking for."

Glancing down at the journal, Arielle sighs. "That would be nice."

Gabby navigates through the leaning towers of boxes. "When Mom told me she sent you up here to clean, I didn't actually think you were going to be up here so long."

"Neither did I." Arielle brushes her hand over the wooden board. "I found a game my mom and I used to play." She looks up at her cousin. "It turns out it had a secret compartment."

The surprise Arielle expected to see flash across Gabby's face disappears as quickly as it arrived. She points to the journal. "With that in it?"

The book lays closed again in Arielle's hands. "Yeah. It's Mom's, but from what I can tell, it's full of...folklore."

That has Gabby stilling. She sinks to her knees and sits beside Arielle. "That doesn't sound like Professor Sierra Reed," she says softly.

Arielle's hands tighten around the journal. "No, it really doesn't."

"What does it say?"

"All sorts of crazy stuff, Gabby." Arielle opens the journal to a random page, glad it's not the one with the drawing of the hellish face. Her finger follows the line of writing. "The obelisks are ancient columns of stone. They appear to be a key of some sort."

Gabby frowns. "A key to what?"

"I have no idea. None of this makes sense." Arielle scans the information again. "For each obelisk, there is a protector. Seven obelisks. Seven souls sworn to protect it."

Arielle flips the page and freezes.

There's another drawing, but this one is different to the first.

An obelisk rises from the soil, seven robed figures circling around it. Seven robed figures with wings.

Her cousin gasps. "Ari. Your dream."

Arielle is stunned into silence, unsure what to make of all this. Her gaze roams to the other side of the page, where the symbol of a seven-pointed star rests.

"What is going on?" she whispers.

Gabby is silent beside her, and Arielle assumes she's just as confused as she is. None of this is making any sense. Since when did her mother take notes on the supernatural?

And since when did Arielle dream about the very same thing?

She leafs through a few more pages, only to find they're blank. She frowns. "That's it. There's nothing more." She turns the book over, flicks to the end, then riffles through the pages again. "Nope. Nothing else."

But just as she says the words, something slips from a slit in the leather cover and falls to her lap. Lifting it up, Arielle finds it's a small metallic star. The same symbol as the one drawn in the journal. She holds it up and it glints dully in the dusty light. "What is it?"

Gabby leans closer. "I don't know, but I've seen that symbol before."

"You have? Where?" But as the words burst out, Arielle realizes she's not sure she wants the answers. If Gabby's seen the star, then that suggests some of this is real...

Gabby chews her lip, seeming to consider the answer. "A few months ago, on a school excursion," she says slowly. "We were on a tour of some old house. This symbol was etched onto the wall of the library."

Arielle blinks. "And what does it mean?"

"I asked the guide, but he told me to keep my hands to myself and took us into the next room. The house is a historic site of some sort that's been turned into a tourist attraction." Her face crinkles in frustration. "I should've paid more attention."

Arielle grips the star, the pointy tips digging into her palm. "You couldn't have known..."

How could any of them when this all feels so impossible?

Gabby is watching her closely. "What are you going to do, Ari?"

If Aunt Shell was answering that question, she'd tell Arielle to stay home. She'd probably point out all the parts of this puzzle that don't fit. Her mother never would've got involved in something as mystical or intangible as all of this. Her mother is firmly grounded in reality.

But... She glances at her boots. Hitsuzen. None of this was a coincidence.

"Mom wanted me to find this journal and this symbol." She looks at her. "In fact, no one else could've discovered it."

Only Arielle and her mother knew the rules of their made-up board game.

"She wanted me to find this." She pushes to her feet. "Which means she wants me to know what it means." She reaches down to help her cousin up, too. "I think we should visit this tourist attraction and check out the library again. See if we can get some answers."

Gabby blinks, then a dazzling smile spreads across her pretty face. "Great idea."

For the first time since her mother's disappearance, Arielle feels a sense of purpose. That she's not quite so lost. She leads the way out of the attic, and they climb back down the ladder. There's a soft thud as the ladder slots back into the ceiling.

"Girls, is that you?" Aunt Shell calls from the living room.

Before she can answer, Gabby grips Arielle's wrist. Arielle turns to find her cousin frowning. "Are you sure?

Yes.

Arielle's about to tell Gabby that even Trinity approves, but her cousin interrupts her.

"Maybe you should sleep on it?"

Now that Gabby seems to be having second thoughts, Arielle finds herself hesitating. Her mother wouldn't want her rushing into anything. But before Arielle can respond, the sound of the news reaches down the hall. Both girls' eyes widen, and they follow the sound of the male anchor.

Police continued to be baffled by the abductions of multiple women across Mercy City. These victims are our mothers, sisters—

The moment Aunt Shell sees them in the doorway, she presses the remote, and the TV blinks off. Pasting a bright smile on her face, she turns to them. "So, do you need more cloths?"

Arielle turns to Gabby, her face resolute. "I'm sure."

CHAPTER II
REIGN

Reign shakes his head emphatically. "No freaking way."
He turns to head back to the hangout, not surprised when Mac doesn't follow him.

She places her hands on her hips. "What else have you got to do today?"

"That's what I told myself yesterday when Darnell and Rico needed a getaway driver," Reign retorts.

"Don't you want an explanation for what's happening to you?"

Reign's hands fly out in exasperation. "I have an explanation!"

Mac pushes her face close to his, her brown eyes flashing. "One that doesn't involve you thinking you're a loser with a one-way ticket to self-destruction."

Reign scowls. "One of us has to be a realist, here."

"The day I was there, the Professor rushed off because she found that Joseph's descendants, and this organization of his, had a headquarters of some sort. It's an old mansion on the outskirts of town that's now been turned into a museum for tourists." Mac jabs her finger into his chest. "I think we should check it out."

"I don't get it, Mac. Since when did you believe in this sort of thing? I mean, we're talking about the stuff of legends here." Reign shoots his arms out to encompass their surroundings. "Our parents are either dead or loved drugs more than us. We're a paycheck for our foster carer. We steal to survive. We don't live in a world of miracles and happy endings."

Reign's almost panting by the end of his tirade. They face off for long seconds, both glaring in a silent battle of wills. Reign knows he's made a point when Mac's dark gaze falters.

For some reason, it doesn't feel like a win.

"You're right. Our trajectory has been mapped out by countless do-gooders." She juts out her chin. "So what have you got to lose?"

Reign blinks, then shakes his head ruefully. "Man, you should study law or something. You're relentless."

Mac shrugs, tucking a stray curl back up into her ponytail. "Why, thank you." She smiles. "I think we'll catch the bus for this trip."

SINCLAIR MANOR TOUTS itself as Mercy City's historical place to be. As Reign and Mac walk up the paved driveway, Reign takes in the manicured gardens. Perfect lawns. Symmetrical lines. Shrubs primped and pruned into perfect domes. Heck, it even has a fountain out the front with a marble angel in the center.

A little part of him wants to kick a few stones out of place.

"Don't even think about it," Mac mutters.

Reign opens his eyes wide. "What? I wasn't going to."

Mac snorts. "Sure you weren't."

They pause as they reach the front of the house. A sign out

the front is advertising a guided tour that starts in ten minutes. Reign's jaded eyes scan the large, stone mansion. A white porch frames the entrance, shading the planters overflowing with flowers scattered on the timber deck. White shutters frame each window, every slat dazzling and...perfect.

Reign crosses his arms. "We don't belong here, Mac."

"But we belong in a decaying house that nightmares could comfortably live in?"

Reign doesn't bother to answer. For him, the question is rhetorical.

A *No Access* sign catches his eye. To the left of the house is what looks like a large stone tower. The circular structure rises several feet above the house, almost reminiscent of a castle turret. Its stonework is darker and more aged.

"Now that's where I'd feel more comfortable," Reign says as he points.

"I'm pretty sure the *No Access* sign is what sold you on it." Mac rolls her eyes. "I wouldn't be surprised if 'rules were meant to be broken' were your first words."

Reign chuckles. "I prefer the word 'challenged.'"

They ascend the steps of the porch and a stand with leaflets greets them in the sweetly scented shade. Mac takes one and quickly scans the information.

Reign shakes his head. "I'm pretty sure your first words were 'take me to the library.'"

Mac throws him a dry glance before returning to the leaflet. "There are fourteen bedrooms. Five bathrooms. A library. A kitchen. A loft. And something called a parlor."

"Did this Professor give you any idea of what you're looking for?" Reign glances at his cell phone. "This place closes in an hour."

Mac chews her lip in thought. She glances at the sign they

passed when they entered and her face lights up. "We should do a tour."

"I most definitely do not want to do a tour." He takes a step back. "We came, we saw this was a bad idea, we left."

"We most certainly did not," Mac huffs. "We came, we proved I was right, *then* we left."

"You are going to be so disappointed," Reign warns.

He's bat shit crazy. It's as simple as that.

A young man with perfectly parted blond hair opens the front door, looking surprised to find them there. "Oh, I was just checking if there was anyone else for the tour."

Mac loops her arm through Reign's and hauls him close to her side. "My boyfriend and I can't wait!"

The man's gaze flicks to Reign then pauses. "Of course." He plasters a smile on his face and opens the door even wider. "Welcome."

Mac's arm tightens around Reign's. She noticed how false the guy's tone was.

And she knows it's already got Reign's back up.

She smiles sweetly. "Thank you." She tugs on his arm and for a second Reign considers connecting with his inner mule. The stubborn one.

"Come on," Mac coos. "There's no need to be shy." She turns to Reign, talking through her teeth. "Or scared."

Reign's spine stiffens. He strides through the door, taking Mac with him. "Bring on the tour."

The man throws them a stiff smile then walks ahead. Reign pauses when he finds himself in an opulent room—probably the parlor—with a group of about ten people standing in the center, their murmurs infused with awe and anticipation.

He shakes his head. "I can't believe I'm doing a tour."

Mac wrinkles her nose up at him as she squeezes his arm. "You can thank me later."

"Good afternoon, ladies and gentlemen," their guide says. "My name is Auden."

"Auden?" Reign mouths.

Mac frowns at him fiercely. "Zip it," she hisses.

"And I'll be your guide for this afternoon." Auden smiles far more genuinely than he did a few minutes ago. "Welcome to Sinclair Manor, one of the oldest mansions in American history."

Reign zones the pretentious guy out, already bored. He scans the room, noting the polished timber surfaces, the thick drapes, the sense of stepping back in time. How in the world did Mac convince him to come here?

Because he saw a man. Heck, he slammed his fist into his chest. And Mac would prefer to believe that something like the Grail Keepers exist rather than admit that Reign's brain is broken.

A part of him admires her for that. No one has cared enough to do that for him.

Despite that, Reign's here so Mac can face the truth. When they learn that the Professor was little more than a kook who showed a girl some attention and fed her love of knowledge, then the facts will be clear. Reign is headed for the nut house or the jail house.

Or dead, like Lance.

The guide's—Auden's—voice pulls Reign out of his dark thoughts. "The stone manor has survived nearly four centuries thanks to eight generations of Sinclairs. The last family owner, after dying heirless, gifted the estate to Mercy City Historical Society."

Reign leans in close to Mac. "I don't think 'heirless' is a word."

Her only response is to elbow him.

"Now, if there are no questions, we shall move onto the kitchen and scullery."

A hand shoots up into the air. "Is it true that the Hudson family were the original owners over those eight generations?"

"Yes," Auden responds warmly to the pretty blonde. He's either thinking of busting a move, or he's excited to have found a kindred spirit.

"Which suggests that Sinclair Manor was named after Henry Sinclair, a Scottish earl who is believed to have been part of an alleged voyage to this continent about a hundred years before Columbus?"

Auden's already straight spine looks as if a ruler just got jammed down it. "That theory has been vigorously disputed."

"It's just that the Templars are thought to have—"

"I'm afraid we only have time for a handful of questions," he says sharply. "You're welcome to discuss this after the tour."

The crowd parts as a few people shift uncomfortably. Reign likes this girl already. That is, until he sees who's standing next to her. Flame blue eyes connect with his and widen.

You've.

Got.

To.

Be.

Kidding.

CHAPTER 12
ARIELLE

Anger flashes through Arielle so fast it makes her fingers prickle and her toes tingle. She skirts around the group of people and makes her way to *him*.

"Ari?" Gabby asks in confusion as she quickly follows her.

Arielle watches the scowl deepen on the face—the one she was hoping wasn't as compelling as she remembered—with each step she takes.

She plants herself in front of him. "Are you stalking me?"

"Yeah," he drawls sarcastically. "I love interacting with angry chicks who don't listen."

Arielle gasps, unable to remember when she felt so furious. She's vaguely conscious of the group moving to the next room, but she remains where she is. "Well, this isn't a coincidence."

She'd point out the word on her boots, but it'll only make her angrier. It's because of him that they're stained.

Gabby moves in close. "Was this guy giving you a hard time?"

A caramel-skinned girl slips in between them, crossing her arms as she places herself in front of the guy. "Ah, I'd like to point out it's your friend who stormed over here, throwing around accusations."

Arielle's cheek flush. "He almost ran me over yesterday. I suspect in a stolen car."

The girl's brows hike up to her hairline. She glances over her shoulder. "Is that true, Reign?"

Reign. Arielle finally knows his name!

Reign.

Trinity seems to roll the word through Arielle's mind, but she ignores her. Now isn't the time to tell her to zip it.

Reign steps around his friend, throwing an amused glance at her. He doesn't strike Arielle as someone who needs protecting.

He looks at Arielle, his gaze hooded. "If I say yes, am I on trial?"

"You should be!" Arielle shoots back.

A throat clears behind them and they turn to find Auden looking at them expectantly. This time, it's embarrassment that flushes Arielle's cheeks.

She smiles sweetly at him. "Sorry. We were just so fascinated by the antique mantelpiece."

Auden waves an arm for them to follow and Arielle quickly does so, Gabby at her side. They need to get to the library, preferably without annoying the snooty guide.

But the moment she sees that Reign and his friend are right behind them, she stiffens. They enter a kitchen area and she waits until Auden starts talking again before turning to him.

"You need to leave."

He arches a brow. "Because you were here first?"

"Because I don't need you to ruin two days in a row," she hisses back.

His friend steps in again, this time frowning. "We have a

right to be here, just like you do." She crosses her arms. "We're not here just to research some history assignment."

Reign places a hand on her shoulder. "Mac, I'll let you know when I need a defense lawyer." He looks to Arielle. "Which may be sooner than I thought."

Arielle narrows her eyes at him, but before she can say anything, Gabby speaks up.

"Then what *are* you here for?"

Arielle startles at the question. She barely registered what Reign's friend, Mac, had said.

Mac crosses her arms and angles her head, the ponytail of curly hair perched high on her head tilting with her. "We think this house is linked to Joseph of Arimathea and a secret organization he established. It's possible their headquarters were here."

Reign groans as he wipes a hand down his face. "Of course, that's what you'd tell them..."

Arielle's mouth pops open. "You what?"

Mac looks at her in triumph. "Put that in your essay."

Gabby is the first to recover. "Except that's exactly why we're here."

"Because of Joseph of Arimathea?" Mac asks incredulously.

They all stare at each other in shocked silence. This is about as far from a coincidence as you can get...

Reign moves first, stepping back and shaking his head. "You know what? I think you're right, Arielle. We should leave—"

"We should work together," Mac blurts.

Arielle is already shaking her head before Mac's finished. In fact, she's shaking it so vehemently, strands of her hair flick her cheeks. "Worst idea—"

"Great idea," Gabby responds cheerfully.

Auden frowns in their direction. "Quiet, please."

Arielle notices that Mac's hand shoots out to grab Reign's

and for the first time she wonders what the nature of their relationship is. She's certainly very protective of him. The frown she didn't realize was stamped on her face deepens. And they're standing very close together.

And now they're holding hands...

Auden seems happy with their lack of response, because he turns back to the group, a dazzling smile on his face. "The dining room is next."

He leads them down a short hallway before Arielle finds they're in a large room furnished with dining table and chairs polished to a glossy shine. Large paintings hang on the wall in gilt frames, and the smell of beeswax hangs in the air.

"The historical society has set the table according to our thorough research," Auden says animatedly. "The crockery is that of the original family."

Arielle tunes him out, noting that Reign and Mac are to their left. And they're no longer holding hands. Annoyed that she noticed that, she's about to look away when Reign glances up.

Their gazes connect and just like the first time they met, the world dissolves away. Arielle's breath evaporates as she feels herself being drawn into the jungle green of his mesmerizing eyes. It's like they're familiar. Yet startlingly new. A contradiction that calms and exhilarates her all at the same time.

Go to him.

Trinity's voice snaps Arielle out of whatever whirlpool she was being sucked into. "Not happening," she mutters.

Gabby glances at her. "What's not happening?"

"I don't think we should work with them," she whispers back as Auden glances at them, continuing his monologue.

"Why not?"

"I don't trust them."

Nor does she trust herself around Reign. He brings out an irrational part of her she hadn't known existed.

"We don't have a choice."

"Why?"

"Something's going on, Ari. I know you can sense it. You need to get to the bottom of it." She glances over to the girl, Mac. "And she knew about Joseph and the Keepers of the Grail."

"The Keepers of the Grail," Arielle repeats softly, staring at the timber floor as she tries to figure out why something doesn't quite fit. Her gaze shoots to Gabby's. "You knew about them."

Although the term was a shock to Arielle, Gabby is talking as if it's familiar.

"You knew the name of the secret organization, didn't you?"

Gabby winces then nods.

Auden claps his hands. "And now, folks. For the library," he announces with a flourish.

He leads the way out a door on the other side of the room and the group dutifully follows. Arielle watches as Reign and Mac do the same. Reign glances at her as they walk past, his brooding face shuttered.

He pauses when he sees she's not moving. "Second thoughts?"

She flashes him an irate gaze. "How sure are you of what we're doing here?"

He blinks, looking a little taken aback. He shrugs. "I'm never really sure of anything, to be honest."

Gabby rests her hand on Arielle's arm. "Shall we keep going?"

The layers in her cousin's question are unmistakable.

She knows Arielle is realizing this is far more complicated than she thought. That it's bigger than she expected. That there are secrets in places she thought there were none.

And Gabby's asking Arielle whether she wants to continue peeling back those layers.

Reign arches a brow, almost challenging her. "Or you could go home and try to get your boots clean."

It would be like none of this ever happened.

Except her mom is missing. Kidnapped. And there's a small metallic symbol burning a hole in Arielle's pocket.

And for some reason, she isn't willing to let Reign see the fact that fear is creeping in alongside the doubt.

She lifts her chin. "I'm not the one who got them dirty."

She stalks past him, and Gabby follows her. Through the doorway, Arielle finds herself in a large circular room almost exclusively lined with mahogany. Mahogany and books.

For a moment, Arielle forgets everything else. This is a room her mother would love. Shelves upon shelves stack high up to the ceiling, each one lined with books and more books. Some are leather bound and embossed, the more modern ones almost looking cheap and lame next to them. Many are thick and heavy, while others' spines are barely noticeable pressed between their more weighty neighbors.

Every book is printed with stories. Information. History. Arielle's mother would've lost a lot of sleep exploring those pages.

"This is where I saw it," Gabby says quietly.

And just like that, the moment is lost. Arielle turns to her cousin, noting the way her hazel eyes have sparked with anticipation.

Gabby knew about the Keepers of the Grail. And she didn't tell her.

Arielle looks away.

What else hasn't her cousin been telling her?

CHAPTER 13
REIGN

Something has unsettled Arielle.

Reign wishes he hadn't noticed it, but he has. And he's pretty sure it's not just his stalkerish presence that's got her off balance.

As everyone—including Mac—disperses through the room, eyes wide as they cautiously run their fingers over spines and shelves, Arielle seems to barely notice her surroundings. As people murmur words of awe and admiration, she's silent.

Even Reign's willing to admit the library is cool. The round walls make it feel cozy, kind of comforting. And he suspects even someone like him could find something to read in here. There are certainly enough books.

But Arielle isn't acting like it's cool. In fact, she looks agitated. As if all the parts of her puzzle don't fit like they used to. And yet her cousin is combing the shelves, looking like she's determinedly searching for a particular book.

Reign drags his gaze away, wondering why he's even still thinking about this. She's probably got a stain on her jeans or something. The denim that hugs those hips—

Frowning, Reign tries to focus on something else. He just

needs to stay here long enough for Mac to realize they're on a wild ghost chase. But before he can stop himself, his eyes are drawn back to Arielle. Not only that, there's a strong urge to go to her.

But as his gaze finds hers, his muscles lock and his breath freezes.

There's someone beside Arielle.

Joseph of freaking Arimathea.

Auden clears his throat from his location beside a velvet covered recliner. "The tower is the oldest part of Sinclair Manor. Some believe it was already standing when the original family settled." He smiles with so much pride, it's like he built the place himself. "The idea to turn the space into a library was conceived quite early on. The family was passionate about documenting history."

For once, Reign puts all his focus on their tour guide, acting like every word is fascinating. Anything is preferable to the imaginary man who's making his way over to him.

Joseph comes to stand beside him. "Who is the possessor of such wealth?" He does a slow spin. "I have never seen so many books in one location."

Reign ignores him.

"Although the stonework was covered over when the library was installed, the seven beams that hold up the roof were maintained," Auden continues. "Those of us in the Mercy City Historical Society like to joke that the family had one section for each day of the week." Giggling, Auden points at one beam. "Sunday." Then the next. "Monday."

Someone in the group titters, which just encourages Auden. He turns, looking like a sprinkler with his arm extended, ready to point at the next section.

"This man is a jester?" Joseph asks.

"I'm not talking to you," Reign hisses.

An elderly lady beside him startles. Clutching her purse, she quickly moves away.

Great. Now he's scaring little old ladies.

"We must talk, Grail Keeper. Countless lives depend on it."

Reign's hands ball into fists. He's about to educate Joseph with another bunch of words he's probably never heard before when he notices Gabby moving within hearing distance. Grinding his teeth so hard it hurts, he tries to hold onto his sanity.

Mac sidles close to him. "He's here, isn't he?"

Reign isn't surprised that she's read him so well. "Yup," he states flatly.

"Cool," Mac says, looking around as if she'll be able to see him. "It's probably because we're getting close."

"Yeah, sure," Reign scoffs. "My hallucination is appearing because we're getting close to the headquarters of your imaginary secret organization."

Mac slips her arm through his. "Oh ye of little faith."

Reign looks up to find Arielle watching them, a small frown scrunched between her brows. Although he's not sure what he's done now, Reign decides this expression is preferable to the worried one he saw earlier.

He sighs, wanting this over and done with as quickly as possible. "What exactly are we looking for?"

"I have no idea," Mac says cheerfully. "Why don't you ask Joseph?"

"No," Reign states flatly.

"You'll want to find the septagram," Joseph offers, still looking around in amazement. "That will show you where you need to go."

"I don't even know what a septagram is," Reign mutters.

Mac straightens. "A septagram? A seven-pointed star?"

Suddenly, Gabby indicates to Arielle to join her with quick

sharp movements. She glances at Reign and Mac, asking them to do the same.

"Oh, Gabby's found something," Mac says with glee as she drags him over.

Gabby's standing beside one of the thick beams that spears up to the roof. "This is it," she whispers. "This is what I saw."

She points to a small carving tucked on the side, about a foot off the ground. Mac instantly squats down. "Is it a seven-pointed star?" She frowns. "Oh, it's a...tower with a wing on top."

Gabby's frowning, too. "I could've sworn it was a drawing of a tower with a cup on top the last time I was here."

"Like the Grail," Arielle adds, the words a statement rather than a question.

"Yeah, like the Grail," Gabby says heavily.

Mac runs her finger over the carving. "What does the wing mean, then?"

There's silence as no one answers. Reign almost shakes his head. Because no one knows the answer.

"Maybe the bored kid who scratched these in put one on every beam just to mess with you all," he offers.

Except, the moment he says it, three sets of female eyes light up.

"Yes!" Mac hisses with excitement. "We need to check the other beams!"

Reign is left standing, pretending Joseph isn't still hovering not far away, as the three girls disperse to the other beams spread around the circular walls. Mac notices him standing there and waves her hands at him, telling him to check the next one along.

Sighing, he wanders to the one, passing a door that's been cordoned off. He's just about to have a look at the base—hoping he'll find someone's initials—when Auden rushes to his side.

"Oh, you can't go in there," he says, hand fluttering toward the door. "It's off limits."

"Sorry," Reign says dryly. "I was looking for the comic section."

Auden lifts his nose an inch. "That's the staff bathroom. It's off limits," he repeats, probably in case Reign is deaf as well as stupid.

Reign pretends to be surprised. "Huh. I wondered what this pretty rope was for."

"The public restrooms are at the entry if you need them," says Auden.

Reign drops to his knee, pretending to tie his shoelace. "I'd better make sure I get there safely, then."

As he messes with the tight knot that he hasn't undone in the life of his sneakers, Reign glances right. He grits his teeth as he sees another tower engraved into the foot of the beam.

And this one has a cup above it.

Auden hovers as he waits, like some Keeper of the Staff Toilets. Reign straightens and walks away, returning to the spot he should never have left.

Mac is already there, and she places a hand on his arm. "Ignore him. He's not even douche status, that's how little attention you should pay him."

Reign doesn't say anything. This is why people like him don't come to places like this. He knows he doesn't belong here. And so does Auden.

Arielle and Gabby return, looking like they have news.

"Mine were two crossed scythes," Mac offers.

Gabby frowns. "Mine was some weird backward 'r' with two dots under it."

"The others were another wing, a cross and a horse," Arielle adds.

They all turn to Reign. "I found the cup," he offers. He refuses to call it the Grail.

"Of course you did, Grail Keeper. It is your legacy."

It's only Reign's years of living in foster care—where being on alert meant never being caught out unawares—that stop him from reacting to Joseph's words. In fact, he stares straight through Joseph as if he isn't there.

Arielle chews on her lip. "That's seven symbols. And they're all different."

"With no way of knowing how they're linked," Reign points out.

Gabby frowns at him. "Not yet, anyway."

Mac grins, elbowing Reign. "I like her."

"That's because she's enabling you," he says under his breath.

Arielle narrows her gaze at him. "You don't believe there's anything to find, do you?"

Something in Reign rises to the challenge in her blue eyes. "Do I think a secret organization exists to babysit the nonexistent Holy Grail? No, I don't. I think you guys all got hit by the same crazy stick."

"Then why are you here?" Arielle asks.

Reign frowns. Of all the questions to ask. He raises his chin, defaulting to his standard defense mechanism—sarcasm. "So I could learn what a septagram is, why else?"

Arielle blinks. "A seven-pointed star." She glances around, eyes widening. "Seven beams. Seven carvings."

"It's here," Gabby breathes.

Reign shakes his head. "Ah, that's not what I meant."

But even Mac is glancing around, now. She looks at each of the beams. "Seven-pointed star..." She turns to Reign and the others. "It's got to be in the center. The place where all the points meet."

The sound of three sharp claps has them all turning to Auden. "The next stop in our tour is the first floor. The antique wardrobes in the bedrooms are something you don't want to miss."

"We need more time," Gabby hisses. "What are we going to do?"

Mac grins at Reign. "It's time for some Mexican food."

"No." Reign vehemently shakes his head. "As in hell no. I never signed up for that."

But Mac's already clutching her stomach as she doubles over. "Sweet lord, why did you let me eat the burrito?" she wails.

For a moment, Reign considers refusing to respond. But Arielle's lips twitch as she realizes what they're up to. And the next thing he knows, his hands are on his hips. "I told you not to, Mackenzie! More than once!" he raises his voice a notch with each word.

"But they're so good," Mac wails.

Reign shoves panicked hands into his hair. "This is exactly what happened last time!"

"Well, you didn't stop me, did you?" Mac grips her stomach, her face twisting. "Worst boyfriend ever!"

Auden rushes over, waving his hands as if that's going to waft away all the noise. "Quiet, please. This is a historical building."

"She needs a bathroom," Reign tells him. "Stat."

Looking a little panicked, Auden pulls back the tasseled cord across the exit. "Quick. She can use this one."

Letting out a howl for good measure, Mac rushes through the door.

Arielle moves in closer, looking at Auden somberly. "I'd take the others to the next part of the tour," she says quietly. "I suspect no one needs to hear what's about to happen."

Auden nods frantically, his perfectly parted hair never falling out of place. "Of course."

"We'll catch up as soon as she's...done," Reign assures him, wondering if he should make a sign of the cross just for good measure.

But Auden rushes away, quickly rounding up his flock and exiting the library. For several long seconds, silence heralds their victory. They have the library to themselves.

Mac appears in the doorway. "That worked faster than I'd expected."

Reign grins. "I think we set a new record this time around."

He turns to Arielle and Gabby, expecting to see the smile that was thinking of blooming on Arielle's face to have grown a little. Gabby high-fives Mac as she climbs over the rope, but Arielle is frowning. A lot.

All business, she strides to the center of the room. "Let's get this over and done with."

Mac and Gabby join her, leaving Reign to wonder if everything he does pisses this girl off. And to think that he just made a scene so she could keep going with her stupid search.

He's more of an idiot than he realized.

"What is this burrito?" Joseph asks as he appears beside him. "A poison of some sort?"

"Shut up, Joseph," Reign growls under his breath.

Mac and Gabby pull back the round rug that covers the center of the room. The stones beneath are steadily exposed, smooth and polished after generations of feet scuffing over them.

They all fall silent as the stones become smaller, forming a circular pattern. The rug is pulled back the last inch and the center is revealed. The female gasps echo around the room.

Reign's brows slam down. Surely that's not what it looks like...

In the middle of the library is a single rock. With a seven-pointed star carved into it.

Gabby claps in jubilation. Mac throws Reign an I-told-you-so look.

Arielle hasn't moved. For some reason, Reign feels a tug to join her, but he keeps his feet rooted to the spot. Joseph just appeared beside the three of them.

Arielle snaps out of her reverie, slipping her hand into her pocket. She pulls something out, light glinting off its metal surface.

"You brought it," Gabby says, her eyes widening.

It's another star with seven points.

"Cool," Mac says with awe. "You have your own septagram?"

"My mother left it for me," Arielle says quietly.

Reign notes her use of past tense. Has Arielle lost her mother? He jams his hands in his pockets, telling himself it's none of his business. If he asks, she'll probably bite his head off.

Arielle kneels, her beautiful face focused and intense as she hovers the pentagram over the carving in the center stone. Even from a distance, Reign can see that it matches perfectly. She lowers it and it slips into place.

Reign takes a step forward only to forcibly stop himself. He waits long seconds for something to happen, his breath held along with the others.

But there's no sound. No movement. No apocalyptic shuddering as the walls cave down around them.

He consciously unwinds his muscles, letting out his pent-up breath. "Well, this was fun—"

A soft *click* echoes through the library. It stops Reign as if he was just shot with a freeze gun. The rock shudders, the dust in the cracks around it disappearing like sand through an hourglass.

And then Reign's moving, leaping across the room and yanking Arielle back. She's hauled to her feet beside him, but she doesn't shake off his arm as her gaze never leaves the unbelievable sight unfolding only a few feet before them.

There's a soft grinding noise and the rock with the septagram dips and slides away. It was a door. A door that's now open, revealing a set of stone steps descending into darkness.

Suddenly, Joseph is hovering beside it. "This could be it! The Grail could be here!" His excited gaze pins Reign. "Your destiny awaits, Grail Keeper."

Reign spins around to face her. "Please, you can't go down there."

The note of vulnerability in his voice tugs at Arielle. She frowns. Surely, she's not so easily suckered in by a gorgeous face? Although he's different with Mac, Reign has mostly been rude and obnoxious to Arielle, and here she is looking for any opportunity to see the good in him! What is wrong with her?

Except Mac doesn't soften. Instead, she raises a brow. "This is the only way to get answers, and you know it."

"I already have answers," he snaps back.

"No, you don't. You have a theory. One I intend on proving wrong." She looks to Arielle. "Did you want to go first?"

Arielle glances from Reign to Mac, struck again at how intuitively these two seem to know each other. No wonder they're dating. "Sure," she says with far more confidence than she's feeling.

But Gabby is already at the top of the stairs that have been revealed. "Actually, I'm going first." She winks, trying to lighten the mood. "If there's a boogeyman, I'll take care of it."

There's no time to ask why Gabby would think she could deal with a boogeyman better than Arielle, because she begins to descend the stairs, the torch on her cell phone already lighting her way. With a quick glance at frowning Reign and smiling Mac, Arielle withdraws her torch from her backpack, and follows her. Mac comes next, blowing Reign a kiss.

"Dammit!" Arielle hears Reign behind them. "There's no way I can let you go down there on your own."

There's a muffled giggle from Mac, and Arielle wonders if she knew this is exactly what Reign would do. She tells herself she's fine with their close relationship. That the twinge in her chest is simply because a little part of her hopes she finds someone who is so in sync with her.

They all fall silent as darkness tries to envelop them, their torches slicing through the black. The stairs curve, the thick stone around them muffling the sounds of their footsteps. The air steadily cools, smelling musty and damp.

Arielle's pulse feels louder and louder the further they descend. Reign was right—they have no idea what they're walking into. What if this place is booby trapped? Her pulse leaps. What if this place has spiders?

"There had better not be spiders," she mutters.

"There are most definitely spiders," Reign calls from behind her. "Ones so fat they probably have cellulite and their bellies drag on the ground."

"Their abdomen," Mac corrects. "And I doubt you could see the cellulite under their exoskeleton."

"Ignore them," Gabby tells Arielle. "I'll protect you, no matter how overweight the spiders are."

Arielle runs her hand over the cool wall to her right, reminding herself she's not in a dream. She gets why Reign is being so flippant—he doesn't believe any of this is more than meets the eye. And Mac seems like the type of girl who's seen too much to be easily rattled.

But she's grown up with Gabby. How is she taking this in her stride so well? Even if she knew about Joseph and the Keepers of the Grail, how can she just forge into the bowels beneath the manor like this?

Suddenly, Gabby stops and Arielle almost crashes into her.

"We're here," her cousin says quietly.

Arielle steps around her, her feet resting on an expanse of stone floor. She senses Mac and Reign come to stand beside them. She can hear harsh breathing and she realizes it's hers. A part of her wants to run straight back up the stairs and pretend none of this ever happened. A part of her knows she's exactly where she's supposed to be, right in this moment.

Fate has brought her here. Destiny is being forged. It's both terrifying and exhilarating.

She lifts her torch and points it into the room and the others do the same. Four beams of light move around the space, traversing and transecting as they scope whatever it is they've discovered.

The room is circular, like the one above, with seven thick beams around the perimeter. Shelves line the walls, less numerous than the library, and gray with age. They appear to hold books and shadowy shapes, possibly artifacts of some sort. The center of the room is an empty stone expanse.

"Look." Arielle points the beam of her cell torch onto the floor. The stones are arranged in a septagram, each tip of the star pointing toward a beam.

"I'm sensing a theme," Mac jokes. She shines her own light around, trying to take it all in. "Man, this place is old."

She's right. The air is heavy with age, the stones feel ancient. Time rests patiently in this place, calm and undisturbed.

"Let's have a look around," Gabby suggests. "See what we can find."

She steps right while Mac goes left. They both walk with purpose, like women at Walmart who know what they want, just not which aisle it's located in. Reign remains by the entrance, his beam of light far more focused on the three of them than what's on the shelves.

Arielle moves slowly around the circular space. The leather-bound tomes dotting the shelves feel like they're old enough to have the answers to the meaning of life. There are vases, statues carved out of stone, a large sword in a scabbard. Arielle's mind struggles to process it all. To grasp what any of this means.

What does this have to do with her mother's disappearance?

"Should we even touch any of this stuff?" Mac asks in awe.

Reign snorts. "How else are we going to hock it to a museum?"

Gabby points her beam of light at his eyes, making him squint and raise his arm. "That's not remotely funny. There's stuff in here humans wouldn't even know exists."

Arielle's about to ask her cousin how she could possibly know that when she passes one of the beams. She stops and retraces a step. Surely it couldn't be...

Just like the ones upstairs, these beams have also been carved. But not with a small symbol. Large, sweeping lines soar up the stone, reaching a point. Strange lines, like rune symbols, run down the length.

Arielle brushes her hand over it. "An obelisk."

Gabby's by her side in an instant. "Did you say an obelisk?"

Her pulse suddenly thrumming, Arielle rushes to each beam. Every one of them has an obelisk carved into it. "Just like the ones in my dream."

"You've dreamed about these?" Mac asks. "How is that possible?"

"I don't know." Arielle frowns. "I don't understand what any of this means," she murmurs, talking to herself more than anyone else.

"I do. Obelisks are keys," Gabby says solemnly. "Keys to the Gates of Hell."

Mac appears beside her. "Did you just say the Gates of Hell?"

Gabby nods. "Open a Gate of Hell and demons will be released onto Earth."

There's a snort from beside the entry. "There are no such thing as demons," Reign scoffs.

"Demons," Arielle whispers, pressing her fingertips to her

temple. "Gates of Hell." She takes a faltering step backward. "It's all too much. All I want to do is find my mom."

"Unless this is what got Sierra kidnapped."

Gabby's words punch through Arielle, her breath drawing in sharply. "What? Why would you say that?"

Her cousin seems to hesitate, but then she squares her shoulders. "Last year, I came back from boarding school a day early. I went to your house to surprise you, but you weren't home. But Sierra was."

Arielle remembers that day. It had been a wonderful surprise. But the flush of happiness she'd felt in that moment doesn't wash through her. There's a note in Gabby's voice that has Arielle tensing. Her words sound like a...confession.

"She quickly shuffled away some papers she'd been reading." Gabby's gaze slips away. "So, of course, when she went to get us something to eat while we waited for you, I peeked. The pages had notes all over them." She looks back at Arielle, her hazel eyes heavy with truth. "She was researching demons. There was even stuff on the first humans."

"No." Arielle shakes her head. "Mom is a history lecturer. She never mentioned any of this."

"Your mom isn't just a historian, she's an occultist, Arielle." Gabby's arm sweeps around the room. "She believed in all of this."

"Demons? The first humans, as in Cain and Abel, Adam and Eve?" Reign asks incredulously. "This is the lamest conspiracy theory I've ever heard," he says angrily. "Shadowy organizations, gates to the underworld, is the Devil going to make an appearance soon?"

"You need to have an open mind," Mac tells him. "Too much weird stuff has been happening, and you know it."

"So far, all you people have are half-baked theories, a bunch of assumptions, and stuff written down by people who believe in magic. You're joining dots that belong in different zipcodes." Reign leans forward, anger seeming to vibrate through him. "You. Have. No. Hard. Proof."

"Zip it, Reign," Gabby snaps. She glances at Arielle. "I can see why he gets on your nerves so much."

Before Arielle can answer, Gabby takes two steps backward. "I know this is all true," she says with conviction. "Because of this."

There's a strange sound of rustling, and in the space of a blink, massive white wings unfurl behind her. Gabby draws a deep breath in, and the wings move with her, impossibly expanding some more as she exhales.

Stunned silence slams through the secret room. Arielle blinks. Everything feels like it just contracted. The space around her. The air. All the things she was sure of in this world.

Because before her are two magnificent wings, and they belong to her cousin. Each feather glistens in the pale beams of the torches, as if it's been dipped in ivory. Luminous, they seem to generate their own light, casting a soft glow around Gabby. Despite the surreal moment, they're undeniably, inexplicably real.

"You know what?" Reign says in disgust. "I'm outta here."

He's gone before anyone can object, Mac rushing after him. "Reign! Wait!"

Arielle is left, alone, with Gabby. Her cousin who just revealed herself to be an angel.

"I..." Arielle starts, only to realize her mind is blank. "I don't know what to say."

"Ta da," Gabby says in a meek, quiet voice.

"You're...an angel."

Arielle isn't sure whether it's a question or a statement. She's not sure whether she's even awake right now.

"I wanted to tell you, Ari. I almost did, so many times."

"How many, Gabby?" Arielle takes a step back, reality hitting her like a tidal wave. "How many lies has our relationship been based on?"

Not giving her cousin a chance to respond, Arielle takes a step back. "I need a moment."

She races up the stairs.

How can she ever trust her again?

CHAPTER 15
REIGN

R eign has just yanked the door to the library open, desperate to get away from this mansion as quickly as possible, when he almost slams into Auden.

Auden rears back, panic spearing across his face. "Did she not make it in time? Is there a mess?" The panic flares. "Has she collapsed?"

"No," Reign snaps, only to modulate his voice. He quickly draws the door shut, conscious the opening to the downstairs chambers of holy-hell-what-did-I-just-see is still open.

"She's...ah, not feeling much better. We're leaving."

Auden slumps with relief. "I think that would be best." He points to a door at the other end of the corridor. "That will take you straight back to the entrance."

Reign nods. "We can make our way out."

Auden smiles at him for the first time since Reign arrived, ironically when he told the tour guide he's leaving. Not that Reign cares. He just saw an—he stops his train of thought. He's pretty sure he never wants to think again.

Auden rushes off again, no doubt off to continue his tour.

Assuming things are normal. Clueless as to what this mansion has been sitting above all these centuries.

Reign almost envies him.

He's about to step away when the door behind him opens. Mac stands there, her caramel skin pale. "What the fu—"

"Outside," says Reign.

She nods, realizing this is a conversation that can't be overheard, and they silently make their way out. Just like Auden said it would, the door leads them to the porch. Reign can't get out of the mansion quick enough.

Once he's down the steps of the porch, he turns right, figuring the gardens will afford them some privacy. Except, he's only made it a few yards when he spins around to face Mac.

"It wasn't just me, was it?" Reign asks in a harsh whisper. "You saw the wings, too, didn't you?"

Even as he asks the question, he isn't sure what he wants the answer to be. If it's a no, then he's more batshit crazy than he thought. He'll need to walk straight out of here and into a straight jacket.

But if it's a yes...

"Yeah. I saw those whopping feathered appendages, too." She sighs. "Gabby's an angel."

There's a low brick wall bordering a garden bed beside him, and Reign sits heavily on it. They need to stay close to the entrance, anyway, for when Arielle exits. And Gabby.

Suddenly, Reign's glad he's sitting down. His legs feel like they just turned into jello. He realizes he hasn't seen Joseph since they went down there. The hallucination had done a recon of the room, slumped his shoulders and disappeared. Reign's relieved. Maybe now that his brain has enough to process with the whole angel thing, it's decided to give him a break. There's only so many times a person can visit wackyville in a lifetime.

Mac flops down next to him. "I didn't see anything that looks like a cup."

"Because there's no such thing as the Holy Grail," Reign snaps.

"I'm pretty sure you would've said that about angels until about ten minutes ago," Mac points out. "You're going to have to face facts."

But Reign is already shaking his head. "Gabby can go be an angel, if she wants." He kicks at a stone. "But I ain't no Grail Keeper."

Mac sighs in frustration. "So you can believe Gabby is one of God's angels, but not that you're a descendant of those entrusted to keep the Holy Grail safe?"

Reign doesn't bother to explain. Some things are in the realms of shit that could happen. Others are just...impossible.

Mac shoots to her feet, pacing. "You can be so stubborn!"

Reign doesn't answer. In part, because it's true. But mostly because Joseph just appeared again.

He stands before Reign, imploring him as he extends his arms. "It is time you listened, Grail Keeper. Angels exist, just as demons do. You must understand what is at stake here."

"Not. Now," Reign grinds out, pressing the heels of his hands into his eyes. "Just leave me alone, Joseph."

"The big J is here?" Mac asks, her voice alive with curiosity. "What's he saying?"

"That you have a great ass."

"I said no such thing," Joseph says, affronted. "This girl has no mule."

Reign squeezes his eyes closed, pressing his hands in even harder. Is this what happened to Lance? Does he fight this, or just accept the inevitable?

"There you are," Arielle says with relief.

Reign jumps to his feet. "We needed some air."

"Tell me about it." She rubs her forehead, looking as strained as Reign feels. "That was intense."

"Yeah, talk about a paradigm shift," says Mac. She eyes Arielle. "You gonna sprout wings, too?"

Arielle shakes her head. "I'm just like you guys. Human."

Mac shrugs one shoulder. "Mildly disappointing, to be honest."

Reign is struck by the way Arielle's flame blue eyes seem to swallow her face. She looks fragile. Lost.

"Your mom is missing?" he asks quietly, conscious that he made some assumptions about her that haven't held up.

She nods. "She was kidnapped. Yesterday."

Reign hides his wince. On the day he almost hit her trying to get away from the cops.

"She's part of the serial abductions?" Mac asks quietly. "That's awful."

Arielle's eyes shine with unshed tears. "I'm an only child. She raised me on her own. All I want to do is find her." She frowns. "And now Gabby's been lying to me our whole lives."

"You two seem pretty close," says Mac. "My guess is she wouldn't have done that without a good reason."

Arielle looks away. "That's not what matters right now. I'm no closer to finding my mom," she chokes.

Reign's heart constricts. He knows how it feels to lose a parent. There's a tear inside his heart that will never be healed. He takes a tentative step forward, wondering if Arielle would accept any comfort from him, but determined to try. The pain in her eyes is almost unbearable.

Except Gabby's voice spears through the aching space between them. "Your mom knew about the Keepers of the Grail. It has everything to do with this."

The three of them spin around, finding Gabby standing only a few feet away, her wings gone. She covers the distance between her and Arielle, swallowing as she looks desperate to be believed. "I confronted your mom. She didn't deny any of it. In fact, she helped me find some crucial information about the Grigori."

"The Grigori?" Mac asks, suddenly piqued. "What are Grigori?"

Gabby looks away. "I'd rather not talk about it," she says, pain flitting across her features. She returns her gaze to Arielle. "But it was your mother who helped me. The supernatural exists, Ari. And it has something to do with these abductions."

"Maybe her mother is an Innocent."

Reign jolts as Joseph materializes beside him. He keeps his gaze fastened on Arielle, pretending he didn't hear him.

She's chewing on her lip, regarding her cousin as she tries to process this.

"She is someone who knew of our existence," Joseph muses. "If she believed, then you must, too."

Again, Reign ignores him. Arielle becomes his lifeline to reality as she opens her mouth to respond.

Except Joseph steps in front of him, his solid body blocking Reign's view. Something a hallucination shouldn't be able to do.

"Grail Keeper, you must accept your destiny," Joseph says urgently.

Reign's head feels like it's about to explode. "Will you just leave me alone?" he shouts.

Joseph instantly disappears, leaving Reign alone with three startled females.

Gabby's spine straightens. "You can leave whenever you want," she says caustically.

Mac steps toward him, shaking her head. "He wasn't talking to you. He wasn't talking to any of us." Her face crinkles with concern. "You okay?"

The answer is no, but Reign's chest is too tight to speak. Mac's looking worried. Gabby is still frowning. But it's Arielle who catches his focus and doesn't let go. Her pretty face softens with something he's seen too many times before. Pity.

He steps backward, drawing his own frown across his features. "Of course I was talking to you. You're all cuckoo and I don't want anything to do with any of this."

He spins on his heel and strides away. The moment Mac calls his name he breaks into a jog. His shoes crunching on the driveway, he works to create as much space between him and them in as little time as possible.

He rounds the bend and a quick glance over his shoulder tells him that Mac didn't follow this time. He's glad. He's about one word away from snapping, and no one needs to see that.

And right now, there are several words that could tip him over the edge.

Angel.

Grail.

Arielle.

Slowing to a brisk walk, Reign finds himself at the gates to the property. He looks left then right, noticing a car heading this way. For a second he considers trying to hitchhike, but then he realizes these people are going the wrong way. They're here to go *to* Sinclair Mansion, whilst Reign wants to be as far from it as he can.

Tucking his head down, he decides to walk to the next bus stop. If Mac or the others pass him in a car, he'll be so obnoxious they'll wish they didn't pull over. Jamming his hands in his pockets, Reign knows he's running, but he doesn't care. It's what he does best.

The approaching car slows as it nears him and Reign moves further away from the road. Surprised to find it comes to a stop beside him, he leans down to talk through the passenger side window so he can tell these good Samaritans he doesn't need yet another person checking he's okay.

He's about as far from okay as he can get.

Except a back door opens, making him step back.

"Hey—"

His words are cut off when a hand clamps over his mouth. Before he can react, a powerful arm drags him inside.

The oppressive hand muffles his scream as the car roars away in a spray of gravel.

CHAPTER 16
ARIELLE

Reign's absence feels like their circle is suddenly incomplete. It seems seeing a girl unfurl her wings inside a secret crypt can really bring people together.

Should Arielle go after him? When he'd shouted to be left alone, he'd sounded more than just angry. He'd sounded freaked out. She could be wrong, but there are moments—split-second flashes—when Reign's jungle green eyes seem like a tangle of pain.

He wasn't talking to any of us...

What did Mac mean by that? Does Reign have voices in his head, too?

Arielle shakes her head. Now she's trying to find common ground with the guy.

Mac sighs. "He just needs to cool off. I'll follow slowly to give him some time, then check he's okay."

"You're a good girlfriend, Mac." Arielle's about to say Reign is lucky to have her when Mac snorts.

"Why does everyone assume that? We're not dating. Reign is my brother from another mother."

"Oh." Why does that answer bring such a sense of relief?

Mac winks. "Although, he is kinda hot, isn't he?"

Heat stains Arielle's cheeks, no matter how much she wishes it didn't. Before she can think of a response that acknowledges that, yes, Reign is beautiful in a way that keeps a girl looking, but no, she's not interested, Mac spins on her heels.

"I'll be back," she throws over her shoulder in a deep, accented voice.

"Good luck," Gabby calls after her.

Once Mac has disappeared around the bend in the driveway, Arielle realizes she's alone with Gabby. Alone since she revealed who she really is.

"Why?" she asks her cousin.

It's one word that encompasses the confusion, the hurt, the deep, penetrating sense of betrayal.

Gabby's hands spear into her blonde curls. "I wanted you to have a normal life, Ari. Do you think it's easy living a lie? Having to hide who you really are?"

"You seemed to cope okay," Arielle shoots back. "Or are all those happy memories together also a lie?"

"Those moments are some of the most treasured ones in my life, bestie of mine. They were the beautiful, normal moments that I craved so much. You kept me grounded in a world of..."

"Angels?" Arielle asks. "And demons?"

And whatever else this supernatural realm she's just discovered contains.

Gabby smiles forlornly. "Yeah. All of those." She sighs. "But then your mom went missing and you started having dreams of obelisks. I thought it was better that you knew." She startles, as if she just thought of something alarming. "You can't tell my mom you know about this stuff."

"She also knows about..." Arielle waves her hand as if Gabby's wings are still there.

Gabby nods ruefully.

"And she didn't want me to know, did she?"

"Like I said, we wanted to keep you safe."

So the three most important people in her life were keeping secrets from her. Big secrets. Arielle feels so foolish. So naive!

"If it counts for anything, I wanted to tell you," says Gabby. "And I just did, even though I wasn't supposed to. And in front of two other humans because I could do it without further witnesses." Her lips trip up. "And just to see the look on Reign's face."

Arielle is rubbing her temples again. "I suppose so," she murmurs.

The truth is, she's not sure of anything anymore.

She looks around, conscious that Reign and Mac haven't returned yet. "So, what's next?"

Gabby shrugs. "You act like nothing has happened."

"You want me to do what?"

Gabby raises a welcome-to-my-world brow. "You have your studies, Ari. Your mom wouldn't want you falling behind, or worse, failing."

Arielle blinks. "I don't care about college right now," she points out. "I don't even know what I want to do with my life. I don't care about anything but getting my mother back."

But her cousin shakes her head. "My mom can't know that you have any idea about what I really am. Or that Sierra's disappearance is linked to the supernatural. You living your life is the only thing that can do that."

"I'm not sure I can do that, Gabby. Nothing is ever going to be normal again."

Gabby slips an arm around her shoulder. "Once your mom is back, all of this will go away. It'll be a weird blip before you discovered your passion and started your dream career."

Except Arielle's cousin will always be an angel. Her mom is an occultist. Demons exist.

Gabby must sense Arielle's hesitation, because her arm tightens. "I only revealed myself to you so that you stop stressing about your dreams and the obelisks. So you would understand what it all means." Gabby levels her gaze at Arielle. "And so you could know how dangerous this is."

Arielle suppresses a frown. Is Gabby trying to warn her off?

The frown almost gains traction across her brow. Should she be listening to her?

Gabby squeezes her shoulder before releasing it. "Aunt Sierra would kill me if anything happened to you," she says jokingly, obviously trying to lighten the mood.

"I miss her, Gabby," Arielle says quietly. "And I'm so worried about her."

Her cousin's face hardens. "We're doing everything we can to get her back."

We? But Arielle doesn't get a chance to ask. The sound of someone running has them both spinning around.

Mac rounds the bend in the driveway, gravel flicking up because she's moving so fast. She skids to halt a few feet away, breathing hard.

"It's Reign," she pants. "I can't find him."

CHAPTER 17

REIGN

R eign does what he's done his whole life—he fights.

And he fights hard.

He throws punches, injecting all the adrenaline thrumming through his veins behind them. Except the man beside him grips his arms with impossible speed and pins them by Reign's side.

With his weapon of choice—his fists—incapacitated, Reign kicks. He aims for groins and knees and shins. But the second man clamps his arm around Reign's legs, holding them easily.

Even then, Reign struggles. He writhes and twists, throwing his body around.

And none of it makes a difference.

The men hold him like he's a four-year-old having a tantrum.

Reign stills, panting hard against the hand still slapped across his mouth. A quick glance out the car window reveals a clear sky—no houses, no buildings. They're heading further out of town. As fight mode slowly fades, fear wraps around his chest like a clamp. Has he just become the next victim of the serial abductions?

"Atta boy," the man behind him murmurs. "If you keep quiet, I'll let you breathe."

The driver snorts, not taking his eyes off the road. "What's the point?"

The man removes his hand. Reign has just drawn in a breath when the man slams his fist into his solar plexus. What little air was in his lungs is forced out as pain explodes through Reign's torso. He doubles over, groaning.

"In case you were thinking of shouting," the man says smugly.

Reign slowly unfolds, half-expecting another blow. When it doesn't come, he cautiously glances up.

And freezes.

A gray-skinned, sunken-eyed Hell-face looks back at him. "Not that there's any point screaming. No one's gonna hear you."

Reign blinks, trying to wipe the image away. But fiery-pits-for-eyes is still there. A quick glance to his left reveals another Hell-face. He knows deep in his gut that another one is at the wheel.

He roars his terror, the need to get out of this car an overwhelming frenzy. He bucks. He tries to headbutt. He throws himself at the door, uncaring that the car is speeding down the road.

The first blow strikes his temple, slamming a tidal wave of pain through his head. The second powers into his stomach, crushing muscles and sending hot nausea up Reign's throat. The third and the fourth and the fifth batter everywhere in between.

They stop and Reign groans. And yet he knows this is only the beginning.

He rights himself, not glancing at either man. "Where are you taking me?" he croaks.

"Somewhere peaceful. Quiet." The man chuckles. "Private."

"This will all be over soon," the second Hell-face croons. He grabs Reign's chin and twists his head so he has no choice but to look at him. He grins, revealing pointed teeth. "When you're dead."

Ice replaces the second burst of adrenaline and Reign almost shudders. Not only is the thing beside him serious, he's looking forward to it.

He releases Reign, his fiery eyes blazing. "In fact, let's stop here."

The driver hoots and slams on the brakes. The car jolts off the road and fishtails to a stop, dust enveloping it.

Surely this isn't how it ends for him. He was so certain he was going to have more choice in the matter. That self-destruction was his fate. That he would follow in Lance's footsteps.

The men get out, hauling Reign with them. Rough hands shove him and he lands on all fours in the dirt, grimacing as gravel scrapes his palms.

"Hurry up," one of them growls. "He'll try to run."

Reign's muscles are already coiled, ready to do just that. He grits his teeth as he holds still, waiting for another blow to come.

"Let him. I enjoy target practice."

Reign braces himself to be just that—target practice. He'd rather die running than kneeling in the dirt.

Suddenly, there's a loud crash followed by the crunch of collapsing metal.

"What the—"

Reign sneaks a peek over his shoulder, seeing that all three men are now facing the car. He catches a glimpse of the boots that just landed on the bonnet before he moves. He drops and rolls, the crack of a gunshot splintering the air a second later. Dust explodes in the space Reign just vacated.

Several more tumbles and he drops into a ditch, rocks painfully jabbing into his back. Reign holds himself there for breathless seconds, expecting another gunshot and hoping this bullet punctures the soil again instead of him.

Instead, he hears a grunt and the sound of flesh hitting flesh. Uncurling to take a peek, he gasps. With wide eyes, he takes in the winged guy crouched on the car bonnet, red eyes glowing in his snarling face.

But these wings aren't white like Gabby's. If hers were ivory, then these are most certainly ebony. Stretched out to their full span, the raven-colored expanse casts a deep shadow over the two Hell-faces that are still standing. Their third comrade is sprawled in the dirt several yards away. The guy stands, his onyx wings rising with him like some avenging angel.

One word whispers through Reign's mind.

Demon.

One of the Hell-faces leaps right and Reign sees that a gun is lying on the ground, a few feet away. The demon must've been expecting it, because he vaults off the car. One beat of his massive wings and he's covered the distance between them.

The Hell-face dives for the gun. The moment it's in his hands he twists and shoots. Reign leaps to his feet, breath trapped in his tight throat.

But the demon tucks his wings and twists, instantly becoming a missile. He slams into the Hell-face and the man's propelled backward, gouging through the dirt. The demon is already punching before they've stopped, his fists like pistons. Except the Hell-face absorbs each blow, desperately throwing his own blows.

The second Hell-face walks toward them, the movement slow and calculated and full of menace. As he approaches, he withdraws a small handgun from behind him. It must've been tucked into his belt.

Reign is already running toward him. "Look out!"

The demon glances over his shoulder, sees the weapon pointed at him and grabs the Hell-face he was pummeling. He hauls the man up and spins just as the crack of the gun detonates.

The Hell-face arches his back as the bullet pierces between his shoulder blades. Reign blinks in amazement, a little awed. The demon just used the Hell-face as a shield.

The second Hell-face never blinks at the loss of his comrade. His outstretched arm changes angle, once again centering on the demon. One pump of the demon's wings is powerful enough to send a gust of wind over Reign as he launches into the air.

The gun discharges again and the second bullet misses the demon. Now in the air, he twists and somersaults, wings fully extended one moment, then contracted and wrapped around him the next. The Hell-face tries to keep his aim on his target, only to find the demon is moving too fast.

The screech of tires on road has Reign spinning around. He watches in horror as a car skids to a halt and Mac, Gabby, then Arielle tumble out.

"Get out of here!" he shouts.

The three girls duck as another shot rings out. Reign runs to them, waving his arm wildly. "Get back in the car!"

Except all three are watching the aeronautics happening behind him in wide eyed awe. Arielle looks terrified. Mac looks scared yet foolishly curious. Gabby is...smiling.

She glances at Reign. "Isn't he amazing?" she asks breathlessly.

Reign isn't sure he heard her right. "He's what?"

"Incredible. And so freaking hot!"

Reign is at a loss for words. She's checking the demon out?

"I mean, look!" Gabby says, pointing.

Reign spins around to see the demon spearing down like a vengeful arrow, one that has no intention of missing its target. The Hell-face aims his gun again and pulls the trigger. It releases little more than an impotent *click*.

Reign gasps, impressed. The demon waited until the Hell-face was out of ammo.

The demon ploughs into the Hell-face and he crumples. Reign half expected him to be pounded into the ground like a pole. One solid punch to the chin and the Hell-face is knocked out cold.

The demon stands, waits a second to make sure he isn't getting up anytime soon, then turns to make his way toward them. He tucks his ebony wings around him as he flicks his auburn bangs out of his eyes.

"Colt?" Arielle asks, her voice full of disbelief.

Reign frowns, wishing the world would slow down a little. "Who's Colt?"

Gabby beams. "My boyfriend."

"Your boyfriend is a demon?"

She nods, pride glinting softly in her eyes. "Yep." She angles her head, arching a brow. "Going to tell me demons aren't real again?"

Reign has no response. That demon just saved his life.

Gabby folds into Colt's side, her face softening in a way that suggests this is where she feels like she belongs. Colt wraps a protective arm around her, pulling her even closer. Before Reign can blink, his wings are gone.

"Ah, thanks," he says haltingly. What the heck are the social rules around thanking a demon for saving you from a bunch of Hell-faces?

Colt shrugs. "No big deal."

Gabby presses a hand to Colt's chest. "Are you a believer now, Reign?"

Reign clenches his hands. "I never said I didn't believe it." He angles his chin, his gaze sliding to Arielle. "Only that I don't want anything to do with it."

Colt glances down at Gabby, eyebrows raised. She shrugs. "He's got a chip on his shoulder," she whispers loudly for anyone to hear.

Colt looks back to Reign. "It's probably safer for you that way," he says solemnly. "We just ask that you don't speak of this to anyone."

Reign makes a cross sign on his chest. "I don't want to be admitted into the loony bin any sooner than I need to be."

Colt glances over his shoulder at the two unconscious and one dead Hell-face. "We need to get going. Others will come looking for them."

"There are more?" Arielle asks quietly.

She wraps her arms around herself, and Reign notes the way Gabby's brow furrows. Arielle has that fragile, lost look about her again. Like her world has been smashed to smithereens and she's worried she'll be next.

He mentally shakes himself. Not that it's his problem.

Colt nods. "But it's not you they want. Once we get home, you'll be safe," he assures her.

Arielle chews her lip as she turns back to the car. Reign follows as the others join her. Mac brushes his hand as she moves in close.

"You okay?"

Reign throws her an arched look. "Just another day on the streets."

Mac shakes her head. "Some weird shit happens on the streets, but nothing like this."

He climbs in the car, sitting beside her, Arielle tucked into the door on the other side. Gabby drives with Colt beside her in the passenger side. Arielle's still pale and quiet.

The drive back is silent, no doubt as everyone tries to process what they've seen today. Reign rests his head back, lowering his eyelids so it looks like he's sleeping, even though there's no way he could turn off his mind right now.

He'd love to forget everything that happened today. The white wings. The black wings. The strange crypt beneath the mansion. But he can't.

Not when he was abducted by Hell-faces. Not when Colt's words to Arielle are on a menacing loop in his head.

It's not you they want.

Arielle may be able to return to some semblance of normality. But for some reason, Reign is on their most wanted list.

A map of Mercy City is on the wall in front of Arielle, seven red pins marking seven locations.

There's that number again. Seven. A part of her is considering writing it on one of her boots, except she doubts she'll be forgetting it anytime soon.

Reign is still standing by the door they just entered through. "You live in the basement?"

Colt shrugs. "I don't like windows."

Gabby squeezes his hand. "More privacy," she says cheekily.

To Arielle's surprise, Colt flushes. Who would've thought this quiet, reserved guy is a demon? Arielle swallows. Who would've thought any of this is real?

She glances around the room again, taking in the cement walls and floor. Gabby and Colt brought them to Colt's hideout, which also turned out to be his living quarters. The small apartment complex above them looked like so many of the common buildings around the city. Square, banal, inexpensive because extras like parking and balconies aren't available.

But instead of taking a lift, Colt had led them to the fire stairs. The descent had reminded Arielle of walking down the stairs into the crypt when Gabby revealed her wings. Is that the moment everything changed? Or was it when she found her mother's journal? Or did all this start long before that, when her mother discovered the occult?

Knowing there's no answer to those questions, Arielle glances at the three people with her in the basement. Colt and Gabby stand close together, pretending they aren't watching everyone else just as closely, probably waiting for someone to finally process all this and fall in a heap. Mac is in the kitchenette, eyeing the stack of pizza boxes to her left and the unmade double bed on her right. She's scoping the place out like she's fascinated by it all, and yet she's ready to fight any second.

Reign is still by the door, scowl in place. His arms are crossed over his chest like a shield. Arielle takes in the stay-the-hell-away-from-me he's working hard to exude, and for once, it's not all she sees. He's staring at her in that intense way of his, emotions shifting in his green eyes. Reign cared that her mother is missing. Reign tried to protect her when the crypt opened.

And lastly, he's still here. Despite everything that has happened, he hasn't run away.

He looks away, breaking the moment. "So, if that's everything, I'd like to get going."

Arielle tightens her jaw. She really needs to get a grip on herself with this guy.

Colt comes to stand beside her, indicating toward the map. "Actually, we brought you here for a reason."

Arielle turns back to study the seven pins, Mac joining them. Reign doesn't move from his place by the door.

Arielle steps in closer as she recognizes one of the locations. "That's where Mom was taken."

Colt nods. "Each of these pinpoints the location a woman was abducted."

"We've been investigating it," Gabby adds. "We've asked around. All we've learned is there was a white, unmarked vehicle fleeing the scene after each abduction took place. And they all happened an hour apart."

"It's not possible for one vehicle to kidnap all seven people in one hour," Reign observes. "Not from different parts of the city."

Arielle resists the urge to glance at him. It seems Reign is paying attention.

Colt nods again. "Yep. There must have been two or three vehicles, maybe even six." He glances at the three people watching him. "This was a coordinated attack."

Gabby sighs. "And Colt detected demonic aura at every location. It was definitely a demon job."

Arielle heads to the small table a few feet away and sits down heavily. "But why?"

Why do demons want her mom? And six other women?

Colt frowns. "We haven't been able to figure that out. I've tried to track them, but I didn't get very far. There's some pretty powerful demon magic involved here."

Mac steps closer to the map. "Maybe I could ask around. I have contacts on the street."

Gabby's face lights up. "You do?"

"We both do," says Reign.

They all turn to him, and Arielle wonders if the others are as surprised as she is. Before anyone can say anything, Mac is shaking her head.

"No. You're still a POI."

"POI?" Arielle echoes.

"Person of interest," Colt volunteers. He angles his head at

Reign. "Seems someone has been messing on the wrong side of the law?"

Reign shrugs. "I may or may not have been the getaway driver for a couple of friends doing a heist." He glances at Arielle, his hands dropping to his side. "It's not my proudest moment, to be honest."

She stills, knowing he's extending an apology.

"Apparently, you're also a POI for demons, too," Colt says. "Any ideas why?"

Reign's arms cross back over his chest. "No idea," he says flatly.

Mac shakes her head even harder. "All the more reason you need to lay low right now."

"I never said I wasn't," Reign points out.

"You didn't need to," she shoots back.

"Seven women have been abducted, Mac. That's seven moms, or seven sisters, or seven daughters."

Arielle notes the edge in his voice. He's talking like someone who cares.

"And what if demons come after you?" Mac demands.

Reign glances at Colt, grinning. "Can I put you on speed dial?"

Colt nods. "Sure. Crushing demons is my all-time favorite pastime."

"Excellent," Reign announces, clapping his hands as if it's all settled. Except the moment he does, he winces.

Mac rushes forward. "Reign, your hands!"

Arielle shoots to her feet but stops herself before she moves. She doesn't need to be beside Reign to see the damage to his palms. Grazed and raw, they're dotted with gravel and streaked with blood.

That's why he had his arms crossed. He was hiding his injuries.

Reign tries to hide them again but Mac won't let him. She opens his hands so she can inspect them. "We need to clean this up."

"It's fine, Mac. I'll just wash them or something."

"It's really not," she counters crossly. She glances at Colt. "Do you have a first aid kit here?"

"Ah...no. Sorry." He shrugs ruefully. "I don't even have crockery here, let alone a first aid kit."

Gabby frowns. "We could stop off at a pharmacy?"

Reign tries to tug his hand away. "Like I said, it's fine. I'll make sure I use extra soap."

Mac huffs as she releases him. "If they get infected and fall off, at least I can say I tried."

"I have a first aid kit."

Three sets of eyes turn to Arielle as she holds up her backpack.

"Of course you do," says Gabby with a laugh. "That bag of yours is like the Tardis. There's probably an entire hospital ward in there."

Arielle huffs in mock offense. "I like to be prepared, okay?" She turns to Reign. "I could clean them up if you like?"

Reign stills. His gaze darts from her to the backpack to his hands. Arielle waits. For some reason, his answer matters. Will he dismiss her offer of help just like he did with Mac?

He sighs. "If it's going to get you all off my back, then fine."

Arielle suppresses a smile as she sets about getting what she needs. Her first aid kit is tucked in the bottom right of her backpack, beside the sewing kit and above the emergency poncho.

Reign slips onto the chair beside hers. "I can do it," he says quietly. Almost nervously.

Arielle rolls her eyes. "We don't have time for that." She holds out her hand. "Come on. Don't tell me you're scared of a bit of antiseptic."

Reign stiffens and plonks his hand on the table, face up. "Bring it on."

"Gabby and Colt," Mac says a little too loudly, tearing her gaze away from Reign. She looks as shocked as she did when she saw an angel for the first time. "Show me everything I need to know about this map."

The two join her and they huddle around the map, their backs to them. Gabby glances over her shoulder and winks.

Refusing to acknowledge it, Arielle flicks open the small sterile mat she's pulled out. She indicates to Reign that she wants to slip it under his hand. He complies, his frown dancing over his dark brows. Arielle picks up a vial of saline, determined to do this quickly. She's being a good Samaritan, nothing more.

She slips her hand beneath his, stifling a gasp as they easily slot together. His skin is so much warmer than she expected, his hand seeming to pulse with a strength that shoots straight up her arm. She ducks her head, avoiding Reign's gaze as she squirts saline over him. A little part of her wonders how steam isn't rising up.

Reign clears his throat. "You really do have the works in that bag of yours."

Arielle flushes his hand, the saline running red as the blood washes away. "Dora the Explorer ain't got nothing on my backpack," she jokes, keeping her gaze on her task.

The streaks of claret wash away, revealing the gravel pocked grazes beneath. The heel of his hand has borne the brunt of the damage, but the cuts don't look too deep. Arielle picks up an antiseptic wipe, hesitating as she realizes she's about to touch Reign even more.

"If you're squeamish, then I can do it." He goes to pull his hand back. "And I promise I'll be quick."

Before Arielle knows she's done it, she's tightened her hand.

She shakes her head. "After what I saw today, this is child's play."

Although the man was trying to kill Reign and Colt, the image of his lifeless form is branded in her mind. She practically felt the bullet that took his life. These grazes are nothing compared to the finality of death.

Reign nods, his arm relaxing. "Yeah. I've seen bullet wounds before, and they couldn't compare to today."

Arielle glances down before Reign can see her reaction to his words. She suspected life hasn't always been kind to him, and that just confirmed it.

His hand tenses in hers. "I don't want your pity, Arielle."

She flashes him an annoyed look, the warm feeling that had been blossoming shriveling a little. "I've noticed."

She's also noticed that he misreads compassion.

She picks up an antiseptic wipe, smiling sweetly. "No pity. Noted."

She wipes at his grazes, keeping her pressure firm but gentle as the remaining pieces of gravel easily come out.

His breath hisses through his teeth. "You're enjoying this, aren't you?"

She flashes him a smile, this one far more sincere than the last. "A little bit."

Reign seems to startle, his eyes widening. His gaze flickers to her lips. Arielle's breath disintegrates in her lungs. One glance from this guy and she's hovering on a precipice she never knew existed.

Reign looks away, glancing at the others over by the map. Jolted back to reality, Arielle looks over, too. Gabby, Colt and Mac are engrossed in their discussion, apparently unaware of the two of them. Arielle returns to her task, placing a large dressing over the heel of Reign's palm. He looked like he was hiding something. Or that he was worried about getting caught. She frowns. Does he have feelings for Mac, after all?

"Other hand, please," she says, not liking the husky note in her voice.

Reign complies, and Arielle experiences the same jolt all over again as she clasps it. She leans over to repeat the process, surprised when Reign does the same.

"I just wanted to say," he says in a low voice, glancing back at the others again. His green gaze, once more full of tangles and mysterious as a labyrinth, returns to hers. "I just wanted to say I'm sorry. About the car." He smiles crookedly. "You know, the whole almost hitting you thing."

Why does Arielle sense that if his hand wasn't in hers, it would be rubbing the back of his head? And since when did such a crooked smile tug at her heart with such intensity?

She smiles back, glad she also has a second chance to get this right. "Thanks. It seems neither of us were having a good day."

He arches an eyebrow, humor glinting in his gaze. "Not so much about the boots, though. That apology I may have to work up to."

Arielle looks down at his palm, noting this one isn't as bad as the first. "Surely you can understand," she says, glancing back up at him. "Haven't you ever owned something that important to you?"

Reign looks away. "Nope."

Realizing what she just said, Arielle's about to take her words back when she stops. Trying to apologize is probably going to sound like pity. And yet...she's not ready for this moment to end. This Reign fascinates her. How is it that he says he doesn't care, and yet it feels like he does?

An idea strikes her and she jams her hand in her backpack, pulling out the first thing she finds.

"Here then," she says, grinning. "Treasure this always."

Reign's brows shoot up as he takes it. "A compass?"

"May it never be splashed with ketchup," she announces with a flourish, placing it on the table beside her.

Reign's mouth twitches but he focuses back on his hand before Arielle can see if those sculpted lips ever make it to a full blown smile. "Gee, thanks," he replies wryly.

A sweet warmth unfurls in Arielle's belly as she flushes the saline. Did they just have a moment? She tears open another antiseptic wipe, suddenly confused. Surely she didn't *enjoy* the moment?

Mac wanders over, peering at Arielle's handiwork. "How's the patient?"

"Grouchy," Arielle says with a smile as she wipes antiseptic over his wound and Reign frowns.

Mac grins. "Wait till you really get to know him."

Arielle holds her smile even though Mac's words strike a chord. Is that what she's doing? Really getting to know Reign?

Because obnoxious, get-out-of-my-face Reign is, well... obnoxious. Arielle can't imagine anyone wanting to spend time with that guy. But there are layers to this guy. And the few glimpses she's had beneath his tough exterior have been...fascinating.

She mentally shakes herself. Her mom is missing, and her angel cousin and her demon boyfriend think the supernatural is involved. Arielle well and truly has enough on her plate right now. She doesn't need the roller coaster of emotions she's experienced around Reign any more than she needs to know that vampires or witches or...or reapers exist right now.

She almost shudders. Surely reapers don't exist.

Reign stands abruptly, his chair scraping over the cement floor. "That's me. Layers of jerk under a thin veneer of asshole."

Arielle blinks as she tries to keep up with the change of mood. "I haven't put a dressing on yet."

He doesn't glance at her as he steps back. "This will be fine." He hesitates. "Thanks."

Mac frowns. "You know that's not what I meant," she points out.

Reign shrugs. "It's something we should all keep in mind." He looks around the room. "Time's a wastin'. Shall we go see what the word on the street is?"

"Sure." Mac glances at Arielle as if she's wondering what just happened.

Arielle drops her gaze. She can't answer that question because she has no idea.

Reign strides to the door. "We'll keep you posted."

"Be careful," Colt calls after them.

"Sure thing," Reign throws over his shoulder, suggesting he has no intention of doing that. Without a backward glance, he and Mac are gone.

Arielle stands there, feeling foolish. She's not sure what she expected to happen, but surely he could've spared her a good-bye? Shown her a little common courtesy?

She turns to her cousin and Colt, trying to find her bearings. She needs something to do. Something to focus on. "So, what do you need me to do?"

Playing her part in getting her mother back, even if it includes acknowledging angels are demons are real, is going to be her sole focus.

Gabby smiles brightly, as if she has great news. "You get a 'get out of jail free' pass. Your job is to go home and pretend like none of this ever happened."

Arielle's about to say she can't do that. Too much has gone down.

But then she sees the compass, still sitting on the table.

Reign didn't take it. Like that moment, along with her silly gift, meant nothing to him. Her stomach bottoms out like she just fell from a great height.

Yep. A rollercoaster.

Arielle straightens her shoulders. "Sure. In fact, I'm going to do everything I can to wipe these past two days from my mind."

CHAPTER 19
REIGN

"**Y**ou like her."

Reign ignores Mac as they step off the bus. He stalks down the street toward their foster home, wishing she'd focus on something else. There's no way he wants to have this conversation.

The bus pulls away, and he's several feet down the path when he realizes Mac isn't with him. He turns to find her standing in the middle of the pavement, hands on hips.

He tips his head back as he lets out a long sigh. "Her mother's missing."

His response jolts Mac into action and she comes to stand in front of him. "Also a relevant fact," she agrees. "But beside the point."

"Actually, it is the point. She has enough to deal with right now."

And she doesn't need some dropkick who's only going to jerk her around. Guys like him don't hook up with girls like Arielle. Not without lying to themselves and everyone around them.

Mac angles her head, peering up at him. "And you'd just add to her burden rather than lessen it?"

With a frustrated groan, Reign turns away. Arielle is beautiful. Smart. A little left of center. And she went through the past twenty-four hours without falling apart once. That makes her impressive.

The moment she smiled at him, her face so close, her flame blue eyes soft and teasing as she'd cleaned his wounds, had taken his breath away. There had been a brief second where he'd wondered what those lips feel like. Whether they're as soft as they look. Whether the fire he senses within her will burn as bright as he thinks it will.

Right before he snapped himself out of his foolish fairytale thoughts. People like him don't deserve happy endings.

Mac catches up and Reign's glad when she doesn't push the point. Instead, she shoves him with her pointy shoulder. "What a day, huh?"

Reign slides a glance her way. "You've been loving it."

"Apart from the part where you were kidnapped and almost killed, it's been kinda cool."

That's probably because she's not hallucinating. Reign realizes that Joseph hasn't appeared since they were down in the crypt. He's glad. Discovering angels and demons are real has been enough of a mind meld.

"I mean, think about it. How much more is there to this world that we never realized?" Mac continues. "And it also means you're not crazy. Joseph is real."

"I'll help with these missing women," Reign states firmly. It's the least he owes Arielle after kicking off the worst day of her life. "And if that means accepting the supernatural, then fine. But I am not"— Reign heavily emphasizes the last word— "believing for a second that my drug induced, weird ass hallucinations have anything to do with it. That was an inevitable slippery slope in the freak show that is my life."

"Reign?" A strident voice carries down the path. "Have you finally hauled your ass back home?"

Mac's shoulders slump. "Avril's in a good mood."

Reign snorts. "She has a different setting?"

They head toward the house and Reign steels himself as he always does before they see their foster mother. He should probably thank Avril for thickening his armor so much.

She's standing in the doorway, hands on her thick hips. "About time."

Reign and Mac glance at each other. Since when did Avril actually want them in the house?

She steps back to let them enter. "I've been praying for your souls."

Reign rolls his eyes, making sure Avril can't see the gesture. She says this every time they come back.

And each time, he responds in the same way. "I don't think it worked."

"I know," she snaps. "Your sins are catching up with you."

Reign and Mac pause in the living room, glancing at each other. The script just changed. Avril always tells them she's willing to help them repent—cleaning each room of this house, one at a time.

Avril's hands are back on her hips. She smiles as she sees she has their attention. "No matter how much I've tried to show you the light, no matter how much I have tried to teach you the way, you invite sin into your life." Avril's working herself up into a Puritan fury. Her greasy hair glistens as sweat beads along her hairline, and her jowls wobble with fervor. "Now, you have invited The wrath of He Who Sees Everything upon yourselves."

"Yep, we know," Reign interjects. "We're paving the way to

eternal damnation. What did you mean when you said our sins are catching up with us?"

"Do not mock me, boy! The sins are real! They are temptations placed in our path by Satan himself!"

"I'm pretty sure I can sin all on my own. I don't need Lucifer's help."

Mac elbows Reign in the ribs. "Do you want this over any time soon?" she hisses under her breath.

Avril's cheeks are turning a ruddy red, as if she's being fueled by the fires of Hell herself. Reign mentally sighs, accepting Mac's right. He just wants a shower and a change of clothes so they can get out of here.

Avril stomps toward them, pushing her blazing face closer to Reign's. "Justice is coming for you, boy. He rang yesterday."

Reign's about to turn away from the sour breath coming at him in puffs when he stops. "You got a call from the dude upstairs?"

"Of course not, you idiot," Avril snarls. "A Detective Kane rang, asking questions about you."

Reign's brows slam down. Seems he's a POI on more than one list. "What did you tell him?"

"That he was wasting his breath because you're never home. That an eternity of damnation awaits you if you don't change your ways." Avril huffs as she crosses her arms over her ample bosom. "I told him a demon of the damned has possessed you."

Actually, a demon saved him today, and he didn't seem very damned, but Reign doesn't point that out. All that matters is that the cops know he rarely comes home. They're not very likely to come looking for him here.

The phone in the kitchen rings, the strident sound piercing the air. Reign glances at Mac, his muscles coiled and ready to run. If it's the cops, Avril will tell them they're here, waiting for the long arm of the law to slap their sinning backsides.

Avril shoves her face close to Reign's again. "That'll be that girl Lizzie, asking for you again. Have you seduced some poor girl to your sinning ways?"

"Actually—"

Reign's words are cut off by Mac's sharp elbow. For a second he considers continuing to tell Avril that Lizzie was far more keen to sin than he was, which is one of the reasons he broke it off. But he snaps his mouth shut.

Instead, he sighs. "I'll call her. She won't bother you again."

Avril harrumphs. "Good." She glances past Reign's shoulder to the hallway behind him. "There are a lot of lost souls I need to pray for."

She'd be talking about all the other foster children she currently has under her care. As she stomps past them, Reign marvels at the fact Avril has convinced herself she's a good person. For people like her, learning of the existence of angels and demons would only solidify that belief.

"So, Lizzie's still hanging around, huh?" Mac asks with a smirk.

"Zip it, Mackenzie," Reign mutters, using her full name just because he knows it annoys her. "She knows it's over."

Mac's smirk grows. "Does she?" She flutters her lashes at him as she heads to the room she shares with two other girls. "You tell yourself that while I go get myself some clean clothes."

Rubbing his temple with one hand while he pulls his cell out of his pocket, Reign sees there are multiple missed calls from Lizzie. He ignored the first few, hoping she'd take the hint, and then the rest of the day...he was busy with crypts, angel wings popping up and demon abductions.

Pressing the button to call her back, he hopes he can keep

this quick. He never stays in this house for long, and with some Detective on his tail, he plans on halving the usual time.

Lizzie picks up after the first ring. "Reign! Where have you been?"

"Sorry, I've had a bit on my plate. What's up?"

The moment he says the words, Reign's gut clenches. He doesn't want a replay of their past few cliched conversations:

Reign, I miss you.

Look, Lizzie, we had some good times—

Some really good times...

True. And you're going to make some lucky guy really happy someday.

"A cop has been at the school, asking about you," Lizzie says in a hushed voice. "A Detective Kane."

Reign's lungs seize mid-breath. The same guy who rang here. "Did he have doughnuts?"

"This isn't funny, Reign," Lizzie exclaims. "He was asking a lot of questions, wanting to know if anyone had seen you recently."

"I don't even go to college," Reign points out.

"Yes, well, the Detective said he's following up any leads." Lizzie pauses. "This could affect your chances of being accepted down the track, Reign."

"I dropped out of high school, remember? College isn't on the cards for me."

"Look, if you've got yourself mixed up with something, I can help. My dad—"

"No, thanks" Reign quickly interjects. He's not owing Lizzie anything. "It's nothing I can't handle."

"Okay." She sighs. "I'm worried about you. Maybe we could meet somewhere, talk about—"

"Thanks for letting me know about the detective, Lizzie, even if he didn't have donuts. You're a good friend." He pulls back the phone. "Coming, Mac!" Returning it to his ear, he injects his voice with as much apology as he can muster. "Sorry, gotta go. Look after yourself."

He hangs up before she can answer, pressing the edge of his phone to his forehead. He never pretended there was going to be anything with Lizzie apart from a bit of fun, and the moment she looked like she wanted more than that, he ended things. Then why does he feel guilty?

He quickly ducks into his room, grabs some clean clothes, and has a hasty shower. Maybe he can wash away the icky feeling that's crawling over his skin. Plus, the less time he can be here, the better. He's out within ten minutes, but he still finds Mac waiting for him in the living room, looking clean and fresh.

Mac looks him over from his still damp hair to the fact he's already wearing shoes. "She took it well, huh?"

It seems some things can't be washed away. "She said a Detective Kane has been asking after me on campus."

"Of course he was," Mac huffs. She wrinkles her nose at him. "You're becoming quite popular, aren't you?"

"Not by choice, let me assure you."

Mac tenses, her head angling as if she just heard something. Reign glances around, suddenly on alert. She's always had a freakishly sensitive set of ears.

"What? What is it?"

But then he hears it, too. The jarring, ominous wails of a police siren.

Mac drops the clothes she was holding. "Avril ratted us out."

Simultaneously, they run to the front windows. A police car slams to a halt in the driveway, three police officers swarming out before the car has stopped moving.

"Run!" Reign says flatly. "The back door."

They've just broken into a sprint when Avril appears in the hall. "What evil have you brought into my house?" she screams, planting herself in their way. "What do they want?"

There's no time to wonder why she's sounding so surprised considering she was the one who called them. Reign feints left and the moment her bulky body tries to block him, he steps right. She bellows as he and Mac zip past her, making a beeline for the back door.

Behind them, the front door crashes open. "Stop!" a voice booms through the house. "You're under arrest."

Like hell, he is.

Shoving the back door open, Reign pulls up short as he finds a uniformed body in front of him. Dammit, the third cop came around the back. The man's face is twisted in an angry scowl as he opens his mouth to speak.

But before he gets a chance to repeat the demand to stop so they can arrest him, Reign plants his fist in the man's jaw.

The cop staggers backward, his eyes rolling back in his head. He crumples to the ground, unconscious as Reign and Mac hightail it for the back fence.

CHAPTER 20
ARIELLE

Arielle stares at the blank computer screen in front of her, feeling like a fool. She promised Gabby and herself she'd act like nothing happened. She agreed this was best.

Except she can't ignore that her world is upside-down and inside out, and angels and demons aren't the half of it.

Her mom is missing.

And the more time passes, the more the ache grows, leaving less and less room for hope. The weight is starting to crush her. She shakes her head, glancing at her boots beside the bed. On the left toe are the words she needs right now.

Hope > Fear

"Hope is the only thing stronger than fear," she murmurs. The moment her mother said those words to her, Arielle had rushed off and scribbled the little equation.

She just never knew she'd need to remember it because her mother would be wrenched out of her life.

And hope and fear were all she'd be left with.

The cursor blinks on the screen, waiting, counting out the seconds she's failing. She told Gabby she'd focus on her studies, just like Mom would want her to. She also told Aunt Shell the same thing when she got home.

And yet, she hasn't written a word.

She rests her head on her desk, closing her eyes. She's so tired, but she admits she's too scared to go to sleep. The nightmare of the obelisk was terrifying when it was a dream. But knowing those stone monoliths have been foretold, that they're supposedly real, turns her blood to ice. For some reason, it feels like the seven robed figures, the ones with wings just like Gabby, are tied to the obelisks in ways she doesn't understand.

Exhaustion clouds her confused mind. Maybe she's overreacting. Her imagination is getting away from her. She's muddling up the loss of her mother with the strange vision.

Her limbs become heavy as she gives into the call of oblivion. Maybe this will all seem better after some sleep...

The obelisk appears the moment consciousness slips away. As if she's picking up from where she left off, the cracks in the monolith flare as if it's in pain. The hand that was clawing at it is gone, but that doesn't matter. The damage has been wrought.

Crimson flares through each crevice, like luminous, blazing blood. The largest crack splinters wider, and the light dims. No. Shadows are squirming out like weightless ink, fracturing the glow. Once the first couple are out, they worm and writhe with more vigor. As each one is let loose, it streaks for the sky, letting out victorious screeches and guttural growls.

Terrified all over again, Arielle tries to break free of the nightmarish dream. She desperately grapples for consciousness, for the safety of reality. The vision is just receding when she sees one final detail.

Arielle pulls herself upright with a gasp. "No," she whispers.

There was one white figure, but she wasn't standing like last time, her wings extended. She was laying at the base of the obelisk, painted in her own blaze of red.

Arielle's throat burns with bile. The wings had been nothing like Gabby's. They'd been lifeless. The woman was dead.

Pushing to her feet, Arielle glances at her clock. It's almost midnight, which means Aunt Shell would've gone to sleep long ago. Arielle tiptoes out of her room, shivering even though it's not cold.

Downstairs, she pads to her mother's chair and curls up in it, trying to contain her tears. "Where are you, Mom?" she whispers brokenly.

Never in her life has she needed her more. Everything is just too...big. And right now, Arielle feels so infinitely small.

Tucking her knees up, she curls even tighter, as if she can physically hold herself together. How is she expected to just sit here and wait?

And yet, what else can she do?

Her head falls to the side, feeling far too heavy as it rests against the back of the chair. Arielle's gaze falls on what used to be the fireplace. Her mother had brought back some middle eastern tiles from one of her work trips and had made it one of her crazy projects, as Gabby liked to call them, to learn how to tile a wall.

Arielle's eyes sting with the promise of fresh tears. Those work trips suddenly take on a new meaning. Was her academic life little more than a facade for her occult research?

How much has her mother hidden from her?

Arielle bites her lip. Of course her mother protected her from this. Arielle is so naive she never noticed a thing. Never questioned her mother's obsession with history and the Middle East.

Arielle's cousin is an angel. Her mother is someone who has dedicated her life to understanding the supernatural. Aunt

Shell...Arielle realizes she hasn't even asked if she's more than human, too.

Maybe her mother suspected that Arielle couldn't handle any of this.

Right now, it feels like she'd be right to think that.

Look closer...

"A clichéd pep talk isn't going to help, Trinity."

If she looks inside, all she's going to find is a lost, scared, unexceptional girl.

Arielle's eyes flood with moisture and the blues and yellows of the tiles blur. A tear escapes and it's barely made it to her cheek before she dashes it away with a frustrated swipe. She may be clueless, but she refuses to fall apart.

The tiles come back into focus and Arielle stares at them with renewed energy. She knows she's being ridiculous, but she doesn't care. If she can hold onto this, then maybe she can hold onto hope.

She frowns. A tile in the center is ever so slightly raised.

Arielle rises and walks over, unsure why it has her so curious. Maybe it's because she's suddenly attuned to the unusual.

Maybe it's because she's learned nothing is a coincidence.

She runs her finger over the tile, discovering that it's slightly, but definitely higher than the others. She grips it with the tips of her fingernails, wondering what in the world she's doing. Even as her mother covered this wall she'd joked that she was far from a professional.

The tile comes away, exposing a hole in the wall behind it.

Arielle stares with wide eyes at the roll of parchment lodged in it. Barely breathing, she gently pulls it out.

Another message from her mother!

With trembling fingers, Arielle unrolls it. In the midnight gloom, all she sees are scribbles. Striding to the lamp, she turns it on. Maybe she's found a clue that could help them find her!

But the soft glow reveals that the scribbles are actually symbols. Hieroglyphics of some sort. A language Arielle has never seen before.

She collapses onto the couch. "Come on, Mom. I could've really used a break."

Two muted knocks on the door have Arielle leaping to her feet, the parchment clapped to her chest. Her pulse flutters in a panic as she realizes it's after midnight.

Who would be visiting at this time?

She makes her way to the door as silently as possible, suddenly wishing she'd taken her phone. For all she knows, the boogeyman is real. A quick peek through the peephole has her letting out her breath.

Arielle opens the door. "What are you two doing here?"

Reign and Mac recoil in surprise at the sight of her. "Ari?" Mac asks incredulously. "What are *you* doing here?"

"Me?" Arielle glares at Reign, his rejection stinging anew. "You're really taking this stalking to the next level."

Mac's eyes widen with realization. "You live here?"

"Yes. This is my house."

Reign's eyes close as he sighs. "Of course it is."

"We'll I'll be," drawls Mac. She grins. "Do you mind if we come in?"

Arielle frowns but steps back. "Just keep it down. My aunt is asleep upstairs."

Mac enters with Reign just behind, and Arielle hates that she notices his proximity as he brushes past. She attributes it to her exhaustion.

"Ari, is that you?"

Arielle spins around, seeing Aunt Shell coming down the steps, holding her dressing gown around her. She stops when she sees Arielle has company, frowning. "What's going on?"

"Sorry, Aunt Shell. We didn't mean to wake you." Arielle's

glad it's dark, because her cheeks flush. "Ah, these are my friends, Reign and Mac."

"You have friends over in the middle of the night?"

Arielle shifts uncomfortably. She's never been good at lying. "Ah, yeah. They've been texting me all day wanting to come over and..." She racks her brain. "To, ah, study! When I didn't answer, they just rocked up."

Even as she says the words, she knows how lame it sounds. Aunt Shell takes the final steps down and pauses as she takes in Mac and Reign.

Neither of them look like study buddies.

Aunt Shell's face breaks into a broad smile. "It's the young gentleman who changed my tire for me," she says with pleasure. "How lovely to see you."

Arielle glances at Reign in surprise. Young gentleman? Lovely to see you?

"We're so sorry," says Mac. She draws up a bright smile. "We can get pretty carried away when it comes to genetics and Mendellian inheritance. Don't we, Reign?"

"Yep, we sure do," he mutters.

Mac elbows him. "What's your favorite part?"

Reign glares at her from under his dark brows and Arielle can't blame him. They can't afford her hastily concocted alibi.

"Probably genetic polymorphisms and their influence on the development of various disorders."

Arielle's brows shoot up as Aunt Shell slides a glance her way. "Handsome *and* clever." Before Arielle can put a stop to the mortifying innuendo, Aunt Shell frowns. "But now isn't the time to study."

"Of course," Mac agrees. "We'll be going shortly."

Reign nods. "We didn't mean to disturb you."

Aunt Shell pats his arm reassuringly. "Of course, you wouldn't have." She glances at Arielle. "Hopefully I'll see you soon, young man." She takes herself back up the stairs, throwing them a baleful glare. "At a more appropriate hour."

The moment she's out of sight, Arielle turns back to Reign and Mac, indicating for them to follow her into the living room. There, she sees the parchment. She quickly picks it up and clutches it to her chest. "How did you find me?"

"Actually, we weren't weren't looking for you," Mac says cheerily. "Reign got into a spot of trouble, so we needed somewhere to hang for a bit."

Arielle glances at Reign. "More stolen cars?"

He shrugs. "Just assaulted a police officer, this time."

Even in the half-light of the hall, Arielle can see his don't-ask expression, so she doesn't probe further. It's none of her business, anyway. "Did Gabby give you my address?"

Mac shakes her head. "Nope. The Professor did."

"The Professor?" Arielle chokes, the air feeling like it just tightened around her.

"I met her about a year ago, at the university library," Mac explains. "She was researching Joseph of Arimathea. It was fascinating."

Arielle blinks. Her mother even told Mac—a girl who was a stranger—about Joseph. And yet, she told Arielle nothing.

"She gave me her address. Said to come see here if I ever needed anything." Mac jams her hands in her pockets. "Your mom's a special woman, Ari."

Pain lances through Arielle's heart. "Yes, she is."

"I haven't needed to take her up on the offer, until today."

Arielle nods then glances over her shoulder. "Come into the living room so we can talk. I don't want to wake up Aunt Shell."

Reign and Mac follow her, Mac whistling quietly under her breath when they enter.

"If I knew how cool this place looked, I would've come sooner."

"My mom travelled to the Middle East a lot. She always brought something home with her."

Reign remains just in the doorway in a manner that Arielle's beginning to recognize. It's like he never quite lets himself fit anywhere.

Mentally shaking herself, she puts the parchment down on a nearby table and crosses her arms. "So, Reign needs somewhere to lay low for a while?"

And as fate would have it, that would be her house.

Reign shifts, his gaze settling on Mac. "I told you this was a bad idea."

Mac ignores him as she moves around the room, occasionally brushing her fingertips over a lamp or a vase. "We were at our foster home when the cops rocked up."

Arielle startles but quickly hides it. Foster home?

"Just after we learned some guy called Detective Kane has been asking after Reign," Mac continues.

Sweet ghosts. Detective Kane was asking about the stolen car on the day her mother disappeared.

"Reign had to punch one of them out for us to get away. Then we quickly learned that Kane's been asking around the street, so we knew we couldn't go back to the hangout." Mac smiles brightly. "We were running out of options when I thought of the Professor." She opens her arms. "And here we are."

Arielle turns to Reign. "I'd imagine you're having second thoughts."

He looks away. "All you need to do is say the word, and we'll be gone."

Except Arielle, fool that she is, doesn't plan on doing that. No matter how rude and taciturn Reign's been, she's not someone who would just turf him out on the street.

"Well, you're not going to be much help from a jail cell," she retorts. "As long as you stay quiet and out of sight, the guest house will work just fine."

He straightens, blinking a couple of times. "Ah, thanks."

It's Arielle's turn to blink. Those two gruff words seem to wrap straight around her heart.

"Whoa," Mac says, something in her voice making them both turn around. She's standing beside the table and holding the parchment, looking at it in amazement. "You have the instructions on how to open the Gates of Hell?"

CHAPTER 21

REIGN

Reign shakes off the weird sensation that just crept into his chest. Few people have offered him somewhere to stay; it's nothing more than that. It has very little to do with the idea of spending more time with the girl who just made that offer as if anything else wasn't an option...

Glad for the distraction—and a little alarmed at Mac's choice of words—he quickly joins her. Looking over her shoulder, he frowns.

"That's written in by a two-year old, Mac. One who had way too many fruit loops for breakfast. It's illegible."

Arielle nods, glancing at it even though she doesn't move. "It's some sort of ancient hieroglyphics. I suspect it's a language that doesn't even exist anymore."

Mac moves the parchment closer to her face, as if she's suddenly become long-sighted. "Really? But it's talking about the Gates of Hell."

Arielle is instantly by their side. "You can read it?"

Reign's stomach drops to his feet. Surely, Mac can't read it...

His best friend moves the parchment back out to arm's

length. "It is most definitely a set of instructions on opening the Gates of Hell. All seven of them."

"Is this because you've spent too much time at the library?" Reign asks, an uneasy feeling wrapping around his spine.

"It must be," Mac says, sounding a little edgy herself.

"What does it say?" Arielle breathes.

For some reason, Reign's pretty sure they don't want to know.

Mac's eyes scan the weird symbols marching across the ancient paper. Her dark eyebrows scrunch down low. "For each Gate an Innocent must be killed."

Seven Gates. Seven Innocents. If someone had told Reign this twenty-four hours ago he would've asked to sample whatever they were smoking. But now...the words coming from Mac make him feel ill.

"An Innocent?" Arielle asks in horror. "What's an Innocent?"

Mac glances at the back of the parchment, as if she's looking for more information. "It doesn't really say." She looks up at Reign and Arielle. "An innocent life taken as a ritualistic sacrifice somewhere? Maybe a virgin?"

Bile is trying to creep up Reign's throat. "That's just sick."

Arielle's blue eyes are wide in the half-light. "If this is real, we need to stop it."

"Whoa, let's slow down here." Reign takes a step back as if to emphasize the point. "We don't know what any of it means. I'm thinking we give this to Gabby and Colt. Get their take on it."

Mac nods, looking pensive. "Where was this?"

"My mother had it hidden in the wall," says Arielle.

"But why?" Mac persists. "Why did Sierra have it here? Why not keep it in the crypt?"

Arielle shakes her head. "I've discovered my mom had a lot of secrets."

There's a catch in Arielle's voice that has Reign glancing at her, but she quickly looks away, avoiding his gaze.

He's talking before he realizes what he's doing. "If I cared about someone, I sure as heck wouldn't have told them about all of this. I'd have tried to keep them as far away from it as I possibly could."

Arielle's brows crinkle as she considers his words. Next, she chews her lip in a way that draws his attention to it.

But Reign looks away before those fire-blue eyes can trap him again. He's not even sure why he spoke. He's not the type of guy who tries to reassure others. He doesn't ask for comfort, and he doesn't hand it out.

Mac rolls the parchment back up. "I'm guessing she kept it separate because if what it says it's true, it could be uber dangerous in the wrong hands."

"*If* what it says is true," Reign adds. "Look, it's late. Why don't we try and get some sleep and talk to Gabby and Colt in the morning? If we're dealing with Innocents and sacrifices and portals to Hell, we can talk game plan then."

A part of him is still hoping this is some sick joke. That maybe there are secret cameras, and a too-perfect game show host is going to jump out any second.

Arielle gasps. "No..." Her terrified gaze bounces between Reign and Mac before settling on him. "What if the people who took my mother believe she's an Innocent?"

Seven women abducted.

Seven Gates of Hell.

Ritualistic sacrifices...

Reign decides to outright reject the notion. "Unless you were adopted, I'm going to make the call that your mom ain't a virgin."

Arielle instantly relaxes. "That's true." She lets out a breath. "Maybe you're right. Maybe we all need to try and get some sleep."

Mac wipes her hands down her face. "I'm liking that idea."

"The attic is this way." Arielle's just taken a step toward the door when a *crash* powers through the house.

Reign is instantly in front of the two girls. "What the freak was that?"

Mac steps around him. "It sounded like it came from the front entry."

Arielle grips Reign's upper arm. "But—"

A tall man strides into the living room. Cold blue eyes scan the space until they fall on the three teens standing in shock. His lip curls in satisfaction. "Give me the parchment."

Every muscle in Reign's body is wired with adrenaline. He draws in a breath and expands his chest, shifting so he's blocking Arielle even more. "Go screw yourself."

The man angles his head, his brown hair messy and unkempt as he extends his hand. "Now. Or I kill you all."

The flat, ruthless way the man says the words has Reign's pulse spiking. It wasn't a threat. It was a cold-blooded promise.

Arielle steps around Reign, her hand still holding his arm like a lifeline. Even though he can feel her trembling, her voice is steady when she speaks. "You're not having it."

Something flares in the man's eyes only to be quickly enveloped by ice. "Very well." He reaches behind to pull something out.

Reign already knows it's a gun.

"What is going on in here?"

The sound of footsteps stomping down the stairs has everyone gasping.

"Run, Aunt Shell," Arielle shouts.

The man quickly steps to the side, remaining hidden as

Arielle's aunt enters the living room. "It's after midnight, Arielle. What—"

She freezes when the man presses the gun into her back, her eyes expanding exponentially.

"I was just striking a deal," he says. "And you've just become my collateral."

Arielle moans in anguish, the sound tearing at Reign's heart. Aunt Shell is now frozen with fear, her terrified eyes pleading with them.

"All I want is the parchment and no one dies." He shrugs. "We all win, really."

Mac steps forward. "Deal." She holds out the rolled up parchment. "Just don't hurt anyone."

The man shoves Aunt Shell forward, snatches the parchment, and is gone.

Reign's about to go after him when Arielle's hand tightens on his arm. "No," she says, her voice laced with panic. "He has a gun."

"So do most people in my neighborhood," Reign points out. If Lance hadn't died by a bullet wound, Reign would probably carry one himself.

"Please don't go after him."

For some reason, Reign knows she's imagining the dead body they saw today. He sighs. The guy would be long gone by now, and Reign doesn't know this part of Mercy City. "Fine, then. But just for the record, I ain't scared of no heat."

Arielle lets out a breath. "Thank you."

The flash of pleasure warms through Reign again

"What...what just happened?" Aunt Shell asks in a thready voice as she collapses on the couch.

Arielle rushes to her. "Are you okay? Do you need anything?"

Aunt Shell shakes her head, still looking dazed. "I just need to know what's going on."

"I found some...paperwork of Mom's. The next thing we knew, that psychopath was crashing through the front door, demanding it."

"What paperwork? What did it say?"

Arielle glances at Mac. "We couldn't read it."

Mac shakes her head. "It was written in gobbledygook."

Aunt Shell pushes herself so she's sitting more upright. She glances around as if she's looking for something. "We need to call the police."

Mac takes a hasty step forward. "Ah, I'm not sure that's really necessary. Everyone's fine."

Aunt Shell looks at her incredulously. "We were just broken into and held at gunpoint. Of course we need to call the police."

Reign's shoulders want to sag, but he doesn't let them. He should've known this wasn't going to be a haven. That he wouldn't get a break.

If the cops are coming, then he can't stay.

CAIN

Cain stands in the center of the circular library, welcoming the burn of Hell as it scorches through his veins. He's known for a long time that this mansion is significant, and yet the why has always eluded him. Learning that the four teens who have captured his interest were here recently, all behaving strangely, only reinforces that.

He smiles, wondering whether he can add trespassing to the list of charges he's accumulating against the boy.

The more leverage, the more likely he is to talk.

Cain wanders around the round room, the angle of his lips turning sour. He's read every book. Scoured every shelf. Analyzed every symbol. He knows the Keepers of the Grail have been here—their septagram is everywhere.

And yet he's found nothing. Despite the thousands of years of searching, despite the lives he's had to take, he doesn't have the answers he needs.

His hands ball into fists as the fires of fury blaze even brighter. He strides out of the room and out of the mansion. Night blankets him, the whisper of a breeze trying to soothe him. But even the wind will die at some stage.

Cain glances down at his arm, turning it until the mark on his inner forearm is visible. The Mark of Cain. The backward seven with two dashes within it is still red and raised. As if he was only freshly branded, as if the punishment of immortality has only just been inflicted upon him.

His hand clenches, the shifting muscles and tendons causing the Mark to twist and ripple. How humans crave the promise of endless life, the fools. They romanticize and fantasize about living through the ages, of seeing what's to come. But they forget that you steadily accumulate everything that has been. Mistakes. Disappointment. Loss. And that you inevitably outlive anything good. In fact, he has seen many things die. Innocence. Hope. The belief that time will heal all wounds.

Because millennia have passed, and Cain is still living with shame and regret.

He climbs back into his car, tamping down the fury of the ages. He has his own way of making this right and that plan has already been set in motion.

The radio crackles. "We've had a one-four-six on Herald Street. Any available units please respond."

Cain's hand is on the volume dial, uninterested in some

mundane break and enter when he stills. He grabs the mic and presses the button. "Detective Kane here. Please confirm address."

"Three Herald Street," the dispatcher clarifies. "Intruder armed but is believed to have fled the location."

The house he was at only a few days before. The house associated with one of the women who have been abducted.

Grinning at his stroke of luck, Cain speaks into the hand-held again. "Copy that. On route."

"Copy that," responds the dispatcher. "Second vehicle on route. Proceed with caution."

Jamming the gas down, Cain roars away in a spray of gravel.

The Keepers of the Grail know about the Mark. They know how to end this. Reverend Daniels told him as much just moments before Cain killed him.

Except their solution will take time. And Cain has had enough of its infinite crawl to nowhere.

He now knows that Lucifer is the only one with the power to end his suffering. He alone can remove the Mark. Releasing him is inevitable.

But until then, Cain is determined to learn every secret the Keepers of the Grail have been protecting. It's possible his liberation is only one more life away.

And according to his research, Reign is the last living Keeper.

CHAPTER 22
ARIELLE

Aunt Shell hangs up the phone, tucking it back into the pocket of her nightgown. "They're sending someone over straight away," she says, trying to sound reassuring. "Don't you worry; the police will take care of everything."

Arielle turns to Reign, speaking quietly but urgently. "You need to run. Hide. Something!"

Except Reign shakes his head. "Not happening. This is an ish-me, not an ish-you."

Arielle frowns, wondering what he's talking about, but Mac steps in closer before she can ask.

"Maybe she's right. You being here isn't going to end well."

Reign rolls his eyes. "Nothing I do ends well. I'm fine. There's a chance they won't recognize me."

Arielle bites her lip. The police will need to speak to Reign. They'll want a statement from him about the man who barged in here, holding a gun.

Aunt Shell hoists her hands on her hips. "What in the world are the three of you talking about? What would anyone want with a lovely young man like Reign?"

"Look, Mrs—"

"Please, call me Aunt Shell."

Reign seems to lose his ability to speak for a second. He shifts uncomfortably. "I've done some things that I regret," he tries to explain.

"We've all made mistakes, Reign." She smiles at him reassuringly. "That's not who you really are and I'm sure they'll see that."

Unsure whether her aunt is being naive or deliberately obtuse, Arielle looks to Mac, hoping she'll try again. Reign can't be here when the police arrive.

But Mac shakes her head. "I think he's the love child of a mule and goat. He's twice as stubborn as either of them," she says resignedly.

"Damn straight," agrees Reign.

"And if he's decided he won't let anyone cop heat because of him, then we won't be able to change his mind."

"Double damn straight."

Arielle arches a brow. "Even if he's wrong?"

Reign's mouth snaps shut as Mac grins. "Yep. Even when he's wrong."

Reign scowls at her. "Not helping."

The sound of a car pulling up has the three of them stilling.

Aunt Shell rolls her eyes as she bustles to the door. "Come on, you three. You're acting more scared of the police than the man with the gun!"

Aunt Shell opens the door and Arielle freezes. Three men stand in the doorway. One in a suit, two in uniform.

Arielle feels Reign tense beside her. She wants to shove him out the back door. Hide him in a closet. Drop a paper bag over his head. Anything that will mean what's about to happen next can be stopped.

"Good evening, Michelle," says Detective Kane. "We've had a call about a disturbance."

Aunt Shell opens the door to let them in. "Thank you for your prompt response, Detective. We've had quite the scare tonight."

Arielle sees the moment Detective Kane realizes Reign is there. His eyes flare. "I can see why." He turns to the two uniformed officers behind them. "Arrest this boy."

Run, Reign! But he just stands there, stoic and silent.

"I beg your pardon?" Aunt Shell asks in surprise. "There must be some kind of misunderstanding. This isn't the man who attacked us. In fact, he was much taller—"

"This boy is wanted for questioning, ma'am. He was involved in a robbery. In fact, he was seen driving the getaway vehicle."

Arielle flushes with anger. There are bigger things at stake here. "A man just stormed into our house and held us at gunpoint!"

"And I'm very sorry to hear that. We'll take your statements shortly." Detective Kane turns hard eyes to Reign. "But you're harboring a suspected criminal. I'm thinking of your safety."

Arielle leaps forward. "No! You can't. He's...a friend."

Detective Kane throws his head back and laughs. "This street scum is your friend?" he asks incredulously. "You need to pick better company. Have you considered that your intruder is someone known to Reign? That maybe they were working together?"

Mac slides closer to Arielle, forming a barrier between Reign and the detective. "Watch who you're calling scum," she spits.

Arielle's blood freezes when Detective Kane reaches into his jacket and pulls out a gun, pointing it directly between her and Mac. The two police officers' hands shoot to their belts as the air congeals with tension.

"He comes with me," Detective Kane says flatly. "Now."

Reign pushes between them, inexplicably stepping closer to the revolver pointed at his chest. "This isn't necessary. I'm not resisting arrest."

"Cuff him," the detective growls, almost as if he's testing Reign.

Reign turns around and places his hands behind his back. His gaze is full of warning, silently telling Arielle and Mac to keep quiet. Arielle winces with each *snap* of the handcuffs.

Detective Kane opens the door. "Let's go and have a chat, shall we?"

Something about the question has shivers spiraling down Arielle's spine. She almost speaks up when Mac grips her arm, shaking her head imperceptibly.

Reign pulls up a cocky grin. "Sure, but I'm going to be honest, I'm not a big talker."

Mac lets out an imperceptible groan as the detective's face hardens. "All I want is the truth," he states flatly.

He goes to lead Reign out, but Reign flicks his hand off his shoulder. "I walk far better than I talk," he growls.

Detective Kane says something under his breath as he shuts the door. Arielle turns to Mac, intending to suggest they follow Reign, when she sees that all the caramel has faded from the girl's skin.

"You heard what he said, didn't you?"

Mac nods, her color returning as her face forms into a frown. "He said that could easily be reversed."

It's Arielle's turn to go pale. *I walk far better than I talk.*

That could easily be reversed.

What sort of questioning is Detective Kane planning? Images of cop shows and police brutality flash through Arielle's mind like they've been discharged by a machine gun, but she pushes them away. They're dramatized stories, nothing more.

Aren't they?

Mac strides to the door. "I'm going to follow them."

Arielle jolts into action. "I'm coming, too."

"Oh no you're not."

Aunt Shell's voice cracks through the air. She's stayed silent through this whole ordeal, no doubt trying to process what's happening. But now, she seems to have found her footing again.

She steps in front of the door. "Ari, you aren't going anywhere."

Arielle glances from her aunt to Mac. She desperately wants to go. But she's never defied her aunt before. She glances at the two uniformed police officers who are still standing in the hall, waiting. If she does storm off, she's going to have to explain why...

Mac steps in between them, facing Arielle. "Your aunt is right. You should stay."

"But—"

"Look, I know Reign makes it a personal challenge to bring out the worst in people," she says wryly. "And yes, that works fine if you want to be loner, but not so well when a detective with a frown for a face is wanting some answers. But neither of us can do much until they're done." Her gaze surreptitiously flicks over her shoulder toward Aunt Shell. "Plus, your aunt's right. It's probably nothing more than a great big misunderstanding."

Mac's telling her that Arielle needs to look like she's not getting involved. That they need to maintain a pretense that nothing big is going down.

That there are no demons.

No angels.

No Gates of Hell.

Arielle lets her shoulders drop. "You're right. This is a big mix up. Everything that happened tonight has got me all jangled." She looks to Aunt Shell. "And these lovely policemen need our statements."

Mac flicks a grateful gaze before walking to the door. She waves to Aunt Shell and the policemen. "I'll give my statement at the station while I'm waiting," she throws over her shoulder before quickly leaving.

Aunt Shell gives Arielle a long look before leading all of them to the living room. There, the policemen take their statements. Aunt Shell didn't get a look at the guy seeing as he was behind her, holding a gun to her back. Arielle, on the other hand, feels like his face has been imprinted on her memory, she suspects because of the terror of seeing her aunt at the end of a deadly weapon.

Just like Aunt Shell said, the man was tall. His light-brown hair brushed over his ears and his eyebrows, looking as if fingers had been threading through it continuously. His eyes were blue, a strange mix of hot fury and cold detachment. And he now has the parchment. The ancient instructions to opening the Gates of Hell.

She told the police the same thing she told her aunt—that she'd just found the parchment amongst her mother's stuff but was unable to read it as it was in some weird looking hiero-glyphics. And she was able to hold the man's gaze the whole time because she was telling the truth. Just not all of it.

The policemen take notes on everything, offering for Arielle to come down to the station to look through some mugshots. She nods, although she suspects this man isn't on any police database. A quick search reveals little evidence—no finger-prints and a broken door. The policemen tell them they'll do everything they can to track down the intruder. For some reason, it feels like an empty promise.

Aunt Shell thanks them as they leave, even offering them

some biscuits before they go. They decline and she sees them out, full of smiles and gushing gratitude.

The moment the door closes, she spins around and crosses her arms. "What in the world is going on, Arielle?"

Aunt Shell's use of her full name tells Arielle that she's mad. Really mad.

"I want answers, and I want them right now."

CHAPTER 23
REIGN

R eign's been questioned before. He glances around the bare room he's in—table bolted to the floor, chair that certainly wasn't built for comfort, concrete walls that are stained with guilt. Everything looks like the other times.

Except for one thing.

There's no microphone and the video camera in the corner of the room is missing a red flashing light. There's nothing to record what's about to go down, and he doubts Detective Kane is planning on bringing anything with him.

This little interrogation is going to be off the record.

Reign keeps his hands clasped on the table and his face blank. It's hard to intimidate someone who has little to lose.

The metal door across the room opens and Detective Kane steps through, holding a sheaf of papers. He's removed his jacket and tie, either trying to look casual, or ensuring he's free to move. Reign suspects it's the latter.

The detective takes the seat across from him, the metal legs scraping loudly over the cement floor. Reign simply watches dispassionately. There's something about this douche that he really doesn't like.

"I'd like my phone call and a lawyer," he states flatly.

Detective Kane snorts. "For a conversation that will have no evidence of existence? That's hardly necessary." He places the paperwork on the table between them, scanning it with great interest. "Petty theft. Unlawful possession of suspected stolen property. Public nuisance. Trespass."

"The first was for a bag of crisps and a six pack of soda. For the second charge, I stand by my signed statement that I found that cell phone and was on my way to return it. As for the last two..." Reign grins then shrugs. "They were the most fun."

Detective Kane continues as if he hasn't spoken. "That's quite the list of misdemeanors you've accumulated, Reign." He angles his head. "The judge won't like that."

"If I cared, that would be mildly intimidating."

Detective Kane's lip twitches as if he's suppressing a snarl. "What was your involvement in the heist that occurred two days ago?"

"What heist?"

"Don't play stupid with me, boy. We have witnesses."

And if they find the Audi, then they'll have his fingerprints. But Reign knows what any other street rat has learned—deny until the proof is irrefutable. Then keep denying.

"I'm happy for you," he says warmly. "I hope they're credible witnesses. It'll make your job a whole lot easier in the courtroom."

Detective Kane doesn't look surprised at Reign's hedging. His gaze sharpens. "I have some information that suggests you were at the Sinclair Mansion today. In fact, two men were found dead not far from there."

Internally, Reign jolts at the sudden change of topic and the mention of the dead men. He arches a brow, trying to buy himself some time. "The where?"

"The Sinclair Mansion," the detective says smoothly, as if

he's willing to play the game. "Large house on the outskirts of Mercy City. Quite old. Belongs to a founding family of the area."

"Yep, just the kind of place I like to hang," Reign scoffs. "When you've grown up with nothing, it's a real buzz seeing how the people on the other side of the tracks live. I'd go every weekend if I could find more cell phones to hock."

Detective Kane's fingers twitch on the paperwork, the only outward sign that he's already had enough of the game.

"Tell me, what is your interest in Arielle Hartely?"

Already expecting another topic change, Reign suppresses the jolt at hearing Arielle's name. He's never heard her surname until now. He tucks away the nugget of information even as he tells himself it doesn't matter.

"She's hot," he says with another shrug. "I suspect my interest in her is similar to any other guy who has a pulse. I mean, those boots..." He leans forward, his gaze on the Detective. "They're cute-sexy. Who can stay away from a girl who can pull off cute *and* sexy?"

Fury snaps across the detective's face as he surges to his feet. He stands over Reign, pressing his face close. "What were you doing in the mansion?"

"Enjoying a spot of tea in the parlor," Reign snaps.

As he says the words, he knows they're a mistake. The flash of triumph in the detective's cold brown eyes only confirms it.

"So, you were there. That house is one of the few mansions in the state to have a parlor." Detective Kane smiles. "So very British of them, don't you think?"

Reign doesn't bother answering. He could point out that he threw out a cocky response, having no idea what a parlor is and whether the Sinclair Mansion even has one, but he'll look like he's arguing too hard. Instead, he goes on the offense.

"You are certainly very interested in the Sinclair Mansion,

Detective. If I were to visit there, is there anything in particular I should check out?"

The smile wipes from the detective's features. He pushes his face close enough to Reign's that he can feel the cold, hard fury that's throbbing through him. "Enough," he grinds out. "You're almost eighteen, Reign. Big boy jail won't tolerate your cocky attitude with the same patience I've shown you." He leans back, jerking his cuffs back down. "Which is why I'd recommend you accept my offer."

Reign waits, his gut clenched. He already knows he won't like what's coming next.

Detective Kane smiles coldly. "I'll drop all charges against you if you show me what secrets Sinclair Mansion hides."

Reign holds very still as those words sink in. The detective knows there's something at the mansion. And he wants it so bad he's willing to give Reign a get out of jail free pass. Now, that's certainly an outcome he didn't anticipate—the promise of freedom.

He glances up, holding Detective Kane's gaze. "Did I mention that I don't like tea? The last place you'd ever find me is a parlor."

The detective shoots to his feet, picks up the chair, and throws it at the wall. The chair shatters, metal legs bouncing off the cement while the plastic seat explodes into shards.

Reign narrows his gaze at Detective Kane. "It seems some people feel strongly about tea."

Detective Kane abruptly steps back. His nostrils flare as he draws in an audible breath. He bangs on the door twice, never breaking eye contact. "How about I give you the night to think about it? Our cells will only give you a taste of what's to come if I throw the book at you with everything I have—which is exactly what I plan on doing if you don't talk—but sometimes a taste is all you need."

The door opens and two uniformed police officers enter. Reign stands and raises his chin, noting the way their gazes shift away from the pieces of chair on the floor. Shaking his head in disgust, he turns, extending his arms to be cuffed again. The hard metal wraps around his wrists, clamping a little too tight before he's yanked away.

Detective Kane holds the door open, waving his arm with a flourish. "Have a wonderful night, Mr. Everson."

Reign ignores him as he's escorted out. Detective Kane is a clueless ass. Reign's life isn't like Arielle, Gabby's, or even Mac's. There aren't a plethora of possibilities waiting for him. His future is mapped out down two paths only. Jail. Or death.

Right now, the detective is showing Reign whether option A is going to be the more palatable one.

He's walked to the back of the station where several cells are sectioned off. Black bars line the front, while more gray cement separates each one. They're all empty apart from the one at the end.

Reign lets out a silent breath of relief. Hanging in a barely furnished room on his own for the night isn't a new experience. In fact, this place is cleaner. Heck, he's willing to bet the food is better, too.

Except the officer shoves him past the first cell. And then past the second. Reign digs his heels in when he realizes they're passing each empty one. "These ones are free," he points out. "You can't legally put me in that one when there are others available."

The officer grunts as he pushes him forward. He clangs a key into the door and yanks it open, shoving Reign in. "Give me your hands," he orders, quickly unlocking the handcuffs. "See, I'm not a total asshole."

The door slams shut, the noise bouncing off the unforgiving

walls. "Just holler when you're ready to talk," says the officer, already walking away.

"You are definitely a total asshole," Reign calls after him.

"Keep it quiet!" screeches a voice from the corner of the cell.

Reign spins around to see a man curled up on one of the concrete slabs they call beds in this place. His clothes hang on his thin frame and his hair is sticking up at odd, greasy angles. He wraps trembling arms around his head. "Too much noise," he wails.

Reign instantly recognizes he's in a cell with an addict, one who's crashing. He takes a slow step to the other bed on the opposite side of the cell. "Sorry, man, I—"

The guy leaps to his feet, eyes crazed in his bearded face. He rushes at Reign, stopping only an inch away and swaying his head erratically. Reign holds completely still, even though every muscle is poised and ready to fight for his life.

"You stay quiet, I'll stay on my half, understand?" the man hisses through brown teeth.

Reign nods. He's seen people like this before, those whose cravings rule their mind. It makes them unstable and unpredictable. And willing to go to extreme lengths to get what their body desperately needs.

The man sways for a few more seconds, eyes unblinking and mouth working, before turning back to his concrete bed. He curls up on the vinyl covered slip of mattress, wrapping his arms around his head again.

Reign moves silently to his half of the cell. He sits on the mattress, grimacing when it creaks under his weight. His cellmate groans and frantically scratches at the scabs on his arms, but he doesn't look up. Resting his back on the cold cement wall, Reign lets out a slow breath.

It's going to be a long night.

He drops his head back, allowing his eyelids to droop as if

he's off to snoozeville. Although there's no chance he'll be sleeping tonight, it's best if his cellmate thinks he is. He notes the cameras attached to the ceiling on the other side of the bars. Detective Kane and his crooked cops can assume he's doing the same, too.

Reign lets his mind drift into what he calls street sleep. One part of his brain hovers close to the rest his body craves, remembering the sensation of oblivion but not quite getting to taste it. The other part is hyper-aware of the man several feet away, noting his irregular breathing, the way he jolts each time he scratches at his cement-colored skin. That part of his brain is waiting for the promise of threat to be fulfilled.

It means the moment the barest thread of smoke creeps across the cell floor, Reign sees it. He desperately tries to pretend it isn't there. Except the smoke grows and thickens, creating eddies that curl around the prison bars and lap at the edge of the concrete beds.

No, not now.

Joseph appears a second later, at first little more than a see-through apparition, but quickly gaining substance. He glances around, seeming to recognize where they are.

"You have been jailed?" He takes a step forward. "You must get out of here," he says urgently.

If Reign wasn't in a jail cell, he'd close his eyes so he could complete the pretense that this isn't happening. He doesn't need to glance at his cellmate to check whether he's seeing this. He already knows he can't. The guy is no longer the craziest person trapped in this cell.

Joseph frowns. "Evil is coming, I can feel it."

Yeah, well, Reign's sanity is leaving. He can feel that, too.

"You must accept your destiny, Grail Keeper. You are our last hope."

Reign chews on the inside of his cheek so hard he tastes

blood. He wants to shout that if he's anyone's last hope, then they've got some serious problems. Of all the hallucinations his mind could've concocted, it had to be one that only reminds Reign of what a disappointment he is.

Actually, it's probably a good thing it's safer that he doesn't move or speak right now. The need to punch Joseph is overwhelming.

The old man's robes droop as his shoulders sag. "I will show you what is fated if you do not stop this, Grail Keeper."

The mists on the ground steadily turn red, as if blood is being spun into cotton candy. Reign's about to turn away, shocked and sickened, when something begins to rise from the crimson smoke. Thick and square, it looks so solid he'd swear it's real. Despite the word barely existing in his vocabulary until a few days ago, he knows instantly what it is.

Obelisk.

The tower cracks and the sound is so loud it almost makes Reign duck. Blazing light streaks through the cell, red and fiery as if Hell itself is breaking free. The crevices expand, the light becoming blinding.

Stop! No more!

But his silent words fall on deaf ears. Joseph watches on, his face a twisted mix of desperation and determination.

Shadows begin slithering out, formless yet very much alive. At first, in ones or twos, but they quickly become a tide of black ink. The creatures that seem to be made of nothing but night spread through the sky like cancer. The soulless beings screech with excitement, the sound as bloody as the red the cell is now stained in.

"No!" Reign roars, leaping to his feet. "Make it stop!"

The vision and Joseph disappear, leaving Reign to stand in the center of the room, breathing heavily. He tries to tell himself what he saw wasn't real, but the fear thumping through his veins refuses to believe it.

Suddenly, something else is before Reign, capturing his attention. It's his cellmate.

And he didn't bring his marbles with him.

"I told you to be quiet," he says, threat laced through his voice and crazy climbing through his eyes.

CHAPTER 24

ARIELLE

A rielle suddenly wishes she'd gone with Mac. Just like every second in the past twenty-four hours, she's in uncharted territory. She's only ever known her aunt to be soft-hearted and mild-tempered. Her sweet nature is the reason she firmly believes Reign is a nice guy.

But right now, Aunt Shell's face is tight with anger, her usually smiling lips little more than a flat line. What's more the police have gone, meaning it's just the two of them. "Let's take this to the living room, shall we?" she asks curtly.

Arielle nods, glad for the chance to get her head around what she's going to say. Whatever it is, it's going to have to be convincing.

Once in the room, Arielle gravitates to her mother's chair, as if it has protective properties. Aunt Shell doesn't sit in her usual place on the sofa, instead pacing several feet one way then back again.

She's the most worked up Arielle's ever seen. "Well?" she demands. "Where did you want to start?"

Arielle shifts uncomfortably. "I...ah..." She clears her throat, jamming some fortitude down her spine as she looks her aunt in the eye, deciding honesty is her best strategy. "I can't really talk about it."

Those words seem to be the very ones her aunt doesn't want to hear. Her hands fly to her chest and she collapses onto the lounge. "Sweet heavens, I've failed again." Her head drops. "Your mother would be so disappointed," she says quietly.

"What?" Arielle whispers, the words punching her straight in the gut.

Aunt Shell looks up. "Why weren't you at school today, Ari?"

"I needed a bit of space," she says, her gaze dropping to her hands.

"And who are Reign and Mac?"

Arielle's spine straightens again. "Reign and Mac are good people—"

Aunt Shell shakes her head. "That's not what I'm asking. How did you meet them?"

"Reign is the guy I ran into at the library. Mac is his best friend. They didn't know anything about Mom and the fact she's missing."

"And the parchment?" Aunt Shell probes. "Why did you have it?"

That question has her hesitating. How much does her aunt know about all of this? Gabby had Arielle promising she wouldn't mention this to Aunt Shell, which suggests she knows very little. Or a whole lot.

"Well?" Aunt Shell asks. "Someone wanted that parchment so bad I was held at gunpoint. What was it?"

Arielle scrabbles for some half-truth so she can ease her aunt's worries.

The sounds of footsteps down the hallway have them both shooting to their feet. Arielle rushes to Aunt Shell and they clasp hands. Her heart thuds against her ribs as she waits to see who their next intruder is.

Gabby appears in the door, scanning the room quickly before landing on her mother and Arielle. "Are you two okay? Mac called, said you had a visitor."

Aunt Shell lets out a relieved huff. "Gabrielle, honey, you just gave us a scare."

"Sorry, Mom." Gabby grins sheepishly. "I should've knocked or something."

Arielle suspects their frayed nerves would've jolted at that, too.

Gabby notes the way her mother and Arielle are still clutching each other. "What happened?"

Aunt Shell recaps everything that's happened, surprisingly calm. Gabby glances at Arielle a few times throughout the story, and Arielle wonders what she's thinking. Is she worried she's told Aunt Shell the truth? Does she know what the parchment contained?

Aunt Shell lets out a breath as she finishes. "I was just asking Ari why she had the parchment in the first place."

Arielle freezes as she turns her expectant gaze to her. She still hasn't come up with a plausible explanation.

"Oh, that?" Gabby says lightly. "It was something I left here for Sierra ages ago."

Aunt Shell's head snaps back to her daughter. "You what?"

"Yep," says Gabby as if it was no big deal. "She thought it was a recipe for camel milk cheese or something."

Aunt Shell's shoulders drop in defeat. "Ari, you should go to bed and get some sleep." She looks at her, the steel in her gaze seeming to flow through to the rest of her. "You need to go back to your studies tomorrow."

Arielle's first instinct is to refuse, but Gabby's eyes widen a notch as she imperceptibly nods. She thinks that's exactly what Arielle should do, too.

Arielle nods. "You're right. Getting back to college is exactly what I need right now."

Aunt Shell visibly relaxes. "Your mom would be happy to hear that. Did you want a hot chocolate to help settle you in?"

"No, I'm fine, thanks," Arielle says with a weak smile. Her stomach isn't up to having anything in there right now. "I'll just read for a bit or something."

Aunt Shell turns to Gabby. "What about you, Gabrielle? Would you like one?"

Although Arielle can't see her aunt's face, there's the slightest pause before Gabby responds.

"Sure, I'd love one."

Arielle turns away, pretending she didn't just see something pass between mother and daughter. "Good night."

Aunt Shell and Gabby chorus their own goodnights before leaving the living room. Arielle walks up the stairs until they disappear into the kitchen. The moment they're gone, she tiptoes back down.

Just as she suspected, there are no sounds of the fridge opening or pots clanging as milk is warmed on the stove. Her aunt and cousin wanted to have a conversation without Arielle present.

"What's going on, Gabby?" Aunt Shell asks in a hiss.

Arielle waits with her breath held. Is Gabby going to give her mother the same story Arielle just did?

"Nothing's going on," Gabby says in a huff. "Camel milk cheese sounded kinda cool."

Relieved, Arielle rests her head against the bannister. Aunt Shell was looking for reassurance, and that's exactly what Gabby's giving her. For some reason, it was important to know that. To know that Aunt Shell is just as clueless about this as Arielle was.

"I don't believe you, Gabrielle."

There's silence and Arielle can just imagine Gabby crossing her arms, maybe chewing on her thumbnail. Her cousin can be pretty stubborn when she puts her mind to it.

"I need to know she's being safe, Gabby," Aunt Shell says quietly. Imploringly. "I owe her mother that much."

Gabby's sigh is loud enough that Arielle hears it through the wall. "I told her Sierra used to research the occult."

Aunt Shell gasps. "Why? I don't understand why you would involve her in this!"

"She's smart and you know it. She was asking questions."

A sick feeling is pooling in Arielle's stomach. Even Aunt Shell knows. Everyone knew...except her.

"And?" Aunt Shell demands. "Sierra never found the Grail! She lost the man she loves for it, and now she's missing! Having Arielle involved is something she never wanted."

Arielle folds over, her arms wrapped around her middle as she clenches her jaw. Nausea is clawing at her throat. Tears are scratching at her eyelids.

They all knew, and they all kept this from her. The three most important people in her life believed she couldn't cope with this.

Gabby doesn't answer and Arielle doesn't know what that means. A part of her wants her cousin to tell Aunt Shell that she's wrong. That Arielle's mother was wrong. That Arielle is far stronger than any one of them realized.

"You conveniently forgot how dangerous this is?" Aunt Shell hisses, as if she's trying to keep her voice down. "A man was in our house with a gun, Gabrielle."

There's silence again.

Tell her, Gabby. Arielle silently whispers. *Tell her I already know who you really are.*

"You promised, Gabby." Aunt Shell's voice has developed a pleading note. "You promised me you wouldn't involve her."

"I just—"

"No, Gabrielle, there is no 'I just' when it comes to this, and you know it. You need to stop before she's in too deep."

Another pause draws out, dragging over Arielle's taught nerves.

Gabby sighs. "Okay, okay. You're right. Ari needs to stay away from all this."

Arielle slams her hand over her mouth as she bolts to her feet. Silently she shoots up the stairs and to her room. There, she shuts the door and leans against it.

The right thing for her is to go to university tomorrow. It's what her family wants.

And yet, what does she do if everything about that feels so wrong?

CHAPTER 25
REIGN

Crazy guy's eyes leap in a way that tells Reign he's about to attack. Reign locks his muscles, hoping this isn't going to hurt too much. All he has to do is get a solid punch and this guy will be out cold.

"Everson! It's your lucky day!"

Reign glances over his shoulder, unwilling to turn his back on the man snarling at him from a couple of feet away. He doubts he's ever heard those words associated with his name.

One of the cops who brought him in ambles over, pulling the keys from his belt. "You're free to go," he mutters darkly.

Reign has no idea what's going on, but he's not going to question it. He quickly moves to the door. "About time. This place has bad feng shui."

The cop opens the barred door and Reign slips through, keeping one eye on his cellmate. The guy goes to rush forward but the clang of the door shutting has him reeling back. He crawls back onto his thin mattress and curls up.

"May as well get clean, bro," Reign says to him quietly. "It ain't worth it."

The man just curls up tighter, the weight of reality too much for him to bear. Reign sighs internally. He knows how that feels.

The cop grips his upper arm and Reign instantly flicks it off. "I know the way out," he growls.

"Seems you know the way in, too," snaps the cop.

They're almost at the front desk when Reign sees who's managed to get him out of this hell hole.

"Hey, Colt," he says warmly. "Long time no see."

Colt indicates with his chin, his body posture looking like he's standing in the middle of a minefield. "Let's go, Reign."

"Stop!" comes Detective Kane's voice as he strides down an opposite hallway. "This young man is under arrest."

The cop who escorted Reign out moves a little closer to him, looking confused. Reign considers jumping the front counter and making a run for it, but Colt must sense it, because he imperceptibly shakes his head.

He levels his gaze on Detective Kane. "Reign is coming with me."

Detective Kane's nostrils flare. "He's not going anywhere."

"Reign is under legal age to be detained without a parent or guardian," Colt states flatly.

Detective Kane's hands clench. "He'll leave. Once I've finished questioning him."

"Questioning him?" Colt's eyebrows flare. "A juvenile? Without a parent or guardian present? Is your superior aware of this?"

The cop beside Reign takes a step away. "Ah, I wasn't there for no questioning," he stammers. Spinning on his heel, he hurries away. "I've got paperwork to do."

Detective Kane takes a threatening step toward Colt. "You wanna play that game, huh?" He crosses his arms as he smiles. "Only a parent or guardian is able to collect him."

Reign stills. There's no way Avril is going to come and get

him out. He could spend days in here.

Colt slaps a piece of paper down on the counter. "I've been appointed his representative by his legal guardian." He angles his head. "And I say he's leaving. Now."

Detective Kane snatches the piece of paper. Reign stays where he is even though he would love to see what's on the document. Surely it has to be forged.

The detective slowly scrunches the piece of paper up in his hand. He turns a furious face to Reign. "I'm not finished with you yet."

Reign recognizes the anger for what it is—impotent rage. He winks at Detective Kane. "But you are for now," he quips.

Quickly making his way around the counter, he joins Colt. By unspoken agreement, they quickly depart. Reign's tempted to glance over his shoulder, wanting to see Detective Kane's tomato-colored face one more time, but he resists. Getting the heck out of here is what he should be focusing on.

Outside the station, a mass of dark curls launches at him. He catches Mac the moment she collides with him, hugging her tight.

After long seconds, she pulls back. "I was worried," she says, the words full of accusation.

"You should've been," Reign says lightly. "That's the cleanest bed I've seen in a long time. I was tempted to stay!"

Mac slaps his shoulder. "You almost did if it wasn't for Colt."

Reign turns to him. "Thanks man, I owe you one."

Colt glances around, clearly uncomfortable that they're still out the front of the station. He starts to stride away, glancing over his shoulder. "That makes us even. You called out earlier when I was fighting those men and one tried to shoot me."

"Great, we're counting," Reign mutters as he and Mac quickly catch up. He glances at Colt as he falls into step beside him. "How did you pull that off? You demons good at forging signatures or something?"

They reach a parking lot and Colt stops beside a cool looking black car. Reign's eyes pop open. "You drive a Mustang?"

Colt nods, a glimmer of pride in his dark eyes. "A 1967 GT."

Reign lets out a low whistle. "Nice."

"Oh wow," Mac says with an eye roll. "It has four tires, an engine, and a whole bunch of metal, just like every other car on the road."

Reign shrugs apologetically. "Sorry, she's not a believer."

Colt grunts as he unlocks the car and climbs in. "She obviously hasn't been to this church."

Mac rolls her eyes again as she climbs into the back seat. "You two disciples can have the front."

Reign climbs in, appreciating the dark leather and well kept interior. Colt starts the engine, and a deep roar throbs around them. They pull out of the parking lot, and Reign's a little disappointed that there was no squealing of tires or fishtailing rear ends.

Colt glances at him. "We're in a police parking lot. Now's not the time to let this baby loose."

Reign grins, deciding that although Colt obviously has a sensible streak, he likes him. Then Colt's words remind him where they're leaving. "So, how did you get me out of there? Have you just committed forgery?"

Mac's head pops between the seats. "Nope. That document was a hundred percent legit."

"Avril signed it?" Reign asks incredulously.

"Yup. I called Gabby, who had Colt come and pick me up from Arielle's. He took me straight home."

The way Mac says home shows exactly what she thinks of the term. As if it's a dirty word.

Colt takes a corner, glancing at Mac from the corner of his eye. "Law is a bit of a personal interest of mine. I knew that you'd need a legal guardian to get you out."

"And when he saw how cray-cray Avril is, he started telling her that he wants to help your troubled soul."

Reign huffs out a half-laugh. "Good luck with that."

Mac slaps his arm again. "He said anyone could be saved, he's seen it." She giggles. "He said he was worried you were starting to hang out with demons."

"She would've signed that piece of paper quick smart," Reign says, impressed.

"Every single one of her chins were wobbling, she moved so fast," hoots Mac.

Colt's lips twitch. "There were certainly a lot of chins."

Reign realizes they're almost back at Colt's apartment. "Well, like I said. Thanks. I'm not on Detective Kane's favorite people list."

Colt pulls up at the curb, frowning as he nods. "I noticed." He turns the engine off. "Let's talk about it inside."

They all climb out and head for Colt's basement. Inside, Gabby leaps to her feet from where she was sitting at the table.

She beams as she rushes to Colt. "I knew you'd get him out."

Reign's not sure, but he thinks he sees Colt's cheeks flush pink. The guy doesn't like too much attention on him. "He was there unlawfully."

"My soldier of justice," Gabby says quietly, her eyes softening as she looks at him.

"Yours, period," he murmurs back.

Mac glances at Reign, making a gagging motion. He grins, pretending to choke himself.

"That's enough from you two," Gabby huffs with her hands on her hips. "One day, you'll find love and you'll be exactly the same."

Reign and Mac glance at each other again, this time bursting into laughter.

"Not in this lifetime," chortles Reign.

Mac shakes her head. "I'm pretty sure that level of puke-inducing connection is reserved for angels and demons."

Reign's laughter dies away as he realizes there's someone missing. "Where's Arielle?"

Gabby's face falls into somber lines. "At home. Where she should be."

Colt takes her hand and squeezes it. "Where she's safe."

Reign feels his brow furrow. "So she's out?"

Why doesn't he like the sound of that?

"I should never have involved her," Gabby says. "This is getting too dangerous."

Reign doesn't point out that it seems like she's trying to convince herself just as much as them. He mulls over what she just said. Arielle's been the poster child of grace under fire throughout all of this, and it's her mother who's missing.

At the same time, they saw Colt kill someone. They were held up at gunpoint in her house. Shit's getting real. If Arielle has a chance to bow out, now's the time to do it. He's about to ask if that's what she wants, when Mac nods sharply, as if she's just reached a decision.

"The best thing we can do for Arielle is find her mother."

Gabby smiles, looking relieved. "Exactly. Which is what we're going to focus on."

Reign crosses his arms, understanding their logic, but unsure how he feels about it. Choice is a privilege life hasn't afforded him very often, so he knows how it feels for others to decide your fate for you. But at the same time, the thought of Arielle getting hurt is like a sledgehammer to the gut.

"Although we still don't have any leads on the white vans used in the abductions," says Colt.

Reign nods sharply. "We were on our way to see what we could find out when the cops turned up at Avril's. We'll get back onto it."

"Hang on a sec, buster," Mac says. "You're not going anywhere."

Reign frowns ferociously. "Of course I—"

"You can't," Colt says flatly. "Like you said, Kane has it in for you. Right now, you need to lie low."

Mac nods. "We got you out once, I doubt that will be so easy the second time."

Reign's jaw clenches so tight his teeth hurt. Dammit, they're right. He's no good to anyone if he's back behind bars. And there's no guarantee that his new cellmate will be as pleasant or easygoing as his last one.

"It's just until things settle down," Gabby assures. "And they don't know you're here, so you've got yourself a place for as long as you need."

Mac skips over and gives him a hug, probably aware that she needs to get going before Reign changes his mind. The threat of trouble on his tail has never stopped him before.

"I'll let you know as soon as I've found something," she promises.

She's gone before Reign can even grunt a response. Conscious he's now in a basement with two people he's met in a pressure cooker, he wonders what he's supposed to do now. The thought of curling up somewhere and getting some shuteye sounds quite appealing.

Gabby frowns at the closed door. "Can we trust her?"

Defensiveness shoots down Reign's spine, any thoughts of unwinding instantly gone. In fact, he was an idiot to have even thought of relaxing. He barely knows these people. "Of course we can trust her!"

She glances at Colt. "It's just that I detect...something about her."

"That she's tough? That she's smart enough to have known about this stuff before you even rocked up?"

Colt ignores Reign, keeping his gaze on Gabby. "Detect what?"

"I can't put my finger on it," she says, frowning slightly. "She's...different."

"And in your white bread world, that's a bad thing, isn't it?" Reign demands. He storms to the door. "Screw this."

Colt is between him and the exit before Reign can blink. His face twists with anger, reminding Reign exactly what Colt is. A demon.

"Gabby's an angel, you fool," says Colt. "She's spent her life being different. Have you thought of losing the chip on your shoulder?"

Reign glares at him. "No. I like it there."

To Reign's surprise, Colt relaxes. Even smiles a little. "I noticed." He crosses his arms, leaning against the door. "I thought you wanted to help Arielle."

"That's what I said, isn't it?"

He owes her after almost mowing her down.

"Good," Colt grins. "Because staying here is how you do that."

Reign grinds his teeth, not liking that Colt's right. He spins on his heel and stomps to the table, flopping down in a chair. "I'm giving Mac twenty-four hours to get some answers," he growls. "If she can't, then I'm outta here."

He's not spending any longer in this basement than he has to.

Not with two people he's yet to decide whether they're friend or foe.

CHAPTER 26
ARIELLE

" I can do this," Arielle murmurs to herself as she stares at the steps leading up to Mercy City University. "I've done this every day since enrolling in my generic social sciences major. Today is no different."

She's about to take a step when she glances at her phone for the gazillionth time. Nothing. No text from Gabby. No news about Reign.

Which is how it was every other morning of her life. No one would need to message her about angels or demons or angry men with guns or detectives who make her skin crawl.

But then again, that was when Arielle could sleep, knowing nightmares weren't waiting to be unleashed. Gabby was human. So was her boyfriend. Reign wasn't a part of her life.

And her mother would've dropped her off instead of Aunt Shell. Because she wasn't missing.

Back when Arielle only had an inkling of how over-whelming feeling lost and confused could be.

"Sure," she says under her breath. "Just another day in the burbs."

Pushing down the anger and the hurt and the confusion,

she stomps up the stairs to the main entry. Staying out of danger is what her mom would want. It's what Aunt Shell and Gabby are trying to desperately do. If that's what Arielle needs to do, then that's what she's going to do.

Heading to class, she acknowledges the odd person who smiles or says hello but doesn't stop to talk. Arielle's never been an outcast, but at the same time, she's never really felt like she's fitted in. She has people to sit with in most lectures, a group she hangs out with at lunch, but she never really connected enough to invite them over. Gabby was always the BFF she had sleep-overs with, giggled with as they messed around with bold shades of lipstick, whispered what they imagined their fathers would've been like.

Arielle tucks her head down, frowning. And Gabby was the one who lied to Arielle her whole life.

She turns to enter her classroom and slams into another body, almost dropping her books. "I'm so sorry!" she exclaims. "I wasn't paying attention to where I was going."

The girl she just bumped into reaches out an arm to steady her. "No, it's all my fault. I was hurrying."

Arielle takes in the blonde across from her. Tall and pretty with perfect hair, she's wearing enough makeup to enhance her fabulous bone structure, but not enough to look made up. Arielle's definitely never seen her before. "Hey, I'm Arielle. I'm guessing you're new?"

The girl nods, tucking a sleek lock of hair over her shoulder. "Lizzie, and this is my first day." She indicates toward the door they tried to enter simultaneously. "I'm hoping this is my history lecture."

Arielle smiles. "Sure is. And it looks like we have it together."

"Well, that's one way to make friends," Lizzie says, rolling her eyes. "Tackling them in the doorway."

Arielle's smile broadens. "You've certainly made an impression. Did you want to sit together?"

Lizzie lets out a breath. "That would be great."

Leading her in, Arielle takes her usual seat toward the back, conscious of the looks they're getting. Lizzie's beauty is sure to turn heads wherever she goes. Lizzie slides in next to her, seemingly unaware, but Arielle suspects she'll make friends easily. Maybe she'll introduce her to some of the others over lunch.

Mr. Rodriguez enters, striding to the front of the class. "I have the results of your papers," he announces, all business like he usually is. "Some of you obviously worked hard on this, others appeared...to have other commitments."

A few people flush guiltily, whilst several look hopeful. Mr. Rodriguez works his way around the room, handing them out, making the odd comment.

He reaches Arielle and passes hers. "Good job, Arielle."

She glances down, seeing the B plus. "My mom helped with this," she says, then quickly bites her lip at the flash of pain that sears through her. That normal world feels so long ago.

Mr. Rodriguez leans forward, his face crinkled with concern. "Any news?"

Arielle shakes her head, her gaze back on the essay. Aunt Shell told her she'd notified the university and her lecturers, but dealing with the sympathy is harder than she thought it would be.

"Well, if you need some time off, let me know. We can work something out."

Arielle's hands grip the paper. "It's fine. Mom would want me focusing on my studies until she's back."

Mr. Rodriguez's eyebrows shoot up only for him to quickly bring them back down. "Of course she would."

He moves onto the next student who groans about getting a D minus, but Arielle tunes them out. Was Mr. Rodriguez surprised that she's planning on staying on top of her assignments? Or her belief that her mother would be coming home...

"What was that about?" Lizzie whispers beside her.

Arielle stills, wondering how she's going to explain the complicated mess her life now is.

"Oh, goodness me," Lizzie exclaims. "I shouldn't be prying. I'm so sorry, I'm supposed to be making friends, not being a nosy newcomer!"

Arielle shakes her head. "No, it's fine. My mom went missing a few days ago."

"Oh god, that's awful," Lizzie says, her hand flying to cover Arielle's. "Please, let me know if there's anything I can do."

"Sure." Arielle tries to draw up a smile. Lizzie is being sweet, but this isn't something she can talk about with anyone.

Mr. Rodriguez clears his throat, and Arielle turns to the front of the room with relief. She should've stuck to going solo, it would've been easier.

"Today, we're going to discuss your midterm papers. For those, we're going right back to Christopher Columbus's discovery of the Americas," he announces with a flourish.

Arielle tries to focus, she really does. But everything that's happened keeps intruding, and for some reason, thoughts of Reign are at the forefront. Is he okay? What happened during the questioning? Have they pressed charges? Arielle frowns. Why does she care so much?

Lizzie lets out a muffled gasp. "You know Reign?"

Arielle glances down, realizing she'd idly scrawled his name on her notebook. "Ah, yeah. I'm assuming it's the same guy." How many Reigns could there be in the area?"

"A body as hot as sin, a face that shouldn't be legal, and the personality of Oscar the Grouch?"

"Yep. That's him," Arielle says wryly. She turns to face Lizzie more fully. "How do you know him?"

Lizzie flushes delicately as she glances at her pink mani-cured nails. "Oh, we used to be...friends."

The layers that are added to the word 'friend' aren't lost on Arielle, although she pretends it doesn't grind right down her spine. Of course Reign has beautiful girls falling all over him. And of course Reign would partake of the goods being offered. It makes no difference to Arielle.

Lizzie looks up, her gaze searching. "Have you seen him recently? Is he okay?"

"I'm not sure," Arielle says tartly. "I haven't seen him since he was arrested."

The moment the words are out, Arielle regrets it. Reign's business isn't hers to share.

"Arrested?" Lizzie asks in horror.

"Look, I have enough on my plate right now with my mom and everything. I don't know anything else."

Mr. Rodriguez's voice rises as he starts to create a timeline on the board and Arielle faces the front again, glad for the distraction. Hopefully, Lizzie will take the hint and the conver-sation will be over. Arielle really needs to focus on how to do well in her term paper.

"Columbus is widely accepted as the first European contact with Central and South America. And excluding a brief Norse habitation several years earlier, the first contact with North America," Mr. Rodriguez says as he continues to scrawl on the board. "Once we've covered the key dates, we're going to explore how accurately the history books have depicted him."

Arielle has just started to take some notes when Lizzie sighs. "Reign was always getting in trouble. Hanging out with those foster kids didn't help."

Arielle hides her surprise at that statement, along with the need to defend Mac. She flips a page in her notebook. This is no longer her business.

"Do you think he's still in there?" Lizzie's hands are twisting in her lap. "Do you think they've got enough to arrest him?"

"I'm not sure," Arielle hedges, keeping her gaze on the board even though her gut clenches. "Maybe."

"That's awful. I mean, I know he can be an ass, but he's a good guy. He doesn't deserve that. If I'd known, I would have..."

Arielle's pen stops mid-word. "You would've what?"

Lizzie shakes her head as if she's already dismissed the idea. "Oh, nothing. I doubt it would make a difference."

"Would what?" Arielle presses. If there's some way to help Reign, she wants to know about it.

"Well," Lizzie says hesitantly. "My dad is the Commissioner. I thought that if I talked to him..." She shakes her head. "It's probably too late."

Arielle straightens, urgency filling her tone. "You should totally talk to him."

"It's just that we're not close. We're not exactly on good terms."

"But he has enough pull to get Reign out," Arielle pushes. "It's definitely worth a try."

Lizzie chews on her lip. "I suppose so." Suddenly, her face brightens. "Reign would be super grateful, wouldn't he?"

Arielle hides her grimace at those words. "I'm sure he'd appreciate it."

Mr. Rodriguez claps his hands. "And that's a wrap, folks. I'm looking forward to learning whether you believe Columbus was a hero or a villain."

The bell rings as if to finish his sentence and the students start to pack up. Arielle starts to do the same but stops.

"So, you'll speak to your dad?" she asks Lizzie.

Lizzie's smile is borderline euphoric. "I'm going to give it a red hot go." She leans forward, wrapping her hand around Arielle's. "You'll let me know if you hear from Reign?"

Arielle smiles through clenched teeth and nods. "Of course."

They swap numbers and Lizzie turns away so fast her corn-silk hair flairs out like some shampoo commercial. With a jaunty wave, she's gone, leaving Arielle to pack up and head to her next class.

Arielle knows she should be happy. This is a sign that she's doing the right thing by being here. If she wasn't at school, she wouldn't have been able to help Reign. Heck, it's possible he'll score not long after he gets out.

But as she tucks her books against her chest, Arielle can't find anything that feels good. In fact, she didn't think it's possible, but she's feeling even more miserable.

CHAPTER 27

REIGN

"You're wearing a groove in the cement," Colt points out from where he's sitting at the table.

Reign keeps pacing across the basement—from the map that pinpoints the seven abductions, to the saggy sofa that he spent the night on. He's missing something. He can feel it.

Gabby shakes her head from the seat beside Colt. "You could've walked to Sinclair Mansion and back by now."

Reign stops beside the map, punching his fist into his hand. "That's it! That's what I'd forgotten!"

Colt pushes upright, his gaze suddenly intense. "Forgot what?"

"So, we know that Kane was mighty interested in Sinclair Mansion."

Gabby nods. "Far more interested in that than your whoopsie on the wrong side of the law."

"Exactly," says Reign. "But we don't know why."

Colt flops back into his chair. "And we have no way of finding out." They spent hours going around in circles last night, each time reaching the same dead end. "We go anywhere near Kane, and he'll find any reason he can to arrest us."

"Except I just remembered something he said when he first started questioning me."

"Illegally interrogating you," Gabby points out.

Reign nods. "Yep. All the more reason this is significant. He flouted the rules so he could find out what he could."

"Well?" Colt asks.

Reign grins. "I'm building suspense, okay?"

Colt raises an eyebrow while Gabby bites her lip, looking like she's trying not to smile.

"Not only did Kane know I was at Sinclair Mansion, he knew two men were found dead not far away. I thought he was throwing that out to intimidate me, but..."

Colt leans forward, his hands on his knees. "Demons clean up after themselves."

"So do angels, actually," Gabby adds. "All supernaturals do."

"I suspected as much," Reign says triumphantly. "They don't want humans asking too many questions."

Gabby gasps. "So, how did he know about them?"

"Bingo," Reign says with satisfaction.

Colt's eyes widen as he turns to Gabby. "He's a demon?"

She shrugs. "It's possible. You guys can cloak your true selves." But then her eyes widen, too. "Do you think he's after the Grail?"

"The Holy Grail?" Reign asks, frowning. The last thing he needs right now is some reference to Joseph and his hallucinations.

"Yep, the one and the same. Sierra has spent half her life searching for it, which is what we suspect had her kidnapped."

"It's protected by the Keepers of the Grail, entrusted to them by angels," Colt adds. His mouth twists. "And wanted by demons for its power."

Reign nods even though he's not sure how his body's moving right now. He's frozen in place as he tries to figure out how he feels about this information. The Keepers of the Grail are real.

Which means...

Reign sits on the arm of the sofa, his legs suddenly weak. Surely not. His stomach clenches painfully, last night's pizza suddenly unhappy to be there. Joseph was telling the truth?

He rubs his forehead, disclosing a piece of information he wasn't going to. "The men who abducted me, they had...demon faces." The same Hell-face Reign saw in the cop car that was chasing him. "They must've been demons, too."

But Colt shakes his head. "They were just men, Reign. Angry, violent men, but just men."

"But..." Reign swallows, wanting to see this conversation through, but also wishing he never started it. "Didn't you just say demons can cloak themselves?"

"Not when they're dead," Colt states flatly.

"Maybe it was the fear of the moment?" Gabby asks gently. "Especially after seeing my wings and all?"

They're suggesting he was too terrified to think clearly. That he was...hallucinating. Reign focuses on the relief that threads through him, growing and amplifying it until it drowns out any other emotion that's trying to gain traction.

This is what he wanted to hear. He can't believe that, even for the briefest of seconds, he was considering the alternative— that he's some Keeper tasked with protecting the Grail. Not only is that ridiculous because street rats like him lack the necessary traits such as honor and integrity for such a task, but Reign already knows how it would end if he did.

He'd screw it up.

Reign twists his face into a wry grin. "Time to lay off the happy juice, from the looks of things." He strides over to the map, keeping his back to Colt and Gabby. "So, in summary, we have a theory, and not much else."

Colt sighs behind him. "Essentially. Although we now have an idea as to why Kane is so interested in Sinclair Mansion."

"A pretty solid idea," Gabby agrees. "It's why that's our next question."

Reign's eyes scan the seven red pins on the map. Each one representing a woman ripped from her life, leaving nothing but fear and confusion behind. "And we have more pressing things to focus on," he points out.

The missing women, one of whom is Arielle's mother.

Turning back to the others, he voices what no one else has. What he'd never say if Arielle was here. "If Sierra's not dead already, then it's only a matter of time before that changes."

Gabby's hand shoots out to grip Colt's. "Sierra's a fighter," she whispers. "She'd do everything in her power to get back to Arielle."

"And we will find her," Colt says firmly, squeezing Gabby's hand. "We have to."

Reign glances at the door, wishing he could be out there doing more than just talking about this. For a moment, he's tempted to leave. To go find the answers they so desperately need. But he crushes the idea the moment it sparks. Kane, a detective who's possibly also a demon, wants him too bad.

His jaw tightens. "Let's hope Mac finds out something useful."

MAC

Mac kicks at a milk crate in the middle of the dingy living room and it crashes into the wall with a gratifying *thud*.

"Where are you?" she huffs into the empty room.

This is the third time she's visited the hangout in her search for Darnell and Rico, and the third time she's come up empty. In fact, the place looks like they haven't been here at all in the past day or so. No new takeout boxes or soda cans, no drug paraphernalia lying around.

It's like they're avoiding the place.

Ducking through the half-hanging door, she stands on the porch, her hands on her hips. In fact, everyone has been avoiding her.

Each person she's run into has suddenly remembered they're supposed to be somewhere, have a drug-induced case of amnesia in relation to the past two days, or have a long story to tell her about some fight they saw between two or three people she's never heard of, never letting her get a word in edgewise.

No one saw or knows anything about a white van, even though one of the women was abducted not far from here. Mac's spent enough time on the streets to know that's a load of crap. Knowing everything about everything is how you stay alive out here.

Mac skips down the stairs, avoiding the one that's little more than a death trap if someone were to put their foot through it, and makes her way to the pavement. She's not going back to Reign and the others without some sort of information.

She's just about to stride away when a noise has her stopping. It's little more than the rustle of a garbage bag, but she's always had sensitive hearing, and she most definitely heard it. Turning to the alley down the side of the house, Mac narrows her eyes. Her eyesight is as sharp as her hearing.

A cat leaps out from behind a dumpster, yowling as it streaks down the alley toward her. The mangy looking feline barely looks at her as it disappears under the stairs of the house. Even though the noise was just explained, Mac waits. If she were to put money on it, that cat looked like it just got shoved. Plus, why would it leave a dumpster and run toward a human?

She goes as still as the rotting building beside her, barely breathing. Just as she suspected, Darnell's head pops up from behind the dumpster a moment later.

Mac stalks toward them. "Lost something?"

Darnell leaps to his feet, shocked fear stamped across his features. "Mac!"

"Surprise," she growls as she stands a few feet away in the middle of the alley, blocking their exit.

Darnell shuffles uncomfortably as Rico does the opposite. His body unwinds as he slouches, his gaze becoming hooded. "Hey, girl. Where ya been?"

Having my mind blown, Mac thinks, in the best way possible. Although learning about the supernatural has overturned Reign's world, for some reason, it was far less of a paradigm shift for her. It just...made sense.

"Having my nails done," she snaps back. She turns her gaze to Darnell, knowing she won't get any answers from shifty Rico. "What were you two doing out here?"

"Dumping anything that's hot."

Mac doesn't point out the stupidity of doing that just outside the house they're using as their hangout. "Why?"

Rico leans a little to the left, shifting subtly in front of Darnell. "Maybe we've seen the error of our ways."

"Wonderful," Mac beams. "Then if you know anything about a white van taking a woman several days ago, you'd tell me."

Rico's face instantly shutters, his relaxed pose gaining tense lines. "Sure we would."

Darnell nods. "If we knew something, which we don't."

Mac strides forward, slamming her hands onto each of their chests and shoving them back against the dumpster. She's had enough of the run arounds, the evasion, the lies. She has enough history with these two for them to trust her.

"People's lives are at stake. Tell me. Now."

Darnell lifts his hands in a conciliatory gesture. "Honest, Mac. If we knew anything, we'd tell ya."

She can't believe she invited these dropkicks to the hangout. "I'm not in the mood for games, Darnell," she snaps. "Reign's in trouble and he needs our help."

Darnell shifts uncomfortably again, but before he can say anything, Rico is knocking away Mac's hand. "Then your lover boy needs to make better choices, don't he?"

He shoves past Mac. "Come on, Darnell. We ain't hanging around here."

Darnell slips past Mac but then hesitates. "The cops are looking for Reign," he says quietly as if trying to explain. "Some detective came looking for him."

"And?" Mac demands. "That's enough for you to turn your backs on him?"

"It's not just that!" Darnell half shouts. "Some girl called Lizzie was also snooping around, asking after him. He's getting a little too popular for our tastes."

Anger sizzles up Mac's spine. "After he gave you a place to stay? After he was your getaway driver?"

Darnell's gaze slips away as Rico shrugs. "He'd do the same."

Except Reign wouldn't. Despite his opinion of himself, Mac knew Reign was different from every other lost and forgotten kid she'd met, and she's spent her entire life in the foster care system. He's not like these two.

"Cowards," Mac spits. "You don't have the balls or the brains to be half the guy Reign is."

Darnell winces as Rico's lip curls. He takes a step forward and Mac draws in a breath charged with anticipation. Rico has no idea what he's up against.

Because Mac isn't just fighting to find these missing

women. Reign may not be her lover boy as this douche has insinuated, but he's still her everything. Her best friend. Her brother in arms against a society that's forgotten them. They're family, one forged by connection, not blood.

And she's going to prove to Reign he's everything she knows he is.

Rico turns his head and spits. "I ain't fighting no girl." He spins on his heel and stalks away, jerking his thumb for Darnell to follow.

Mac snorts. "Now you're going to pretend you have standards?"

They ignore her, not even glancing over their shoulders as they reach the end of the alley, leaving Mac frustrated and fuming beside the dumpster. She looks around, considering throwing something at them. It won't get her the answers she needs, but it'll give her a little burst of joy.

And right now, she suspects she won't have anything to smile about for quite some time.

"Hey, Mac," Rico calls from the street. She looks up, hoping maybe he's discovered a shred of conscience in that selfish head of his.

He grabs his crotch as he jerks his hips. "I guarantee my package is twice what your lover boy's got. Let me know when you want to play with a real man." He hoots with laughter even though Darnell doesn't join in, sauntering away. With a last look at Mac standing alone in the alley, Darnell hurries after him.

"Assholes," Mac mutters.

There's a gust of wind from behind Mac, grabbing at her clothes as it wafts past. She frowns. The alley is a dead end. How could a gust of wind come from that direction?

She turns around, fists by her side, muscles ready to fight or flight. A man steps out of the shadows at the end, walking steadily toward her. Mac narrows her eyes, quickly taking stock. He's young, probably her age, with ebony skin and closely cropped hair. But that's not what has Mac tensing. Broad shouldered and tall, he's not wearing a shirt, revealing layers of finely-honed muscle. His whole body exudes strength in a way she hasn't seen before, but it's even more than that. It's the steady, predatory way he's walking.

"I agree with your analysis," he says, continuing his measured, unflinching approach. "Assholes is the appropriate term for those two specimens of human."

Human. Whoever this guy is, Mac instantly knows he's supernatural. Possibly another demon. And there's no way of telling whether he's in the Colt-I-got-ya-back category, or the killing-frenzy-is-my-pastime type. "Who are you?"

The man's dark gaze flares, anticipation flooding his strong features. "Hello, Mackenzie. My name is Dumah."

CHAPTER 28

ARIELLE

"He's free."

Arielle spins around, hand flying to her chest. "Oh, Lizzie. I didn't hear you."

She works to steady her pulse, wondering how long she'll be walking on this knife edge of fear. Probably until her mother is home, safe and sound...

Lizzie flicks her glossy blonde hair as she giggles. "Sorry, I guess I was excited to tell you."

Arielle glances around. The front of the university is almost empty now, all the students rushing off with somewhere to go. Unlike her... She knows she needs to study—that's what she promised she'd do—but she's loitering. As if she's avoiding going home.

In fact, she's already texted Aunt Shell that she'll walk back.

Then, she realizes what Lizzie just said. "Reign's out?"

"He was released that night," she beams.

Arielle nods, pushing away the thought that she had to find out through a girl she just met. "Well, that's good news."

"Yep!" Lizzie glances around as if to check they're alone. "Are you going to see him?"

Arielle's hand tightens around the strap of her backpack. "Ah, we're not exactly that close."

"Oh." Lizzie scuffs her foot over the pavement. "I was hoping you'd take me to see him."

Take Reign's ex-hottie to visit him? Does the universe think Arielle is a saint? She shakes her head. "Sorry, but I can't," she mutters, glad she's telling the truth.

Reign is likely staying with Colt, and that location is top secret.

Lizzie's face drops with disappointment. "Are you sure? I wanted to talk to him." She twirls a lock of glossy hair. "We have some...unfinished business."

"Sorry, Lizzie. But as far as I know, he's staying with a friend. And that friend is very private, he doesn't give out his address."

Lizzie's shoulders join her face in trying to brush the pavement. "Oh. Okay."

Arielle takes a step away. "Anyway, I'd better get going." She smiles a little. "It seems I have a date with Columbus."

But Lizzie's hand snaps out to grab her arm. "You could give it to him!"

"I beg your pardon?" Arielle asks, a little uncomfortable with the way Lizzie's fingers are digging into her arm.

Lizzie flushes, releasing her. "I gave him something once, but he left it at my place."

Arielle glances at her feet. "I know that feeling," she mutters under her breath.

"Pardon?"

"Nothing," she says brightly. "Look, I'm not sure when I'll be seeing Reign next. Maybe you're better off waiting."

Lizzie looks perplexed. "But you'll be seeing him at some stage?"

Arielle stills as she considers the question. It's not like she'll never see Reign again...is it?

"Of course, you will," says Lizzie, all bubbles again. "That smile of his is like heroin."

Except Arielle has rarely seen Reign smile. She seems to inspire a permanent scowl in him.

"I really don't think—"

Lizzie leaps forward, clasping her hands together. "Please?" she begs. "I really want him to have it. And I only live a block away. We'll be real quick."

Arielle hesitates, swayed by the pleading in the pretty girl's eyes. "Fine," she sighs. "But there's no guarantee I'll get it to him soon."

Lizzie squeals as she jumps up and down. "Thanks! You're the best!"

No, just a pushover, Arielle thinks wryly.

Lizzie loops her arm through Arielle's and tugs her across the road. "It's really not far," she assures her.

Arielle allows herself to be drawn along, noting that Lizzie seems to be very comfortable to touch someone she's only just met. She must be really keen to make new friends.

Lizzie draws her down a quiet street. "I love your boots, by the way. They're so cool!"

Arielle glances down. "Thanks. My mom gave them to me."

For some reason, the reminder of her mother has her wishing she hadn't agreed to this. She should've gone straight home. She should be studying.

She notes the three scrawled words down the side of her laces. *Kindness is power.*

That's why she's doing this. Because it's Lizzie's first day and she needed a friend.

"Your mom sounds cool," Lizzie says brightly.

Except Lizzie seems to have already forgotten that Arielle's mom is missing.

A quick tug and Arielle's pulled down a quiet cul-de-sac. "Almost there," Lizzie chirps. "Reign is going to be so surprised."

Arielle notes that the houses are now smaller, the yards a little messier. Didn't Lizzie say her father was the Commissioner of Police? Surely, he'd have a nicer place in a more up market area?

She stops, pulling Lizzie to a halt. "Are you sure you live down here?"

Although she knows the question is a silly one—of course Lizzie knows where she lives—Arielle voices it anyway. Something isn't right.

Lizzie releases her arm, flicking her hair as she rolls her eyes. "If I lived a block away, don't you think I would've been attending Mercy City University a little sooner?"

Arielle flushes, feeling foolish and naive and thoroughly duped. She flushes an even deeper crimson as she realizes they're all the reasons Aunt Shell and Gabby think she's better staying out of everything that's going on.

Before she can ask what this is all about, a shadow moves behind her. Arielle spins around, heart shooting up her throat and clogging the scream that was trying to escape.

Detective Kane angles his head. "Hello, Arielle."

She takes a compulsive step back, only to crash into Lizzie. She quickly side steps, glancing over her shoulder. "You set me up?"

Lizzie shrugs, glancing at her manicured nails. "I was helping a friend."

Arielle hates the flash of betrayal that spears through her chest. Lizzie owed her nothing. It's her own stupidity that let her down.

Detective Kane casually tucks his hands in his pockets. "I need you to take me to Reign."

"Sorry, I don't know where he is." Even Arielle isn't stupid or naive enough to do that.

"So polite," Kane purrs. "Even when you're lying." His face hardens. "What did you find in the Sinclair Mansion?"

Although the change of topic is unexpected, Arielle is already shaking her head. She has no intention of telling this guy anything. "Some very pretty crockery. You should totally check it out."

A muscle twitches in the detective's cheek as he angles his head. "If you were to help me, I could help with the search for your mother."

Arielle doesn't know if she's more shocked or angry. What the heck has he been doing up until now? She throws back her shoulders. Truth be told, she has more faith in Gabby, Colt, Reign and Mac. "Go suck a duck."

Fury flashes across Detective Kane's face a split-second before he moves. Although Arielle registers the ferocity of the emotion, she never gets a chance to react.

Kane moves too quickly.

His arm lashes out and the back of his hand slams across her face.

Then there's nothing but black.

GABBY

Gabby's never seen so many emotions jammed into one person as she has with Reign.

Anger. Determination. Resentment. Guilt. Fearlessness.

Rage. Way too much self-loathing. And beneath it all, deeply repressed hope.

Feeling others' emotions is both a blessing and a curse. In fact, it's the hardest part of being an angel. After everything they've been through, Colt understands that, which is why he simply nodded when she told him she was going on a pizza run.

His steady gaze told her he understood she won't be going to the local place at the corner. Nope, Gabby needs more of a break from being cooped up with Reign than that. Colt knows she won't be back for an hour or so.

In fact, he even offered for her to drive his precious car. And if that's not love, Gabby doesn't know what is.

Brushing her hand over the black glossy paint, she decides she'd rather walk so she tucks the keys in her pocket. Her legs need a stretch after spending so much time inside. She draws in a deep breath and tilts her face to the sun. Yep, a walk is just what she needs.

Something flickers in the clear blue above her and she stops mid breath. The barest flash of light, it was probably a satellite. Or a weather balloon. Maybe someone's flying a drone.

But still, Gabby waits. In her world, she's learned the usual explanations aren't the only possibilities. She needs to make sure.

The flicker grows, becoming a sparkle, then a glowing ember. It streaks down, leaving a tail of shimmering pearl behind it. Gabby gasps as the vein of brilliant white tumbles to Earth like a falling star.

She yanks the keys back out and unlocks the car. "I'll be careful, I promise," she says aloud.

Colt never intended for her to take his baby very far. But she has to find out why an angel just descended to Earth.

And why now.

Although she taps the steering wheel with impatience,

Gabby drives carefully through Mercy City, heading in the direction that the angel would've landed. Even the car seems to want to go faster, leaping away at lights and purring eagerly every time she accelerates. But she contains their restlessness. Not all angels are friends.

Gabby soon finds herself in the River District, the poorest suburbs of the city. She's just about to consider turning around when a familiar jolt runs down her spine. She's close.

She pulls over to the curb and locks the car. Then she double checks she locked the car. A scratch Colt could probably forgive...eventually. Someone stealing his pride and joy would surely test their relationship. Looking around, she finds she's parked outside a derelict house with a saggy porch and the door hanging sideways by a single hinge. It looks like no one has lived there for a very long time.

Following her instincts, Gabby steps into the alleyway down the side of the house. She can sense this is where the angel landed. Cautiously, she enters, everything on high alert.

But there's a dumpster to her right, some garbage cans to her left, and little else. The alleyway is empty.

Not willing to give up yet, Gabby closes her eyes, breathing in deeply. Yes, there it is. The pure scent of divine grace. This is where the angel landed. Her eyebrows twitch as she senses something else. Someone else has been here.

Gabby's eyes fly open. Mac.

The trace is faint, but the girl's signature stubborn passion is there. Mac was definitely here. And now she's not.

Although there's something odd about Mac, a muted flavor to her emotions that Gabby can't put her finger on, Mac has done nothing but help. And her loyalty to Reign is something Gabby respects. That sort of love can never be born from evil.

Except, Gabby's too late. She's certain Mac's presence and the angel's aren't a coincidence.

"Dammit," she growls as she slams her hand into the dumpster, then instantly winces as a resounding *boom* echoes down the alley.

Gabby pulls her hand away, flushing guiltily when she sees the crater she just punched into the metal. Even now, her powers can still surprise her. Even now, after everything she's been through, she has trouble controlling her emotions.

"Hey, what's going on?"

Two teens appear at the mouth of the alley, frowning. The dark-skinned larger one glances around suspiciously as his smaller, lanky friend hitches up his saggy jeans as he saunters in.

"Well, hello there," he purrs, revealing teeth that really shouldn't be that yellow on a kid that age. "What do we have here?"

Gabby takes a step forward, trying to block their view of the dented dumpster. "I'm looking for a friend of mine. Mac."

The dark-skinned guy frowns but doesn't respond. Saggy jeans shrugs his bony shoulders. "Never heard of her."

Gabby angles her head. "But you knew I was talking about a female?"

The guy's face twists as he takes a menacing step forward. "We don't want no trouble."

"Me neither," says Gabby, holding her ground. "I just want to know where Mac is."

Saggy jeans spins on his heel, shoving his friend as he walks past. "Come on, Darnell. We got better things to do."

Gabby takes a step forward but quickly stops herself. Maybe she should go back to Colt and Reign, see if they can make contact with Mac. Something about all of this feels off.

Saggy jeans storms out of the alley, kicking a trash can on his way for good measure. His friend, Darnell, pauses though.

He turns back to Gabby, concern swimming in his dark eyes.

"A guy took her. No shirt, pretty buff looking. Said his name is Dumah."

Even before Darnell has finished saying the name, Gabby is running, panic climbing up her throat.

Dumah has escaped.

CHAPTER 29
REIGN

When Reign's cell phone rings, he almost doesn't answer it. When he glances at the screen and sees it's Lizzie, he strongly considers turning it on silent. Lizzie never calls just once.

As if to prove him right, the ringing stops only to start right back up again. Colt slides an unimpressed glance at Reign from where he's studying the map. It's what the guy's been doing for the past hour, as if he's turned into some statue of a scholar.

Reign rises from the couch and takes the call. Maybe if he tells Lizzie he's at the library and can't talk, she'll leave him alone. He moves to the other side of the room, tucking the phone up to his ear.

"Hey, Lizzie—"

"Reign, thank god you answered," she says in a rush. "It's Arielle."

Reign freezes. "How do you know Arielle?"

"I ran into her this afternoon. I stopped to comment on her boots. They're the coolest pair of Converse I've ever seen."

Dread trickles down Reign's spine like tar. "Why are you calling me, Lizzie?"

"Oh, Reign, it was terrible," she says, her voice thick with tears. "I walked with her for a bit—she's so friendly, you know?—when a man appeared out of nowhere."

"What man?" he demands. "What happened?"

Lizzie dissolves into sobs. "He took her, Reign. I tried to stop him, but he was too strong."

Reign's heart feels like it's stopped and is pounding out of control, all at the same time. "Where are you? I'm coming right now."

Lizzie gives him an address and Reign hangs up. He finds Colt standing a few feet away, eyes narrowed.

"Who was that?"

"Lizzie, a friend of mine," Reign says, already heading for the door. "She said she saw someone take Arielle. I'm meeting her there."

To Reign's surprise, Colt doesn't move. In fact, he crosses his arms like he's about to turn into a statue again. "We should call Gabby. Come up with a plan."

"You're kidding, right? Arielle's in trouble and you want to think about it?"

"I don't like this. It could be a trap. How do you know you can trust this girl?"

"What? You get a bad feeling about Lizzie, too?" Reign half-shouts. "Just because she's associated with me?"

Colt shakes his head. "We'll call Gabby," he says again, this time with more force. "Then we can go together."

Reign strides for the door and yanks it open. "Go back and stare at your map," he shoots over his shoulder, taking the stairs two at a time.

No wonder those seven women are still missing. Colt needs to meditate on everything first.

Outside, Reign breaks into a run. Luckily, the location Lizzie sent isn't far away. As he weaves around irate people telling him to slow down, Reign pushes himself to go faster. He should never have agreed to keep Arielle separate. It's her mother who's missing. She has more to lose from this than any of them.

Plus, when they left her alone, they left her vulnerable. If Reign wasn't intent on breaking the sound barrier with his sprint, he'd kick himself. Arielle needs to make her own choice as to whether she's part of this.

Reign reaches the location several minutes later, breathing hard as he sucks in great lungfuls of air. Deciding oxygen is for chumps, he takes stock of the house he's now outside of. Large and square, his criminally inclined mind registers it wouldn't be an easy place to break into with its thick brick walls, ornate bars over the windows, and minimal shrubbery to hide in.

He frowns, suddenly wondering what Arielle would be doing around this area. The quiet street is nowhere near her home or any shops. Nowhere to buy cute boots in sight.

Trying to get his breathing under control, Reign approaches the front door, wishing Colt's words didn't decide to take this moment to whisper through his mind.

It could be a trap. How do you know you can trust this girl?

Rapping on the door, Reign notes the curtains are drawn on the windows on either side. There's no way to tell what he's walking into. He tells himself to get a grip. The worst trouble Lizzie ever got into was for chewing gum in class. She's the daughter of the Commissioner, for crap's sake.

The door opens swiftly and a hand shoots out to grab Reign by the shirt. He instantly morphs into a flurry of punches and kicks, his fight instinct taking over. Although several of his blows hit flesh, he's dragged into the house, doubling over when it feels like a sledgehammer just slammed into his gut.

Although his screaming stomach demands that he crumble, Reign doesn't stop swinging. But first one fist is trapped, then the other, and his hands are yanked painfully behind him.

"Hello again, Reign."

The smooth voice slices through his adrenaline, making Reign fight even harder. But whoever it is behind him, holds his hands tight, no matter how hard he jerks. "Go to Hell, Kane!"

The detective chuckles. "Been there, done that. Although it's not that much different to this existence, to be honest."

Panting, Reign sees they're in a hallway bare of furniture. Belatedly, he realizes he didn't even tell Colt where he was going. The knowledge that he's done what he does best—screw up—tastes as bitter as it feels.

He angles his chin. "Don't I need a parent or guardian here for this?"

Kane's eyes narrow as he takes a predatory step closer. "Tell me what you found in the Sinclair Mansion and I'll let you go."

Reign glares at him. "You really expect me to believe that?"

Kane nods to the man behind Reign and his arms are jerked painfully upwards, yanking a groan out of him. He arches his back, agony screaming through his arms and down his spine. Reign focuses on locking his knees and staying upright. Damned if he's going to give Kane the satisfaction of seeing him collapse.

Reign raises his head. "That's really not the way to get a guy to talk."

To his surprise, Kane steps back, adjusting his cuffs. "You and me are more alike than you realize, Reign." His gaze flickers to the man behind him as he nods.

Reign's arms are jerked higher as he's shoved forward. Despite the pain, he still struggles as he's maneuvered down the hall and to a closed door.

Kane opens it then steps back as Reign is shoved through. "Maybe this will help change your mind."

The door slams behind him and Reign's about to turn

around and do his darndest to break it down when he stops. There's a body crumpled in the corner of the bare room.

Arielle.

MAC

"This will do nicely," Dumah says coldly as he shoves Mac through the door of the warehouse.

She stumbles but quickly rights herself. She looks around the gloomy space, instantly seeing that it's much bigger than she hoped. The only windows are those high atop gun-colored steel walls. A few doors are dotted around, but they're all closed. It's like a giant, metal cave.

"Running will be a waste of energy," says Dumah from behind her. "I will catch you before you've even decided which locked door you're going to try."

Mac spins around, jutting her chin. "With your demon power?"

Dumah throws back his head and laughs, the cold sound ricocheting around the cavernous walls. "I hail from a much loftier realm. In fact, my orders come straight from Heaven."

Dumah's an angel? Unless he's lying... Mac clenches her hands, knowing she needs to keep her wits about her. "What orders?"

"Why, to kill you, of course."

Mac takes an involuntary step back. "Look, I was hungry, the pack of gummy bears was there, I made the wrong call. I don't think I need to die for that."

Dumah stalks forward, maintaining the too-close space between them. "Oh, my dear Mackenzie, you have done far more than steal some candy."

Mac frowns, her eyes darting around the massive warehouse. There's not even a milk crate she can throw at this guy. "I think we have a case of mistaken identity. I've never hurt anyone."

Well, not on purpose. Or only in self-defense.

Dumah moves before Mac has a chance to blink. He grabs her by the throat and drives her backward until she slams into the wall. She grabs his arm, trying to pull away the clamp around her neck. Except the corded muscles feel like steel, and the more she struggles, the more he tightens his hold.

Her chest is burning with the need for air and her throat feels like it's being crushed in a vice before Mac gives up. She falls limp against the wall, her hands slipping away from Dumah's arm. There's no point, he's far stronger than she is.

Dumah's lips trip up in his ebony face as his hand relaxes. He leans forward, coming close enough that Mac can see that the smile never reaches his black eyes. "Disappointing," he hisses. "I would've liked a fight. Now I'm obligated to kill you quickly."

"How very gracious of you," Mac sneers past her constricted throat.

In an explosion of movement, she tries to knee him in the groin only to connect with his thigh. Just because there's no point fighting, doesn't mean she isn't going to. Dumah grunts in pain and a second later, a set of massive white wings erupt out behind him.

But Mac doesn't have time to process how something so beautiful could be attached to something so deadly. Dumah roars with fury, his hand once again becoming a vice around her throat.

"You act tough, but I can feel your fear," he taunts. "It will be the last thing you remember as your filthy soul is extinguished."

Dumah straightens his arm and Mac slides up the wall. She struggles, kicks, scratches at the arm pinning her, but none of it makes a difference. Steadily, inescapably, she rises. She can no longer breathe as her feet leave the floor, dangling uselessly in the air. Her neck feels stretched and crushed all at once.

Pinpoints of night dance across her vision as Mac feels consciousness slip away. She's dying, and she has no idea why.

"Release her, Dumah!"

The effect is instantaneous. Mac drops to the floor as Dumah spins around.

"Gabrielle," he says, venom dripping from her name. "I see one abomination has come to save another."

Mac draws in deep lungfuls of air as she clasps her throat. From her crumpled place on the floor, she sees Gabby stride toward them, stopping a few feet away.

"The child of an angel and human deserves to live as much as this one does," he says, waving a dismissive arm at Mac.

Gabby hoists her hands to her hips. "You should've stayed in Heaven, Dumah. The last time I saw you, I made sure you were punished for siding with the Grigori. You were languishing in a cell where you belong."

Dumah laughs, taking a few measured steps to the side. "No cell in the three worlds can keep me captive. Heaven is as corrupt as your mortal realm. There were those who wanted to see me free." He expands his wings. "Those who know I'm doing what needs to be done."

Gabby takes several corresponding steps in the opposite direction, creating a slow moving dance. "And what's that, Dumah? What twisted, righteous scheme are you planning?"

Dumah shrugs. "Simply to bring Hell upon Earth."

Gabby frowns, her hands clenching by her side as they continue to move in a slow circle. "What have you done?"

"Research, daughter of Gabriel. I asked the right questions

of the right people." Dumah opens his arms in an expansive, generous gesture. "And learned the name of the first Innocent. It's only a matter of time before everything you know and love will be plunged into chaos."

"Not if I stop you first," Gabby says, her voice as hard and cold as ice. She leaps, her wings unfurling behind her, and with one massive beat, she soars into the air.

Dumah vaults up, too, and the chilling dance is played out, several feet above the ground. The two angels circle slowly, taking measure of their opponent. Dumah's exposed chest glints softly in the gloom of the warehouse, his pearly wings a powerful contrast. Opposite him, Gabby looks smaller and far more fragile, but Mac knows that doesn't mean a thing. It's the size of the fight inside that counts.

Please let it be the size of the fight inside that counts.

As Mac stands there, head tilted back and breath held, she realizes Dumah was wrong. She's not scared. She's terrified.

She doesn't understand everything that was just said, but she gets the gist. Dumah wants Hell on Earth.

And just to add another layer of holy-shit to that, it seems Heaven wants Mac dead.

"**A**rielle, wake up."

Reign's voice trickles through the pounding in Arielle's head. She goes to raise her hand to her temple and the sound of metal clanging makes her wince. What's more, her hand stops midair, something preventing it from going any higher.

"Bastards," Reign growls.

She opens her eyes to see her hands are cuffed to short chains that are attached to the floor on either side of her. She yanks on them in disbelief. "They most certainly are."

He shuffles closer. "Are you okay? Did they hurt you?"

"I'm okay, I think." She looks up, finding him right beside her, his labyrinth eyes clouded with concern. "How did you find me?"

Reign studies her for a few more seconds and she almost flushes. She probably looks a mess, and with her hands in chains, it's not like she can fix her hair or anything. "Lizzie called me," he huffs. His eyes widen as if he just realized something. "She also rang me when I was at my foster home. The cops turned up not long after."

"She's off my Christmas card list," Arielle mutters. "I can't believe I tried to help her."

Sitting down cross legged, Reign extends his hands. "Here, let me have a look at those cuffs. I might be able to jig them open."

She draws herself into a sitting position and extends her wrists. The chains aren't even long enough for her to bring them together. Reign frowns as he shuffles to her right hand, leaning over to inspect her shackle.

She clears her throat, suddenly aware of how close he is. "Where are we?"

"Some house in the burbs. Lizzie gave me the address so I came looking for you. Kane and his goons nabbed me and here I am." He looks up, giving her a crooked smile. "Ta da."

Her breath evaporates. Lizzie was right, that smile is like heroin.

And now that Arielle has had even a tiny taste, she wants more.

"Why?" she asks, working hard to stay focused on the topic at hand—the fact they've been kidnapped with who-knows what's in store for them. "What do they want?"

Reign's fingers lightly trail below the metal on her wrist, sending tiny shivers dancing up her arm. "Kane wants to know about the Sinclair Mansion. He said he'd let us go if we tell him everything."

She snorts. "What a load of poppycock. Of course he won't let us go."

He pauses, glancing up at her. "Did you just say poppycock?"

"Yes, I did," she replies, raising her chin. "So?"

Laughter flashes in Reign's eyes, and she can't tell if it's at her or with her. "No reason," he says as he returns his focus to her bonds. "Just checking."

"My mom always said I'm an old soul," she blurts before she can stop herself. She doesn't need to explain anything to him.

"Yeah, well, I'm going to need a few more lifetimes to figure things out," he says, keeping his head down. His hands still. "Sorry I came running like a wounded bull. I should've brought Colt and Gabby with me."

"Hey, I'm the one who befriended the enemy. We wouldn't be here if it weren't for me."

Reign glances up, his dark eyebrows low. "You didn't do anything wrong. You were being kind. The world needs more of that."

"And you were trying to help someone." Reign was trying to save Arielle. "You didn't do anything wrong, either."

His frown only intensifies as he ducks his head to focus back on his task. "That's different."

She leans closer. "Poppycock," she says quietly but clearly.

His shoulders still, the muscles under his black t-shirt tensing. This close, she can see the way his raven hair brushes his neck, the way he seems to have stopped breathing just like she has. She wills him to look up at her.

But instead, he pulls back. "Dammit, I can't get them open." He glances around the room. "I need something to break one of the links."

He paces around the room like a caged lion, stopping at the window. He pushes it open, giving Arielle a brief moment of hope. Maybe he could go get help. Except the frosted glass reveals what's on the other side. Ornate, wrought iron bars.

Reign grips them and shakes them. "Dammit," he growls again. "They're welded in place."

Arielle stares at the door, reality finally sinking in. "We're trapped." She's chained to the floor. "And we have information they want."

His hands clench. "I won't let them hurt you."

She nods, awed but also a little intimidated by the fierce intensity vibrating through him. She bites her lip. "And I'll do everything I can to protect you, Reign."

Reign's eyes widen imperceptibly, even his tight jaw seeming to loosen. She wonders if anyone has ever said those words to him. The thought makes her sad and all the more determined, at the same time.

Before either of them can say anything, the door is pushed open and two men storm into the room. Reign is standing in front of her before they've fully entered. The men seem to expect it, because they converge on Reign like they knew he'd be there. Reign runs at them head down like a human battering ram. He ploughs into one of them, drawing out an oomph.

"No!" Arielle screams as the second brings his fist down on the back of Reign's neck.

He crumples immediately, sprawling on the ground. Reign pushes himself to all fours only to be kicked in the stomach. He groans as he's propelled onto his side. The first man grabs him by the shirt and slams him against the wall to her right. Although Reign's face is twisted in pain, he comes up swinging.

But the men are too fast. Too strong. In a blink, they pin Reign against the wall, one with his arm across his throat, the other immobilizing his hands. Still, Reign fights with the force of a hurricane, twisting his body and flailing his legs.

"Hello, Arielle."

Arielle turns to find Detective Kane in the doorway. He walks toward her and squats down. On the other side of the room, Reign stops struggling. "Stay away from her you Hell spawn!"

Kane ignores him, his gaze remaining on Arielle. "Would you like to talk? I'd imagine your bedroom is far more comfortable than this old place. All you need to do is answer a few questions and you'll be back there in no time," he practically purrs.

"Tell him to f—" Reign's words are cut off as the man with his arm across Reign's throat pushes in sharply, making Arielle wince.

She jerks on her chains. "Don't you think if I knew something, I'd tell you? Leave Reign alone!"

Kane pushes to his feet, his lips thinning. "Very well. We'll do it the hard way."

He steps around Arielle and she twists, trying to keep him in view. Behind her, Kane grabs her face and jerks it back against his legs. "Keep still and this will be practically painless," he growls.

There are more sounds of scuffles from Reign but Arielle can no longer see him. Her neck is stretched tight as Kane keeps it tipped back.

"What are you doing?" Reign screams. "Get your hands off her!"

There are more muffled movements followed by a soft groan.

Fear is spiking through Arielle as she realizes Kane has something in his other hand. "There's just a little something I'd like Arielle to drink."

Keeping her pinned with one hand, Arielle watches in horror as he brings a vial of liquid into her line of vision. She tries to wrench her head away but Kane's grip is like a vice. Next, she clenches her teeth in an effort to keep her mouth shut, only to have Kane dig his thumb into her jaw. She squeezes her eyes shut, trying to block out the pain radiating from that one pressure point.

"Come on, Arielle," Kane grunts. "All I need is one little opening."

His thumb digs in harder, feeling like it's going to punch

right through her skin. The pain multiplies, streaking up her skull. The muscles of her jaw crumple under the agony and her mouth pops open.

"Yes," Kane hisses. He brings the vial to her lips.

"No!" Reign roars. "Give it to me. I'll drink it."

Kane looks up, a slow smile spreading across his face as his grip on Arielle's chin instantly relaxes. "I was hoping you'd say that."

He releases Arielle and stalks over without a backward glance. He holds up the vial to show Reign. "How would you like to do this?"

"On the rocks," Reign spits.

Arielle yanks on her restraints. "No Reign, don't do this!"

Kane's hand snaps out to grab Reign's jaw and pushes his head back into the wall. Reign holds Kane's gaze as he opens his mouth. Wasting no time, Kane accepts the invitation and pours the clear liquid into his mouth.

He steps back, adjusting his shirt. "If you spit it out, then your girl will pay the price."

Fury sparks from Reign's eyes as he swallows.

"What did you just give him?" Arielle asks, her hands trembling so hard the chains softly *clink*.

"Thiopental," says Kane, a quiver of anticipation running through his voice. "Otherwise known as truth serum."

GABBY

Dumah makes the first move, just as Gabby expected him to. He's always been driven by the need to win, no matter the cost.

He launches at her, a black and white arrow thirsting for death. Gabby vaults forward, determined to meet him halfway.

She has to stop him. The alternative isn't one she wants to consider.

Dumah's face twists as he lets out a roar. His hands clench into fists. He injects speed so he can crash into her with as much force as possible.

So Gabby does the same.

They slam into each other, a shock wave blasting through Gabby's muscles as Dumah tries to power through her. She pushes back, but the split-second head start he got has her propelled backward. He grapples and punches as Gabby ducks and weaves, throwing her own blows at any opening she gets.

There's a resounding *boom* when her back is battered into the wall of the warehouse. A groan is yanked out of her as agony explodes down her spine and across her shoulders. She channels the pain as she thrusts her wings, using them as leverage to push off the wall.

She shoves Dumah away, shooting after him so she can return the favor. This time, she slams him into one of the metal beams, his wings crumpling as his back arches. He grunts, his face warping with an unholy mix of pain and fury.

"You are not strong enough to stop me," he half-growls, half-screams.

One contraction of his powerful wings and he's free, throwing himself at Gabby with all the hatred that's vibrating through his heavenly body. They clash again, fists trying to strike anywhere they can. Gabby blocks and punches, but for every time she connects with flesh, a blow batters her body. This is a fight neither of them are willing to lose.

They pull apart, breathing heavily as they take stock.

"It's only a matter of time before the first Gate of Hell is thrown open," Dumah growls.

"Or it's only a matter of time before I kick your ass," Gabby snaps. "Again."

This time, Dumah soars high, which means Gabby does, too. They're almost at the ceiling of the warehouse when they clash again, wings outstretched as their bodies become weapons. Gabby throws a punch, enjoying the jolt of satisfaction when it connects with Dumah's shoulder. She throws another in quick succession, but he blocks it and grabs her arm. One yank and their bodies collide. One sharp movement and he has her by the throat.

Dumah's wings tuck in as he launches into a dive, taking Gabby with him. She struggles, trying to pry his fingers loose, trying to wrench his arms away. This was his plan. To spear her into the unforgiving concrete floor.

They tumble through the air, the ground rushing at them. Dumah twists so Gabby is beneath him, but she uses the momentum to jerk him back around. Over and over they turn, each wanting the upper hand before they hit ground zero.

It's then, as the wind whips through her and the warehouse becomes a blur of gray lines, that Gabby realizes they're too evenly matched. This fight could go on for hours, a war of attrition until one of them tires out.

The only way she can win is to give him the advantage.

She stops struggling, bracing herself. This is going to hurt. A second later, Dumah slams her into the cement floor, shards of concrete exploding into the air as the floor cracks. Gabby gasps as the air is forced out of her crushed chest. Dumah's fist flies for her head and she turns away at the last moment. More concrete explodes as a crater is carved out.

Dumah's lip curls with the taste of victory. "I wonder which Sin will be the first to be released onto the world."

As his next punch aims for head once more, Gabby reaches into her pocket. If she misses, her face is going to look like the concrete on either side of her.

A split second before Dumah's fist ploughs through Gabby's

skull, she slaps a metal cuff around his wrist. Dumah yanks it back in shock, but Gabby already has the second clamped around his other wrist. Metal clanks as Dumah wrenches on them, screaming out his rage.

Gabby pushes him away and rolls to her feet. A second later she slams her fist through Dumah's jaw. He collapses, unconscious before his body hits the floor.

Mac rushes over to her. "Holy heck, that was some fight!" She peers at Dumah. "What's with the cuffs?"

"Divine chains," she says, breathing heavily. A gift from her father. "Angels can't escape them."

"What do we do with him now?"

Gabby frowns. "We'll have to take him back to Colt's place. We need to learn what he's planning."

What he's already put into motion.

An Innocent has been named. It is their grace that will open the Gate of Hell. Shock ricochets through Gabby as she realizes something else.

The obelisks. They are the monuments guarding the portals.

And Arielle has dreamed of them.

She's foreseen the Gates of Hell opening.

The question is, why her?

CHAPTER 31

REIGN

Reign's popped some pills in his time, but none of them have felt like this. As he sits on the floor, his head feels like it's full of steel wool—muddled and uncomfortable. His body is strangely disconnected. And yet, there's a pleasant buzz filtering through the parts he can feel, making him warm and strangely content.

Kane doesn't look as scary as he did a few minutes ago. Their situation doesn't seem so dire. In fact, a part of him just wants to take a nap.

Despite all that, he doesn't like these feelings, he just can't really remember why. Although contentment is a feeling that's eluded him his whole life, this strange sense of serenity feels... wrong. For starters, he's never wanted to nap. Sleeping involves nightmares or being vulnerable for long stretches of time. Reign isn't a fan of either of those.

He looks around, trying to understand what he should do next. He sees Arielle, tears streaking down her cheeks, the flame blue of her eyes subdued. She sits on the ground, hair disheveled, her shoulders drooped with helplessness. Something shifts in his chest, a truth that has wanted to be said from the first moment he saw her.

"You're beautiful."

Arielle blinks, for some reason the words only make her look sadder. "Reign," she whispers. "You shouldn't have done this."

"I disagree." Detective Kane steps in between them, dragging Reign's groggy gaze up to the man's face. "The serum is working wonderfully."

The serum. Kane made him swallow it. And yet Reign didn't want to. He frowns as he tries to think of why. "I don't think I should be talking to you."

Kane smiles as he squats down, bringing himself to eye level with Reign. "But you will, nevertheless." He angles his head. "What did you see in the Sinclair Mansion?"

Reign frowns. "A lot of stuff. Including a guy who thought he was better than me."

"I don't want to know about your petty insecurities, Everson," Kane growls. "Did you find a hidden room in the library?"

"Don't answer him," Arielle calls out. "He's evil!"

Reign tries to get a glance of her, hearing the desperation in Arielle's voice and wanting to understand it, but Kane shifts his weight, blocking her. "All I'm asking is a few questions." He smiles reassuringly. "Some women can be quite neurotic."

Reign rubs his forehead, confusion whirling through his mind. "That's sexist," he points out.

"Sorry," Kane says, not really sounding it. "Now, did you find a hidden room in the library?"

The answer wells up in Reign, wanting to be told. He goes to stop it only for it to tumble out anyway. "We sure did. It was quite the surprise, let me tell you."

Kane's dark eyes blaze open wider. "How?"

"A pentagram-thingy," says Reign, the words now tumbling

out unfettered. "In the center of the room, under the rugs. It opened a door to a crypt beneath it."

"No, Reign," Arielle moans.

Reign tries to get up, no longer okay with sitting there and not being able to see Arielle, but Kane shoves a hand into his chest and pushes him back against the wall.

"What did you find in there?"

Irritated, Reign glares at him. The fuzzy-everything-is-good feeling is starting to wear off. "Nothing much. A lot of old, dusty stuff. We didn't really have a good look around." He shoves Kane's hand away. "Now leave me alone. I need to check if Arielle is okay."

"The serum is wearing off already," Kane muses. "Interesting."

The serum... Flashes of a bitter tasting liquid squirming down his throat has Reign trying to push to his feet.

But Kane pushes a hand into his chest, keeping him where he is. "She's not going anywhere, I promise. One last question." He leans close. "Are you the Grail Keeper?"

"No." Reign's answer is instant. There's no way he could be someone as important as that. "Sorry, you've got the wrong guy."

For some reason, Kane looks disappointed. He pushes to his feet. "Very well." He strides to the door. "I'm going to go get all that 'dusty old stuff.' Until then, why don't you two hang tight, as you like to call it."

Kane leaves, and Reign notes there are two men on the other side. He draws in a sharp breath when he sees their faces.

Hell-faces.

He rushes to Arielle and stands in front of her. "Get away from her!"

But the door is already shut. Reign remains where he is, heart thundering as adrenaline thrums through his veins.

Those bastards are only feet away and there's no way he's letting them anywhere near Arielle.

"Reign, are you okay?"

He turns around, intending on telling her he's fine. "No, I'm not." He startles, wondering where that came from. "Those freaks scare the shit out of me."

He takes a step back, clamping his mouth shut. That was far more honest than he intended. He rubs his temple, realizing it's the truth serum. It must be wearing off—he's no longer feeling like he connected with an inner Care Bear that he never knew he had—but he's obviously still a little bit more uninhibited than he'd like. Actually, a lot more than he'd like. Control is what keeps Reign's world...controlled.

"Me, too," Arielle says gently. "They're evil and they're dangerous."

Reign walks over and crouches down. They need to focus on more important things than his unstable mind. "Did they hurt you?"

She shakes her head. "You made sure they didn't. You had the serum instead of me."

"And then I told Kane exactly how to get into the crypt," says Reign, disgust at his weakness burning in his belly.

The chains clink as Arielle moves her hands only to be stopped short. Her hands clench. "Because you're under the influence of truth serum," she points out. "You had no choice."

Before Reign can answer, there's a thump at the window. He leaps to his feet, once more standing in front of Arielle. A second later, there's another thump, followed by the whine of metal bending.

Reign's hands form fists as he tries to shake off the lingering effects of the drug. He can't afford to have dull reflexes. Arielle's life could depend on it.

The window opens just like he knew it would, revealing the intruder.

Reign's fists drop to his side. "Colt? What the freak are you doing here?"

Colt jumps through the window, revealing the bent iron bars behind him. "Saving your asses." He sees Arielle chained to the floor and he strides over. "I went after you not long after you left, Reign, but I lost you." He kneels down beside her. "But then I sensed demon magic and followed it here."

"Thank you," says Reign.

Colt studies the chains. "Which means I'm now one up on you."

"Actually, there's no one I'd be happy to owe more," blurts Reign before he can stop it.

Colt glances over his shoulder, surprised.

"He was forced to drink truth serum," Arielle explains.

"Which means I also told Kane how to get in the crypt," Reign adds bitterly.

Colt grips the cuffs. "Just hold still, Ari," he instructs. His grip tightens. "And don't worry about the crypt, we cleaned it out the day we found it. The contents are now hidden at another location, cloaked by demon magic."

Arielle gasps as the metal around her wrists crumbles. She draws her hands up and rubs her skin. "Thanks."

Colt stands and walks straight back to the window. "Quick, we need to go."

Reign waits for Arielle to join Colt, then hesitates. "There are demons out the front."

"They weren't demons, but yes, I've taken care of them."

Reign strides to the door and opens it, seeing that the men are indeed lying unconscious on the floor.

"You didn't trust my word?" asks Colt.

"To be honest, I don't really trust anyone," Reign mutters. Including himself.

Because both men still have sunken, gray faces and black lips, and Colt just said they're not demons.

Colt helps Arielle climb through the window then indicates for Reign to follow, but he shakes his head. "In the order of who jumps ship, you go first. If anything happens, you can protect her better than I can."

Colt frowns, but quickly follows Arielle. Reign's right behind him. He finds they're down the side of the house, the sounds of the street not far away.

"I didn't see any other guards," Colt says urgently. "But we don't want to risk it."

The three of them break into a run, leaving the yard and sprinting down the pavement. Reign glances over his shoulder repeatedly, but no one follows them.

They managed to escape.

Back at Colt's basement, Gabby meets them at the door. "Where have you been?" Her eyes widen when she sees Arielle's with them. "What is she doing here?"

Colt arches a brow. "Is it okay if I come in?"

Frowning in consternation, Gabby takes a step back. "I suppose so, it is your place..."

They file in and Mac rushes toward Reign, giving him a hug. Unsure what's going on, he hugs her back. "Are you going to make a habit of this?"

She pulls back, smiling. "Have I got a story to tell you."

"Ditto," he responds. "You go first, though."

"Not yet," Gabby says loudly, her hands on her hips. "I thought it was agreed that Arielle wouldn't be involved in any of this."

Arielle angles her chin in a way that's starting to become

familiar. "Yes, you did." She takes a step forward. "But I'm in this, whether Aunt Shell agrees or not."

"She was just abducted and kept prisoner," Reign points out.

Gabby gasps, but quickly recovers. "It's too dangerous."

Arielle shakes her head. "This is my mom, Gabs." She glances at Reign. "I'm not sitting back and watching others risk their lives for this."

Reign suppresses the startle her words trigger. Surely she's not talking about what happened in that room.

Gabby's shoulders drop. "Okay." She sighs. "I just don't want to be there when you tell my mom."

"Right now, they need to lay low for a bit," says Colt. "I think we should go and see if that house has any links to the abductions."

"Yes, good thinking," Gabby agrees. She turns back to the others. "We shouldn't be long. Keep an eye on Dumah."

Reign glances around the basement, but as far as he can tell, they're the only ones here. "Is he a leprechaun? A fairy?"

"Nope," Mac says, her voice hard. "He's the angel who tried to kill me."

MAC

Mac pushes the door open to the small bathroom that's on the basement floor. "This is the asshat."

Reign and Arielle enter, staring at the man trussed up in the bath, glaring at them.

"Shouldn't we have him somewhere else?" Arielle asks cautiously.

"He can't move. Gabby slapped divine bonds on him."

"Is not wearing a shirt an angel thing?" Reign asks. "Cause I need to know before we see Gabby next."

Mac rolls her eyes at his poorly timed humor. "He tried to kill me, said something about being sent to do it. If it wasn't for Gabby, he would've succeeded."

That sobers Reign. He takes a step forward, looming over Dumah. "That's not a very angelic thing to do."

Arielle crosses her arms. "Why would he do that?"

Mac's hand tightens around the doorknob. "That's exactly what I'd like to know."

Why does Dumah have some sort of personal beef with her? She's little more than an orphan who's spent her life jumping around the foster care system. Heck, no one even wanted to adopt her.

She joins Reign, her stomach a storm of fury and fear. "Why me?"

Dumah curls his lip, regarding them with derision. Maybe some hatred. "You're focusing on the wrong thing, fools. The first Gate of Hell is about to be opened. And once that happens, your precious world will be consumed by demons."

His words punch through Mac. He's right. They have bigger things to worry about.

"Where?" she demands. "Where is this going to happen?"

Dumah's face hardens, resembling smooth obsidian. "Did you know my name means silence in Aramaic?" He clamps his mouth shut, telling them he has no intention of saying anything else.

"The scumbag isn't going to talk," Reign says, turning away in disgust. "If only Avril was here."

They leave the bathroom, Reign leaving the door ajar. If Dumah finds a way to move, they'll hear about it.

Back in the kitchen, Mac paces. "He's so sure," she mutters, dread like a rock in her gut. She turns to the others. "He said he knew the name of the Innocent."

"That's why he's so cocky." Reign frowns. "He's found the key that will open the Gate of Hell."

Arielle collapses onto a chair. "No," she moans.

Reign shoots to her side. "Arielle?"

Mac wonders if he's noticed he's barely been more than a few feet away from her since they returned.

Arielle looks up at him, her gaze clinging to his. "I think I know who the Innocent is. This is why they've been abducting the women."

Reign stiffens as something strikes him. Realization shoots through Mac a second later.

Arielle's lip trembles. "It's my mother."

CHAPTER 32

ARIELLE

The obelisk punches through the night air, the runes carved into its sides pulsing softly. There's a hooded man beside it, his arms are held high, a curved blade glinting in the dark.

It's then that Arielle sees he's beside a stone table, and that a woman is strapped to it.

No!

He plunges the knife into the still body of the woman and she convulses. Blood courses down from her chest, drawn to the obelisk like a magnet. The moment the rivulets of crimson reach it, it cracks. Although the dream is as silent as it is vivid, the sound is a shockwave through Arielle. That monument protects a Gate of Hell.

She jerks awake before she can see the rest. She already knows how it ends. She's foreseen it.

Tucked up in the corner of Colt's couch, she glances around as she tries to get her breathing under control. Reign and Mac are on the other side, Mac's head on his shoulder, both asleep. On the other side of the room, Arielle can make out Colt and

Gabby wrapped around each other on the bed. Gabby's soft snores fill the air.

Arielle wipes a trembling hand down her face. Colt and Gabby returned from the house Arielle had been held in, saying it was empty, with no signs or clues as to where Kane had gone. It was as if he'd never been there. Even the chains were gone. They ate pizza that Arielle barely tasted before Gabby pointed out they all needed to get some sleep.

Arielle had tucked herself into the couch, the knowledge that her mother is the Innocent crawling through her chest. She'd sat there, eyes stinging with exhaustion and unshed tears, as the breathing in the room progressively evened out.

She hadn't meant to fall asleep. She tried not to. But fatigue must've won.

And now another nightmare is forever branded in her mind. Arielle couldn't see who was strapped to the table, but she didn't need to.

She knows it's her mother.

The nightmares were terrifying and sickening before, but knowing her mother is the one being sacrificed makes it feel like her rapidly beating heart is being torn out of her chest.

Arielle pushes to her feet, then pauses. No one in the room stirs. Good, because she needs some answers. She now knows why she's been having these night terrors. It's because it's her mother who's the Innocent. Their close bond has meant Arielle is being warned.

She refuses to believe her dreams are foretelling an inevitable future.

She pads to the bathroom, peeking through the cracked door. Cramped and chained, Dumah glares at her from the bath. Heart thumping, Arielle slips in.

"Where is she?" Although she says the words quietly, there's steel laced through them.

This man, no, this angel, knows where her mother is. He's the one who signed her death sentence.

Dumah regards her for long moments, his head angled. "Does it really matter?"

"She's my mother!" Arielle hisses. "Yes, it matters!"

Dumah's face softens as it settles into lines of satisfaction. "Ah yes, I believe this one is a mother."

Arielle takes another step in, so much anger pulsing through her that she's trembling. "Tell me where she is."

"You cannot stop it," Dumah says, his voice laced with contempt. "We have the Innocent. We have the blade forged in the bowels of Hell itself. The Gate of Hell *will* open."

He turns his head away, letting her know he has no intention of talking. Frustrated and near tears, Arielle leaves the bathroom. She meant what she said. She's not going to sit back and let this happen.

She's going to do everything she can to save her mother. She needs to stop her nightmares from becoming reality.

Back in the main room of the basement, Arielle pauses. No one has moved, meaning she didn't wake them up. Except she's not going back to sleep, the last terrifying visions are too fresh.

Heading to the door, Arielle decides she's going to do what her mother would do. Research. She's just grabbed the doorknob when a hand lands on the door above her. She spins around to find Reign behind her.

"Ah, what are you doing?"

Arielle presses a hand to her thumping heart. She's not sure if it's from the surprise she just got, or because of the way Reign looks in the barely-there light—brooding and sexy. He keeps his hand on the door, which means he's standing far too close for her equilibrium.

"I thought you were asleep," she says, glad for the need to

whisper. It covers up the breathlessness that's suddenly overtaken her.

"Sleeping isn't one of my strengths. But you didn't seem to want an audience." Reign glances at the door. "Except then you decided to leave."

"I'm going home," Arielle says, keeping her voice quiet but firm. She won't be talked out of this. "I want to look over my mother's journal again."

Reign pauses, glancing back at the others. "Good idea." He removes his hand, and Arielle unwinds. Not only did he just create some space between them, but she doesn't have a fight on her hands. "I'm coming with you."

"What?"

"You heard me. It's not safe for any of us to be out alone right now."

Arielle chews on her lip, considering his words. Dammit, he's right. "Fine, then. But if Aunt Shell sees you, you do the explaining."

Reign grins, making Arielle's heart trip. "I'll tell her I really wanted to study again."

Flushing at her ridiculous lie, Arielle spins around and opens the door. They slip out and silently pad up the stairs. Outside, Arielle hails a ride. It's not until she and Reign are in the back seat that she realizes she's alone with him for the first time since her abduction.

She glances at the driver, keeping her voice down. "Reign, about what happened back at the house with Kane—"

"Yeah, Colt's really something, huh?"

"No, that's not what I'm trying to say. When—"

"As in, I doubt those two boof heads even heard him coming. Do you think he knocked them out with his, you know..." Reign glances at the driver then makes bird wings with his hands, fluttering them.

"Reign," Arielle huffs, frustrated. "I'm talking about—"

His brow rumples quizzically. "What do you think that guy can bench press? I mean, to bend those bars like that, it would have to be at least eight hundred pounds."

Arielle frowns, realizing Reign is being deliberately obstructive and obtuse. He doesn't want to talk about the fact he volunteered to drink the truth serum.

"We're here," the driver announces.

Arielle pays him and they climb out, Reign practically leaping to the curb like his seat was electrocuted. She decides to let the topic go, for now. There's no way this conversation is over.

Unlocking the door slowly and carefully, Arielle creeps in, Reign right behind her. She doesn't want to have *the* talk with Aunt Shell right now. There's no way she's going to take Arielle's decision to be a part of all this well.

But the house is silent as they make their way to the living room. Arielle turns on the lamp beside the couch, creating a pool of soft light. She indicates for Reign to sit down.

"The journal is on the bookshelf."

Reign sits, his eyebrows hiking up. "Hiding in plain sight and all that?"

Grabbing the square timber box, she returns to sit next to him. "Not exactly." She places it on her lap, opening the drawer with the pieces.

Reign draws back. "I'm not a fan of board games."

"Then you don't know what you're missing out on," Arielle says as she arranges the pieces on the carved squares. Egg in the center. Four pigs around it.

The pieces sink down, followed by a soft *click*. Reign's mouth snaps shut as the secret compartment pops open.

Arielle withdraws her mother's journal. "I'll teach you how to play another time."

She opens the leather-bound notebook and is quickly assaulted by words and images. Joseph of Arimathea. Obelisks. Demons with sunken eyes and black holes for mouths. Arielle quickly flicks past them. They're too similar to her dreams.

Except the pages are blank. Although she knew they were—like her mom never got to finish whatever she was documenting here—Arielle's still disappointed. They're going to have to read what little information there is, even though she's already combed through it. Even though it will only describe everything she's already seen.

She flicks through the pages right to the end, knowing it's a desperate act of avoidance, but doing it anyway.

"Hey," says Reign. "There was something on the last page."

Arielle opens it to see he's right. A handful of lines have been scrawled on the last slip of paper.

Reign leans in closer, his scent filling her lungs. "Your mom had a reference section in her journal?" he asks incredulously.

"She was an academic." Her face softens. "And a little kooky."

"That explains a few things."

Arielle stills, but there's no mockery in Reign's tone. In fact, there's a strange softness. As if he likes kooky.

Telling herself there's kooky, and there's delusional, Arielle reads the first two words aloud. "Infernal Damasicus."

Below is a location. *Veritas Library*.

"I've never heard of it," Arielle muses.

And below the location is an address. *67 Argyle Street. Mercy City*.

"That's not too far from here," Reign observes.

Arielle taps her finger on the page. "We need to go check it out."

"It would be shut now, but we'll go first thing in the morning," agrees Reign. He pulls back, something flickering in his eyes. He clears his throat. "You should probably get some sleep."

Arielle glances at the door. The steps that go up to her bedroom are just beyond it. Except she has no desire to go there. She'll be alone...with the nightmares.

She shakes her head. "I'm fine."

"Arielle, you need to sleep. You've had a big day and tomorrow isn't looking like it's going to be in the small category, either."

She shakes her head again. "Seriously, it's okay." She glances at the bookshelf. "In fact, I might read something," she adds brightly.

She goes to shoot up only to find that Reign has trapped her hand. "You're scared to sleep, aren't you?"

Her shoulders sag. "Is it really that obvious?" Could she be any weaker? Gabby would probably *want* to see the visions so she could kick some ass. Mac would've just kicked ass in the first nightmare and they never would've come back.

Reign sighs. "Only because I know the signs all too well."

Arielle glances at him. Reign doesn't like to sleep? That would explain why he knew she was sneaking in to see Dumah...

He fluffs up the pillow next to him. "Here. Why don't you just rest? If it looks like you're going to sleep, I'll poke you."

She chews her lip. "Won't you need to sleep?"

"Not my strong point, remember?"

Arielle hesitates. The thought of the two of them together, here, alone, is...intimate. What's more, it feels safe.

She lies down on her side, her head on the pillow that's beside Reign's thigh. She imagines she can feel his warmth radiating onto her scalp. He shifts a little as if he's getting comfortable, one arm coming to rest across the back of the couch.

Silence fills the living room, heavy and warm. Despite everything that's happened, Arielle finds her muscles unwinding, her body sinking into the couch.

"Do you think—"

"No talking," Reign mumbles grouchily. "I've done enough of that today."

Arielle chews on her lip. Who is this guy? He's gruff and reckless. And yet gentle and loyal. A guy who does nothing but push the world away, at the same time as he helps people he's only just met. The guy who said she's beautiful in such an achingly honest way that she couldn't help but believe him...

The guy who makes her feel safe. She jolts as she realizes she was drifting to sleep.

"You didn't poke me," she accuses in a whisper.

"I lied," he says softly. "Go to sleep, Ari. I'll keep the boogeyman away."

Ari... His use of her nickname has something sweet and warm flowing over her. She snuggles into the couch a little deeper, feeling like a cat curled in a stretch of sunshine. Beside her, she hears Reign let out a breath. It sounds as relaxed as she's feeling.

As exhaustion creeps over her dropped defenses, Arielle knows there's one more thing she has to say. "Reign, about today."

"Seriously, it wasn't a big deal," he murmurs.

"You had no idea what they were going to give me, and yet you took it anyway."

It could've been poison. He could've died.

"The world would've gone on without me, Arielle." She notes the way he uses her full name again. Reign's putting his serious pants back on. Or his defenses. "It's really not a big deal."

Except it is. But for some reason, Reign doesn't see that.

Which is a puzzle that, suddenly, Arielle very much wants to solve.

GABBY

When Gabby wakes up the following morning, she's not surprised to find the couch is empty. There's so much restlessness in Reign and Mac that she doubts either of them remain in one location for very long.

And Arielle seems to have found a new center of gravity with Reign. Although Gabby can sense Reign's draw to her cousin, she's not sure whether his darker side will overshadow that...

Colt rolls over, his sleepy eyes blinking at her beneath tousled auburn hair. "They're gone, aren't they?"

His demon hearing would've already ascertained that there's only two of them in the room. Gabby cocks her head, sensing Dumah's simmering frustration in the bathroom. Their prisoner is still with them. Colt has probably heard his breathing by now.

She leans closer to Colt, breathing in his warm, sleepy scent. "It's just the two of us and—" she wrinkles her nose—"him."

He frowns. "Why don't you just kill him?"

Gabby presses her forehead to Colt's chest, absorbing his strength. "I'm not sure I could ever kill again," she says, her voice barely above a whisper. "Not after what happened with the Grigori."

Colt's hands cup her head and nudge her to look at him. "You have a beautiful soul, Gabrielle," he murmurs.

He leans down to kiss her and Gabby melts with everything

she feels for this demon of hers. Their bond should've been impossible. It spans the abyss between Heaven and Hell.

Which is what makes it all the more amazing. Wonderful. Sacred.

Colt pulls back, his cinnamon eyes as soft and gooey as her heart feels. "We'll deal with him later," he promises. "For now, we need to find Sierra."

Gabby nods, reality dousing her like ice water. She rolls off the bed and walks over to the map. "Except we haven't found any more leads," she says, frustrated.

Colt comes to stand behind her and she leans against him, enjoying the feeling of his bare chest. He sighs as he wraps his arms around her. "If only we could trace just one of the vans."

Gabby leans closer to the map, her eyes narrowing. "Maybe it's not just the vans that are significant."

"We've looked at the locations of the pins from every angle. There's no rhyme or reason to them. They don't create any pattern that we know of."

Gabby steps out of Colt's hold, pointing to the pin that marks the place Sierra was taken. "Maybe it's more about the last place they were seen," she says, her voice heavy with implication. "The location they were taken from."

Colt leans closer, his eyes widening. "Argyle Street," he breathes. "Why would Sierra be visiting Veritas Library?"

They look at each other, their glance full of the implications of that question.

Gabby turns to go grab some clothes. She's going to miss seeing Colt's naked chest, but they have a lead. "There's only one way to find out."

CHAPTER 33

REIGN

"Well, isn't this just downright cozy?" Mac says in a way too chirpy voice.

Reign jolts awake, disorientated for long seconds. He glances down, seeing tousled blonde hair spread across his lap, his arm draped over the smooth curve of a female hip. The smooth curve of Arielle's hip!

She snaps upright a second later, her head barely missing his chin. "Oh." She glances at Reign as he withdraws his arm, her eyes widening. "Oh."

Mac chuckles. "Yeah, oh."

Reign shoots to his feet, scowling. This is why he doesn't sleep. You never know what you might wake up to. And a smug best friend is one thing he could do without. "We came here to look at the journal."

"Ah ha," she says, crossing her arms. "I came here because I woke up and my cushion had run off."

Reign takes another step away from the couch. He can't believe he fell asleep. With Arielle's head on his lap...

He keeps his gaze firmly focused on Mac. "Have you heard of the Veritas Library?"

"The Truth Library? Veritas is Latin," she says, even more smug. "And nope, never heard of it." Her face brightens. "We're going to a library?"

One no one has heard of, not even his nerdy best friend. Interesting.

Arielle smoothes her hair. "It was at the back of my mom's journal. With an address."

Mac leaps for the doorway. "Then what are we waiting for?" A cheeky sparkle glints in her eye. "Unless you two wanted to discuss anything?"

Reign strides past her, wishing he didn't notice the way Arielle's cheeks just turned pink. "Zip it, Mac," he mutters under his breath.

Her chuckle follows him all the way to the door.

The ride to Argyle Street isn't long, but there's enough time for Reign to ruminate on what just happened. He's glad Arielle got some sleep. In fact, that was the whole idea of getting her to rest.

It's his own shuteye that surprises him. In fact, he feels more rested than he has in a long time. He glances at Arielle in the front seat. Her hands are clasped in her lap as if she's nervous. She'd be totally focused on where they're going, this Veritas Library that no one seems to have heard of even though it's not far away. And so she should be. She doesn't need a drop-kick like him on her mind.

She flicks a glance over her shoulder as if she could sense his gaze. Reign freezes when her eyes meet his. She smiles slightly and mouths two words.

"Thank you."

She turns away before Reign can react. In fact, he remains frozen where he is for long seconds. Two words.

And he wants to do something that he does as often as sleep. Smile.

"Sixty-seven Argyle Street," their driver announces as the car draws to a halt.

Arielle pays the driver, something that has Reign's teeth on edge. Right now, he has two-dollar bills in his back pocket and little else.

The driver stares at their destination. "You sure you got the right place?"

She nods, opening the door. "We're sure."

They climb out and as the car leaves, Reign realizes what the driver is talking about. They're facing a stretch of brick wall, two old wooden doors chained shut in the middle. There's a barber shop on one side, number sixty-six. A pharmacy on the other, number sixty-eight. Both have shut down, and from the looks of the dirty windows and peeling paint on the signs, they have been for some time.

"Your mom must've written down the wrong address," he suggests. He steps forward and peers through the gap in the old timber doors. "It's dark, but it looks empty."

But Arielle shakes her head, her brow scrunched. "She wouldn't do that." Maybe this is like Sinclair Mansion. There must be a hidden door or something.

"Cool," Mac breathes as she stands in front of the brick wall. She takes a step back as if she's trying to survey the entirety of the view.

Reign joins her, noting there's nothing exceptional about the red bricks and gray mortar. "Your latest interest is the art of bricklaying? Is there some impressive pattern you're not seeing?"

She looks at him quizzically, indicating toward the wall. "What are you talking about?"

Reign narrows his eyes. "What are *you* talking about?"

Mac takes a step back, schooling her face as she averts her gaze. "Ah, nothing."

260

Except, he knows Mac. Whatever's going on is most definitely something. But before Reign can ask, another voice joins them.

"What in the world are you peeps doing here?"

They all turn to find Gabby and Colt walking toward them. Once they reach them, Gabby plants her hands on her hips.

"You two are supposed to be lying low," she says to Reign and Mac.

Mac glances at Reign. "Do you remember agreeing to that?"

He scratches his chin. "Nope. No recollection whatsoever."

She wrinkles her nose. "Although, in all fairness, even if we did agree, we wouldn't have done it."

"Also true," Reign acknowledges.

Gabby huffs as she turns to Arielle. "I'll go back to my original question. What are you doing here?"

"Mom had a note about Veritas Library in her journal." Arielle indicates toward the brick wall they're standing beside. "This is the address."

Gabby's eyebrows shoot up with surprise. She glances at Colt. "Should we?"

Colt crosses his arms, studying the three of them. A little part of Reign wants to move closer to Arielle. He can sense the weight in Colt's gaze.

Finally, he nods. "Let's tell them."

Tell them what? Reign tenses. He'd rather know what the heck is going on before Colt goes making those sorts of decisions.

"Arielle. Reign. Mac," Gabby says with a flourish. "I'd like to welcome you to Veritas Library."

Reign glances at the brick wall, about to point out that this Truth Library must be for mice, only to freeze.

"What the..."

His eyes progressively widen as his mouth slowly drops

open. The brick wall ages before him, some areas fading away completely. No, not fading. Morphing. Long, narrow windows appear on either side, a large ornate door coalescing in the center. A curved arch appears over it, one word etched into the ancient building that's now before him.

Veritas.

Mac leans closer to Reign. "You see it now, don't you?" she asks smugly.

Reign doesn't have time to answer, because Gabby pushes open the wooden door. "Shall we?"

Mac is the first to enter, practically skipping through the door. Arielle follows, throwing a questioning look at her cousin.

"Yep, it's a supernatural library," Gabby says proudly. "Humans can only see or enter it with an invitation."

Reign quickly follows Arielle, tense at what they're going to find on the other side. Colt and Gabby look like two parents who are about to show their children a secret shortcut to the North Pole.

Reign blinks as the door closes behind them. He swallows. Then blinks again.

The area before him is colossal. Magnificent. Possibly a little pretentious. A soaring ceiling is somewhere above him, glittering chandeliers hanging in the room that seems to be holding its breath. Mahogany bookshelves line the walls, countless candles flicker in wall sconces, looking as if they stretch forever, rows upon rows of books stacked as far as the eye can see. When he finally draws in a breath, his lungs fill with the scent of aged leather and paper.

"It's Hogwarts meets the Tardis," Mac breathes. "But a library, which is even cooler."

Arielle turns to Gabby. "My mother knew this was here," she says quietly.

Gabby nods. "She must've. Maybe as part of her research."

Arielle looks back toward the shelves. Hundreds and thousands of books, most leather-bound and worn, reach as far as the eye can see. "I need to find Infernal Damasicus."

"Infernal Damasicus?" comes a strident voice from their left.

Reign spins around, his shock and awe replaced by his usual state—preparedness to fight. His gaze drops as he sees a woman coming toward them. A woman in camo pants and a white tank top, dog tags and all, in a wheelchair.

"Veritas is run by witches and seers," Gabby whispers.

Reign almost rolls his eyes. Of course it is. What's next, vampires in roller skates, chewing gum?

The woman's dark eyes roam over each of them, her pageboy hair slicked back. "Who's interested in the Infernal Damasicus?" she asks haughtily.

Reign decides he doesn't like her. Anyone who goes all I'm-better-than-thou tends to tick him off.

Arielle steps forward. "I am. I'd like to have a look at it, please."

"I'm afraid that's not possible."

"Look," Reign grinds out. "We don't have time for supernatural red tape. All she wants to do is check it out."

"Well, she can't," the woman announces, her black eyebrow raised. "It was borrowed yesterday."

"By who?" Colt asks quietly.

"I'm afraid I can't share that information," she says, raising her snooty nose an inch even though she's no taller than four shelves high.

Idly, Reign wonders whether she's a witch or a seer. Then he decides he doesn't really want to know.

Arielle takes another step forward. "Please, this is important."

The woman's mouth opens only to snap shut again. She

wheels a little closer, her eyes narrowing. "You look like someone I know." She draws back in shock. "Sierra."

"Yes, Sierra is my mother."

Reign moves a little closer to Arielle. "You know her?"

"Oh yes. She's different to many others who come here. They all want the usual stuff—love potions, curses, how to kill a ghost, that sort of thing." The witch waves a hand dismissively. "Sierra wanted something rare. Something no one has seen for centuries. The Holy Grail." She sighs. "Never got very far, though. She told me she even found a cloaked grave once, which is impressive, but never anything about where the Grail could be located."

Reign doesn't point out that it's probably because the Grail doesn't exist.

"My name is Nim," says the woman, smiling a little. "I like your mother. She's determined."

"She really is," Arielle agrees quietly, her grief palpable in those three words.

Suddenly Nim straightens in her wheelchair, her eyes widening. "Something's happened. Sierra would never have allowed her daughter to come here."

Arielle's shoulders tense. "So I've heard," she says, a strange hitch in her voice. "That changed when she was kidnapped several days ago."

Nim's hand flutters to her throat. "Great ghosts," she murmurs. She spins around and wheels toward a desk the size of a billiard table. There, she opens a large book, running a black fingernail down a ledger.

They follow, and Reign once again shifts closer to Arielle. No matter how cool this place looks, none of this can be easy for her to hear.

Nim glances up. "I remember now. He was a dark-haired,

strong looking man." She points to the book. "His name was Mr. Kane."

Reign curses at the same time Gabby does. They glance at each other, spitting his name like it just joined the ranks of the first word. "Kane."

"He must be supernatural," Colt muses. "I doubt anyone invited him in."

"A demon?" Reign asks pointedly.

"Possible," Colt concedes. "The longer we spend on Earth, the more adept we become at masking ourselves."

"A demon has the Infernal Damasicus?" Nim asks in horror.

"Why?" Reign asks, his stomach filling with dread.

"It has several references to the Grail," she answers, her face looking as pale as her tank top.

Mac stills. "Do you think he's had something to do with the abductions?" She blinks. "That he's trying to raise Hell on Earth?"

"Maybe," says Colt. "Demons want the Grail as much as angels do. Why else would he abduct Arielle and Reign and go to such lengths to learn about the crypt?"

Reign frowns. "Did Sierra ever come here with anyone?"

Nim shakes her head, then stops. "A long time ago, she did. A man called David. I believe he was a Grail Keeper."

The final two words slam through Reign. Someone else knows the term. As if it's a thing. He stops himself from glancing around and looking for Joseph, his stomach churning. It's not supposed to be a thing.

"I believe he had a child," the witch continues, unaware that Reign has just had the floor sucked out from beneath him. "He stopped coming and Sierra was doing everything she could to find him. Spent hours scouring the grimoires to find the right location spell."

Arielle's mom was casting spells? He shakes his head.

There's too much to process. It's getting too hard to sort fact from fiction.

Nim's face brightens. "Although I just received a message from Blaise." She zips around the desk, sifting through some papers. She lifts one up triumphantly then clasps it, her eyes closing. "Yes, it's something important."

Reign waits, no longer caring who the heck Blaise is or that it seems Nim is a seer. All they want is a lead.

Nim unfolds the message, her eyes scanning the page. She looks up.

"It's an address for David."

CHAPTER 34
ARIELLE

As Arielle stands in front of the address Nim gave her, she knows that even as tenuous leads go, this one is as flimsy as rice paper.

This David guy hasn't seen her mother in over seventeen years. He could've moved. He may not even remember her. He may be even grouchier than Reign.

But it's all she has.

Arielle checks the piece of paper again. "Yep, this is it."

The house is barely distinguishable from any other house in the suburbs. Double-story, green lawn, manicured garden. Arielle tries to look for anything about it that may look special, a hint that someone called a Grail Keeper might live here.

Except it's innocuously average.

"There's no car in the driveway," Reign observes.

"If we get here and there's no one home..." Mac mutters,

Arielle frowns. "We'll just have to come back."

"I suppose we'll have Gabby and Colt with us, then," Mac offers.

Arielle nods, wishing her cousin was still with them. As

they'd left the library Gabby and Colt had paused. "We're going to look for Kane."

Colt's face had hardened. "I'd like to have a chat. Demon to demon."

Those last few words had sent a shiver down Arielle's spine.

Reign rubs his chin as he surveys the house. "What do you think a chat between two demons even looks like?"

Mac shudders. "If it's anything like angel v angel, then it's worse that you can imagine."

Arielle looks away. She's not sure she wants to start to guess at what it will involve. From what she saw when Reign was abducted, Colt is a formidable foe.

But then again, so is Kane.

"So, are we waiting for anything in particular?" Mac asks.

Arielle goes to move only to find her feet are glued to the pavement. Suddenly, the thought of going up and knocking on that door doesn't sound like such a great idea.

Reign moves in a little closer. "Arielle?"

"What if..." She swallows, not wanting to finish the sentence.

If this lead turns out to be nothing, she has no idea how to find her mother.

Reign studies her in that intense, brooding way of his, but there's no way she's saying this out loud. It makes her ill to even think about it.

He glances at the door as understanding dawns across his face. "There's no such thing as a dead end, Ari." He shrugs. "Think of it more as narrowing down our options."

Arielle blinks. "I like that." She smiles, suddenly feeling lighter. "I might even put that on my boots."

Reign glances down, raising an eyebrow. "I think I've ruined them enough."

Arielle lifts her right foot, pointing to a small scrawl near the heel. "See that? It says 'bitter trials are often blessings in disguise'. It's an Oscar Wilde quote."

Reign's eyebrow hikes up even higher. "Except there's no way to tell the difference when life's just being a bitch."

Arielle rolls her eyes, unwilling to buy into his grouchiness. "Well, I'm not writing that on my boot."

Reign blinks, and it's as if the motion is a minuscule double take.

Mac walks past them, heading to the door. "Atta girl, Ari. Don't take his crap."

Arielle follows her, leaving Reign muttering something about being ganged up on. She wonders if traitorous Lizzie ever got one up on Mr. Push The World Away.

But as she comes to stand beside Mac, Arielle sobers. The door is before her. A door that will either provide the information she desperately seeks. Or...they'll be narrowing down their options again.

She lifts her hand and knocks. "Please, please, be home David," she says under her breath.

Footsteps approach from the other side. "Someone's home!" Arielle whispers.

"I'll get it, Mikki," calls a female voice.

Arielle frowns as recognition jolts through her. "But that doesn't make sense."

"What doesn't?" Reign mutters, suddenly tense as he glances around.

The door opens and the smile falls from Aunt Shell's face. "Arielle?"

Arielle tries to understand what's going on. "What are you doing here?"

Aunt Shell grabs her by the arm and drags her inside. Reign and Mac are just behind her.

"I should be asking you the same question, young lady,"

Aunt Shell mutters furiously. She looks over her shoulder. "Just some kids playing a prank, Mikki," she calls in a falsely chirpy voice.

She glances at Reign and Mac. "More studying, huh?"

Reign grins. "What else would I be doing?"

Aunt Shell frowns. "You're lucky you're a nice boy, Reign. Otherwise I'd be suspicious." She turns back to Arielle. "Now, what are you doing here?"

Arielle lifts her chin. She's not going to lie. "I'm looking for my mom."

Although she obviously suspected it, Aunt Shell draws back as if she was slapped. "We discussed this. You can't." She grips Arielle's arms "You need to leave, now. For your own good."

"No," Arielle says, shaking her head. "I'm not going to do that."

Reign steps forward. "And she won't be alone."

Mac steps around Arielle's other side. "No siree, she won't."

Aunt Shell is speechless for a second. To be honest, so is Arielle. The support from these two is...humbling. She's not totally sure what she's done to deserve it.

Aunt Shell steps back, releasing Arielle's arms. "I see." She tucks a stray strand of hair behind her ear. "I've been doing my own research, you know. That's why I'm here."

Arielle glances around the hallway they're in. "At David's house?"

"Yes, I remembered how close he and Sierra were when we were young. She used to tell him everything." She twists her hands as she looks at the three teens. "I think I know why Sierra was abducted."

"So do we. Angels and demons are looking for the Grail."

Aunt Shell's hands flutter restlessly as she hears exactly how much Arielle knows. She frowns, shaking her head. "No. I've discovered these abductions have happened before."

"This has nothing to do with the Grail?" Reign asks quietly.

"I'm not sure. All I know is that forty-five years ago seven women were abducted." Her eyes fill with tears. "It was a ritualistic sacrifice so a dark witch could resurrect her mother."

"That's just wrong," mutters Mac.

Aunt Shell nods. "The sacrifice required the murder of seven women with similar features and same age."

Reign shifts a little closer to Arielle. "And Sierra?"

"She and the other women who were abducted are blonde and the same age. I did some digging and it turns out they're all distantly related."

Arielle's head is reeling. "They're relatives?"

"Yes, descending from the same bloodline," Aunt Shell says, her voice trembling. "And according to the text I read, they will all bear a mark on their shoulder in the shape of a star. Apparently it cannot be seen by men."

Arielle's knees go weak. "Like the one Mom has."

Aunt Shell nods. "Yes." Her face scrunches up. "It always looked familiar, but I could never place it."

Suddenly, anger shoots through Arielle, strengthening her. "Were you going to tell me any of this?"

Aunt Shell's face turns fierce. "This is why Sierra never wanted you involved in this. She was protecting you." Her anger dissolves as quickly as it flared. "Please Ari, let this go."

"I can't do that," Arielle says quietly. Firmly.

And those four words feel good. They feel like the truth.

Aunt Shell's shoulders sag. "Well, I've told you all I know." She glances over her shoulder. "You should get going."

"We came here to talk to David," Arielle says stubbornly.

"Please," Reign adds with a smile.

Aunt Shell's face crumples. "Oh Ari, David's—"

There's a knock on the door behind them. Aunt Shell glances at the three of them. "Is Gabby joining us?"

Arielle frowns, glancing at Reign and Mac. "Maybe they couldn't find him?"

Aunt Shell gasps. "Who? Who were they looking for?" She marches to the door and yanks it open. "Gabrielle Hartley, I'd like to have a word with you—"

The hooded man standing on the porch snaps an arm out and grabs Aunt Shell, yanking her toward him.

"No!" screams Arielle.

She launches forward, but Reign is faster. Just as he leaps, the hooded man raises his other hand, pointing it at them, palm out.

Reign is propelled backward by a blast of crimson energy a split second before the explosion hits Arielle then Mac. Arielle slams into the wall, watching in horror as Reign crashes into the hallway cabinet, timber splintering everywhere.

Arielle slides to the floor, gasping for breath as pain ricochets through her. Blackness overwhelms her, stealing the consciousness she's desperately trying to hold onto.

Aunt Shell.

Mac.

Reig—

CHAPTER 35
REIGN

Reign feels like a freight train has tap danced on his head. For a split second he figures he must be hungover.

And then he remembers.

He shoots into a sitting position, and his surroundings tilt at crazy angles. Clasping his head, he wills it to stop. There was a man. He took Aunt Shell.

And Mac and Arielle were blasted with the same explosion of energy that had Reign doing a Superman into the cabinet.

Reign stumbles to his feet, holding his head with one hand. He needs to make sure they're okay. He's taken two staggering steps when he realizes there's another woman here. She's kneeling over Ari and Mac as they start to stir.

"Get away from them!" Reign hurls through numb lips, the words not coming out nearly loud enough.

The woman looks up. "It's okay, I'm David's wife. My name's Mikki."

Reign falls to his knees, still trying to get his bearing before he decides whether he can trust this woman.

Arielle sits up, holding her head. "What happened?"

Mac props herself up on her elbows. "We got smashed by a power ball," she mutters. "A freaking big one."

Arielle shoots to her feet. "Aunt Shell!" she cries, panicked. "We need to find Aunt Shell!"

She stumbles and Reign quickly catches her. She grips his shirt, looking up at him. "They took her, Reign."

Reign's heart constricts and his arms instinctively tighten. "I know. We'll do everything we can to find her."

Arielle tugs on him. "We need to go. Now."

"We will, but I think you should call Gabby and Colt first."

Mac stands up, too. "He's right. That was some pretty powerful magic."

Arielle chews on her lip then nods. She pulls out her cell phone and calls Gabby. "You need to come to the address Nim gave us. I'll explain when you get here."

She hangs up, her flame blue eyes flickering with pain. "Now her mother's been taken, too."

As the shock of the energy ball or whatever it was wears off, anger starts to simmer in Reign's veins. Not only has Arielle's mother been taken, but now her aunt, right as they stood here. Gabby is going to be devastated. That's two good souls who have been hurt by whatever it is that's going on.

Mikki steps forward, and Reign notices she's shaking. A small woman with her brunette hair in a stylish bob, he wonders if she's some kind of supernatural, too. "Did Shell have the mark, too?"

Arielle's eyes widen as the question hits her. Her brow quickly furrows as she sifts through her memories. "No, I don't think so. Well, I never saw one."

Mikki nods, looking relieved. "You're Sierra's daughter?"

"Yes. I'm trying to find her."

"We all are," Reign adds.

Mikki turns to him. "And you are?"

"Reign. I'm, ah, sorry about your hallway thingy."

Mikki shakes her head. "David hated it, anyway."

"Is he here?" Arielle asks. "Could we talk to him?"

Mikki's arms wrap around herself. "David died seventeen years ago."

"Oh," says Arielle. "I'm so sorry for your loss."

Waving away the apology, Mikki smiles. "I used to be so jealous of David and your mother. They were very close." She shakes her head. "I thought they were crazy, chasing after the Holy Grail."

Reign's stomach contracts as if he was just punched. This wasn't supposed to be about the Grail anymore.

"David said they got close," Mikki continues. According to some book called Infernal Damasicus they learned that the Grail was buried somewhere. Somewhere deep. They tried a location spell to find it."

Her arms tighten around her midriff.

"Something happened, he never told me what. They parted ways." She shrugs and her soft features turn wistful. "And in the end, he chose family."

Reign suspects Mikki didn't ask too many questions after that. She had the guy she loved and that would've been enough.

Arielle mirrors Mikki, her arms wrapping around herself. "I think my mom did, too."

There's a knock on the door and Reign instinctively leaps in front of the others. His trust in that innocuous sound is forever fractured.

"Ari? It's me, Gabby."

Arielle steps around Reign and opens the door. Gabby frowns the moment she sees her cousin. She opens her arms and engulfs her in a hug. "What's happened?"

Arielle pulls back and lets Gabby and Colt in, shutting the

door behind them. Their gazes dart around the four still-stunned faces and the smashed furniture.

"What happened?" Colt asks grimly.

"Gabby," Arielle says, her voice strained. "Your mom was here. She was telling us what she discovered when a man appeared." She grips her cousin's hands. "He took her and then knocked us out with some sort of magic."

Gabby blinks, then blinks again. "Mom's been taken?"

Colt steps closer, wrapping an arm around her shoulder. "What color was the energy?"

"Red."

"Demon magic," he growls. "Kane must've taken her."

Reign rubs his head, trying to untangle everything that's happened. Is this about the mythical Grail? Or something else?

"That's not all," Arielle says. "Whoever's doing this is planning a ritualistic sacrifice."

Gabby goes stiller and progressively paler as Arielle outlines what they've learned. The hand gripping Colt tightens more and more.

There's a flicker out of the corner of his eye and Reign stiffens. Joseph materializes at the end of the hallway, extending his hand as if he's reaching out to him.

Reign's breath is pushed out of his too-tight chest. He was hoping he'd gone. He was hoping that keeping busy would keep Joseph away. So far, that had been working.

"She's an Innocent," Joseph says gravely.

Reign turns away. He's not going to ask who Joseph is talking about in front of all these people. Sierra? Shell? Heck, is he talking about Mac or Gabby or Arielle?

"You cannot save her without the Grail."

Reign focuses on Gabby. She's the picture of a composed daughter. If she can hold her shit together after learning her mother was just abducted by a demon with plans of ritualistic sacrifice, then he can ignore an annoying hallucination.

Gabby clears her throat. "We need to find Kane."

"Did you find any clues?" asks Mac.

Colt shakes his head. "He's disappeared. Without a trace. Even the precinct hasn't seen him."

Mac's frown is ferocious. "We don't have time to chase all over Mercy City, looking for him."

"We could try a location spell," says Colt, although he doesn't sound like that's much of a solution.

"Of course we could," Reign mutters. "Let me guess, it's filed under L at Veritas?"

"As much as I'd love to build my forever home among those shelves," says Mac. "We don't have time to do that. It could take days."

Mikki raises her hand as if she's in a classroom. "I can help you with that."

"You're a witch?" Colt asks, hope unmistakable in his voice.

But she shakes her head. "No, but I know someone who is. She's the one who helped Sierra and David all those years ago."

Mikki disappears and returns a moment later with a slip of paper. "Her name is Blaise. She doesn't live too far away from here."

Arielle takes it. "Thank you, Mikki. This is very helpful."

They all glance at each other, the sense that things are getting real hanging heavily in the air.

Seven women are fated to be sacrificed. Sierra and Shell are probably two of them.

And somehow, they have to find them before it's too late.

CHAPTER 36
ARIELLE

Arielle knocks on the faded door of the dilapidated brick house they're standing in front of, conscious there's no time for hesitation or worries or doubts. Two words have been a drumbeat pounding through her from the moment they left Mikki's house.

Ritualistic.

Sacrifice.

Out of all the words Arielle has heard—abduction, angel, demon, Grail, Hell, magic, supernatural—those two are the most terrifying. Especially when in the context of her mother and aunt.

There's no answer, so Arielle knocks louder. Unlike David's house, it hasn't occurred to her that no one would be home.

"We don't have time for this," she mutters.

Mac strides past her and thumps on the door. The pounding almost makes the aging porch rattle.

"Great," Reign sighs. "Now the witch is going to think the feds are after her."

Except there's no answer. No one opens the door.

"What do we do now?" Arielle asks quietly.

Colt crosses his arms. "We wait."

Except they don't have time... Her mother is slated to be sacrificed, Aunt Shell, too!

Reign steps back, craning his neck as he surveys the second floor. "There's a window up there. And it's open."

Arielle looks up, realizing he's right, but the flare of hope is short-lived. "It's the second floor." She glances at Gabby and Colt. "And no, those two are not flying up there."

Colt looks over his shoulder as a car drives past. "Too risky. We can't afford to be seen."

Reign rolls his eyes. "I wasn't talking about those two getting those oversized wings of theirs out."

He jogs back several steps, assessing the front of the house. Arielle frowns. The sagging porch has a gabled roof, but the posts holding it up look like they might be built out of cardboard. The house itself is brick, a second floor with two windows, one of which is open.

"You can't climb this porch, Reign," she says sternly.

"Wasn't planning to," he responds cheerily. "That porch is about as stable as my sanity."

A few more steps backwards and Reign breaks into a sprint, running straight for the brick wall.

"He's not..." Arielle breathes.

"He most certainly is," says Mac, her voice alive with anticipation.

Reign leaps and hits the wall with one foot, instantly using it to launch upwards. He lands a few feet up and does it again, his arms reaching high. His fingertips hook into a barely noticeable ledge on the first floor and he draws himself higher.

Arielle holds her breath as she watches, worried he's going to fall...impressed with the play of muscles across his shoulders.

"Reign has been running all his life," says Mac. "He's been determined nothing will get in his way."

Not even a two-story house.

Dragging his bodyweight up with nothing but his hands and arms, Reign swings his leg up and hooks it on the porch. Arielle takes an involuntary step forward, conscious of how flimsy the structure is. Reign keeps close to the wall as he slowly pushes to his feet. He reaches right and jimmies the window open the rest of the way.

With a grin and a wave, he slips inside.

Mac turns to the others. "You should see him climb apartment blocks."

The images that come to mind terrify and exhilarate Arielle.

Suddenly, a high-pitched scream echoes from within the house.

Arielle's heart jolts with alarm. "Someone's home."

"He'll be fine," Mac says complacently. "That scream was female, for one."

There's a crash as something heavy falls. Arielle shoots forward and knocks on the door. "He could be in trouble."

Mac crosses her arms with a sigh. "I'm telling you, he's fine."

Colt frowns. "This is a witch, Mac. I suspect a powerful one."

She rolls her eyes. "Even as a toad, Reign will be hot."

Arielle knocks again, desperation climbing through her chest. Mac is being far too relaxed about this, even if she's right and Reign could pull off handsome amphibian.

The door opens just as she's about to rap again, a tall woman on the other side. Her sleek violet hair cascades down her shoulders and torso, flowing over her purple boho dress. "Can I help you?"

"Where's Reign?" Arielle demands. "What have you done to him?"

The willowy witch steps back to show Reign right behind

her. He grins. "I hope purple is your favorite color, too," he says cheerily.

"Which is the color of what?" the witch says.

Reign lifts up his hand, ticking off each finger. "Psychic powers. Opening of the third eye. Wisdom. And spiritual knowledge. All qualities I recognized in you the moment we met, Blaise."

The witch snorts. "As you climbed into my bedroom."

"Sorry, Blaise." Reign rubs the back of his head. "I explained why."

Arielle watches as Blaise's lips twitch with humor. First Aunt Shell, and now the witch—Reign has managed to charm them both. He broke into Blaise's house, for poppycock's sake! And yet, he's been a human Oscar the Grouch with Arielle. What does that even mean?

Blaise turns back to Arielle and the others. "You require a location spell. To find your mothers."

Arielle nods, her stomach tangling in knots. "And five other women. If we don't, they'll die."

Blaise opens the door wider. "Come in."

The inside of the house is dark and old and smells like incense. It opens straight into a living room unlike any Arielle has seen before. The floor is covered in Oriental rugs, while cushions are scattered in lieu of chairs or a couch. A large altar is at the opposite side of the room and covered in purple velvet, adorned with a multitude of candles flickering among jars and herbs and crystals.

"Cool," says Mac.

Blaise stands in the center of the room. "Reign tells me Sierra is missing."

Arielle's heart jolts. "You knew my mother."

"Your mother and I are good friends. We have been for a long time."

Arielle knows she shouldn't be surprised by this new information. She knows she shouldn't feel betrayed. But both emotions slice through her whether she likes it or not. Her mother led a whole other life she never told her about.

Shoving away the thoughts, Arielle focuses on Blaise. Everything hinges on the next question. "Can you find her?"

"Location spells can be...obstreperous. But it will be made easier by the fact I am close to Sierra." She narrows her eyes. "I will need a drop of your blood. It will make the spell stronger."

Arielle nods. "Anything." She'd give a limb if she had to. Even her life.

Blaise studies Arielle for long moments. "Your mother did the same for you."

Before Arielle can ask what that means, Blaise turns to Reign. "Men cannot be present for this spell."

Reign frowns. "Then let's not classify according to gender, huh?" He moves closer to Arielle. "We'd rather stay here."

Blaise crosses her arms. "He reminds me of your father," she says to Arielle before returning her gaze to Reign. "The spell cannot be done with you here. Sierra's daughter will be perfectly safe with me.

Arielle stills. Blaise knew her father?

Reign opens his mouth but Blaise raises a hand, long purple fingernails and all. "I will call you in the moment I'm done. You can even climb through the window again if you'd like."

Mac grabs his arm. "Come on, I'll keep you company." She pulls him back toward the door and Colt follows.

Gabby blows him a kiss. "This will be just like being back at boarding school."

Once they're gone, Blaise heads to a door at the other end of the room. "I just have a few supplies to collect."

Now alone with Gabby, Arielle rubs her forehead. "Being in a witch's house, casting a spell, is just like school?"

Gabby has the grace to look a little flustered. "I went to the Academy of the Arcane. It's a school for supernaturals."

Arielle blinks, unsure whether she can process this, too. It's like her mind is too full of revelations. Of truths that have been kept from her. "I see."

Gabby reaches out to clasp her hand. "I know you're hurt because we kept all this from you. I'm truly sorry for that."

Swallowing the desire to yank her hand away, Arielle can't hold her cousin's gaze. "I know you are."

Gabby frowns, her hand tightening around Arielle's. "Something's bothering you."

"Everything's bothering me!" Arielle explodes. "Apart from the fact angels and demons and witches, heck, even the Holy Grail, are real, my mom has been kidnapped for a ritualistic sacrifice to resurrect who knows who. Come to think of it, who knows what!"

Gabby remains silent and still throughout Arielle's rant. Her eyes narrow ever so slightly. "There's something else."

This time, Arielle does jerk her hand away. She doesn't need her cousin to be so perceptive right now. "How can you be so calm about this?" she huffs.

Her mother has been taken, too.

Gabby's face tightens. "I learned the hard way that emotions need to be controlled." Her gaze flickers away. "I swear I'd tell you about it if I could, Ari."

Because Gabby doesn't think she can handle it. Just like Arielle's mom and Aunt Shell.

That's what's really bothering Arielle. The knowledge that as she desperately tries to save her mother, the people she trusts are expecting her to fall apart at any moment. Probably because she's only human. There's nothing special about her. The girl who's never done anything extraordinary like her mother, who isn't an angel like her cousin, who blindly accepted every lie she's ever been told. Heck, she doesn't even know what she wants to be when she grows up.

Gabby frowns and opens her mouth, no doubt her perceptiveness is ringing alarm bells.

But the door at the other end of the living room opens. Blaise appears, completely transformed. Gone is the violet hair and purple dress. Her hair is now as raven colored as the flowing raven dress she's wearing.

It seems this witch changes wigs along with her outfits.

As if to match her black hair and black dress, she's carrying a black candle. She nods solemnly. "It is time to start the spell."

CHAPTER 37
REIGN

Reign paces out the front, eyeing the window he just climbed through. Blaise may have done little more than throw a crystal ball at his head the first time, but he suspects the witch will be less understanding the second instance he broke into her home.

"You're going to have to wait," Mac points out from where she's sitting on the steps of the porch. She indicates toward Colt, who strode to the edge of the street the minute they exited the house. "He doesn't seem too worried."

"I don't know about that," says Reign, studying the tense shoulders and too-still stance. "He looks pretty worried."

"Are you worried?" Mac asks quietly.

Reign spins to face her. "Aren't you?"

Mac angles her head as she watches him. "Only if this locator spell doesn't work."

He doesn't point out there are far more than just that point where this could go wrong. Even if they find the location of the sacrifices, they have to stop them somehow. That's if they're not too late...

She shrugs. "But then again, I don't *like* like any of them—"

Reign stiffens. "We're not having this conversation."

"Far more than I'd like to admit," she finishes.

"Mackenzie…" Reign growls low in his throat.

She puts her hands up in a sign of surrender. "Okay, okay. I won't poke Grumpy Bear." She glances around. "So, is the Big J here?"

Reign sighs, not sure he likes the change of topic. "Not yet, but they'd better hurry up with the locator spell. It seems if I sit still too long, he appears."

"What has he said?"

"Oh, only that one of those women is an Innocent, and I need to find the Grail to save her."

"And what if he's right?"

Reign starts pacing again. He knew he shouldn't have let Mac humor his hallucination. "You heard Arielle's aunt. This isn't even about some mythical artifact that doesn't even exist. This is a ritualistic sacrifice to raise the dead." As he says the words, a tremor ripples down his spine. He can't believe those words just came out of his mouth as if they're normal.

Mac wraps her arms around her knees, placing her chin on them. "But it doesn't make sense. Why was Kane so interested in Sinclair Mansion?"

"Because he's into antiques."

"And Dumah," she continues as if Reign hasn't spoken. "He believes the Gates of Hell are opening."

"He's also handcuffed in a bathtub."

Mac pins him with a determined glare. "And why has Joseph appeared? Why do you think you see him, Reign?"

Reign stops his pacing, his stomach painfully flip flopping. It's because a part of him wishes he was a Grail Keeper. He wants to be someone who people believe could be a hero. Someone…important. Someone a person like Arielle could respect.

He looks away. "Because I've done a damn good job of screwing up my brain chemistry. Because I've learned the supernatural is real." He pulls up a cocky grin as he glances back at Mac. "Because it turns out I've got quite an imagination."

He also sees Hell-faces and apparently they're not a thing.

"Except, you're forgetting something," Mac says quietly. "You saw Joseph before any of this started."

Reign almost doubles over as the truth he's been avoiding slams him in the gut. Joseph appeared in the alley before angels and demons became part of his daily vocabulary. As if to add salt to the wound, Joseph himself appears beside Mac.

Reign scowls and turns his back. "Let's focus on getting Sierra and Shell back, shall we?"

He finds Colt striding toward them. "We need a plan B."

Grudgingly, Reign turns back to Mac, relieved to find Joseph gone. Maybe he's getting a better handle on his delusions.

Mac pushes to her feet. "You don't think the locator spell will work?"

Colt shakes his head. "We're hoping it will work. We can't pin these women's lives on just hope."

They glance at each other. And if the location spell doesn't work...

Reign rubs his temples. "Did you want a unicorn, too?" He doesn't bother to ask if they're real as well. He doesn't want to know.

Colt sighs. "It may be easier. Kane has disappeared, most likely because the time is drawing near." He glances over his shoulder. The sun is disappearing over the suburban skyline, as if it's slinking away because it doesn't want to see what's coming, either. "It will be soon."

As if on cue, the door to the rickety house opens. Reign has to check twice that it's Blaise standing there. She's changed from purple witch to black witch, and the transformation feels ominous.

She steps onto the porch. "The spell is done."

Arielle and Gabby appear behind her, their faces somber.

"Did it work?" asks Reign, his muscles heavy with dread.

"Of course, it worked," Blaise snaps. She holds out a burnt piece of map. "This is where Sierra can be found."

Reign takes it, shock slicing through him as he registers the location. He looks to Arielle, seeing that she already knows where they have to go.

He nods, holding her gaze.

"Sinclair Mansion, here we come."

CHAPTER 38
ARIELLE

The curved driveway to Sinclair Mansion is muted and silent in the evening air. Arielle wants to run down it, taking all the rage and fear that are like fire and ice in her veins and using them to make this right.

Her mother is there. So is Aunt Shell. Taken so they could be sacrificed.

Except, as she climbs out of Colt's car along with the others, Gabby grips her shoulders. "Colt and I are going to take care of this."

Arielle frowns. "But—"

"There are likely to be demons there," Colt says gravely. "And we don't know how many." He reaches into the car and pulls out three handguns. He passes one to Arielle. "If they come for you, use this. The bullets are coated in lead, which is poisonous to demons."

Arielle takes the gun, her stomach contracting at the cool weight in her palm. She's never held a weapon like this. The thought of shooting it has bile burning up her throat.

Reign and Mac take theirs. Mac frowns. "I've never liked these things."

Reign pulls something back as he checks out the weapon, obviously familiar with it as the gun makes an ominous clicking sound. "They're deadly, dangerous and worse in the hands of the wrong people." He clicks it again and tucks into the back of his jeans. "But they reach further and do more damage than a punch, which is preferable when dealing with winged evil."

"Wait here," Colt orders quietly. "We'll call when it's clear."

"Sure thing," Reign says as he leans against the car.

Mac nods. "Be safe."

Arielle frowns internally at their easy acceptance of being left behind. She reminds herself this isn't their fight, it's not their mothers trapped in Sinclair Mansion, but she can't help feeling disappointed. Like Reign just let her down.

Gabby and Colt step away, the early evening cloaking them in muted black. They look at each other, nodding. A moment later, two sets of wings appear, one ebony, the other ivory, and they head for the sky. In a blink, they're gone.

Arielle lets her breath out, wondering how in the world she's going to wait. Her nerves are already at snapping point.

Reign pushes off the car. "Let's go. We're not waiting here."

"No freaking way are we waiting here," agrees Mac.

Reign turns to Arielle, and she tenses. Is this where he tells her it'll be safer for her to stay here? This may be her mother and aunt, but Arielle doesn't have the fighting experience they do. Her clothes have always been washed and clean, she's never gone hungry, and she's never ever spent a night on the street. She's never had to fight for anything in her life.

"What do you want to do, Ari?"

He holds her gaze, telling her with all the turbulence in his jungle green eyes that this is dangerous. That they have guns they'll probably need to use. That she's risking her life.

And yet, he's asking her. He's giving her the choice. Something softens and hardens within Arielle all at once.

She squares her shoulders. "I want to fight."

For her mom.

For Aunt Shell.

For the hope that she's stronger than she feels.

Reign draws in a deep breath. "Okay. Fight it is." He indicates toward the driveway with his chin. "We'd better get going. Those two have a head start." He flaps his hands as if they were wings.

Arielle feels a smile tripping up her lips, despite everything they're facing. "Unfair advantage if you ask me," she says as she falls into step beside him.

Mac appears on her other side. "It would be kinda cool to have wings," she muses. "What do you think is their maximum speed? Do you reckon they ever get itchy? And how in the world do they clean them? It's not like they'd fit in the shower."

Reign rolls his eyes. "Only you'd think of all that stuff, Mac." His handsome face sobers. "Now, we need to be quiet."

Silence descends in the same way night is—steadily and absolutely, multiplying with each passing second. The driveway snakes ahead of them, the road that will take her to her mother. As Arielle walks beside Reign, her heart starts up a steady thud.

Who is she to think she can storm a mansion full of demons and rescue eight women?

They come around the final bend and Sinclair Mansion looms dark and ominous ahead. Mac points to a tree nearby. "You two wait here. I'll scout the place out."

"Mac—" says Reign, but she's already gone, her body swallowed by the night. He takes Arielle's hand and draws her behind the trunk. "Dammit."

Arielle jerks her hand away but it's too late. Reign turns to her. "You're scared.

He noticed how slick her palms are. Heck, he may have

noticed that her pulse has been taken over by a freight train. "I'm terrified," she admits. She holds her breath. Now is the moment he recognizes bringing her was a bad idea.

"Good," he whispers. "You should be. This is dangerous as shit."

"I know what I'm getting into, Reign." Arielle sighs. "Are you going to tell me we'll find them both, too?"

That it's not too late.

Reign shakes his head, his eyes unfathomable in the dark. "I don't make promises I can't keep."

Although the blunt words should shock Arielle, they don't. In fact, they're strangely comforting. It means she can trust Reign to tell her the truth.

"Look, I don't know what's going on here, but I do know you have people around you who will do everything they can to save your mother and her sister."

Including Reign...

"Why are you here, Reign? Why do you even care?"

"Why does it matter?" he shoots back.

"I don't know. It just does."

Arielle stills, her breath held as she waits for one of Reign's flippant responses. She tells herself she'll be okay with that.

He sighs. "Because this"—he waves his arm wildly in a vague arc—"matters."

Arielle slowly releases the pent-up air in her lungs. Was he talking about the mansion and her mom and the women? Or was he talking about the sweet tug she can feel in her chest, wanting her to step closer?

He huffs out another breath. "I'm only here until I screw it up, okay?"

Arielle takes his hand. "That could be quite a while," she says softly.

Reign freezes. "Ari..."

Mac materializes beside him. "There's eight of them guarding the place." She shrugs. "Only seven of them are conscious."

Reign turns abruptly. "So, there's an opening."

Mac glances around the tree trunk. "We'd have to go now."

And then they're running, feet crunching over gravel, heading for the shrubbery around the house. Arielle's lungs feel too tight as they crouch down. She clamps her hand over her mouth when she discovers there's an inert body next to them.

Mac and Reign's heads move in short sharp movements, each seeming to look in one direction as the other scans the opposite. A shadowy outline appears to their left and they all duck down. A breathless moment later he's gone.

Reign grabs Arielle's hand as they run toward the door, still crouched. They've just made it up the final step when another figure steps in front of them, gun raised.

Arielle jolts back in fright just as Reign leaps and slams his fist into the man's face. The man grunts, shaking his head as he tries to right himself. Reign grabs the gun and jerks him forward. Mac's leg shoots out, her foot powering into his torso. He folds over with another grunt and crumples to the ground.

"Quick," Reign hisses as he opens the door. "The others could've heard."

"Hey!" shouts a voice from somewhere to their left.

Arielle darts through and Reign and Mac follow, shutting the door behind them. A body slams into it a second later. By unspoken agreement, they break into a run, making their way to the library.

The crash of the door being smashed open echoes behind them, followed by heavy boots thundering over the timber floor. Arielle runs desperately through the dark hallways and rooms, hoping she's remembered the way. Her heart feels like it's stampeded out of her chest.

She reaches the door and pushes it open, relieved to find the circular library on the other side.

There's a crack and the doorframe beside her head splinters. They're being shot at!

Reign pushes her inside, his own gun held at arm's length. He lets off a couple of shots before he and Mac join Arielle in the room. Reign slams the door shut as Mac leaps around, scanning the room.

The library is empty, the trap door to the crypt standing open.

"Dammit, there's no lock," says Reign.

The door smashes, wood splintering everywhere as a man barrels through. He shakes off the impact, looking around the room.

Arielle gasps as she sees his eyes are a glowing, hellish red.

"Locks won't help you, boy," growls the demon.

"But this will," states Reign.

He lifts his gun and pulls the trigger. The demon jerks backward, slamming into the second one who was just coming through the door. The second one shoves his comrade away, roaring.

"Thanks for the clear shot," quips Mac as she pulls her own trigger.

The demons sink to the ground, a wisp of black smoke curling up from their mouths.

"Are they dead?" Arielle asks in a whisper.

"It was them or us," says Reign darkly.

Mac rushes toward the open trap door. "And I'd much prefer it to be them."

Arielle follows her, her mind reeling. She scrabbles to understand what just happened. Two beings lie lifeless only feet away. And yet, the threat to her mother's life is painfully real.

Reign is watching her closely, his face shuttered, as she nods decisively. "You're right."

Mac disappears down the stairs and Arielle follows, Reign right behind her. A strange red glow emanates from below, as if they're descending into the bowels of Hell itself. Arielle clutches her gun, knowing she'll use it if she has to, but really hoping she won't.

They reach the crypt to find the stone room completely empty. No books. No artifacts. No demons.

Reign spins around one way then the other. "This had better not be a trap..."

Arielle tries to control her breathing. A trap will mean this ends before she even had a chance to save her mom. If it's not, then they've just reached a dead end.

Except...

She inches forward to the shelves across from them. The red glow seems to be coming from behind it. She pulls on them, gasping when they move. Silently, the massive slab of stone opens like a door.

Revealing a large room beyond it with seven stone beds. And seven lifeless women lying on them.

Arielle rushes in, her heart lodged high in her throat. "Mom," she chokes.

The first woman's blonde hair is splayed down the altar she's lying on. Arielle rushes to her side, registering the pale face and unmoving body. "It's not her."

Reign is beside the woman as Arielle rushes to the next one. This woman is just as still and pale, and also not her mother.

Mac lifts her hand from a third woman's neck. "She's dead."

"So's this one," says Reign heavily.

"No, no, no." Arielle dashes to the next one, and then the next.

It's the second last one who's her mother. Any joy that tries to gain life is quickly guillotined by the sight of more pale skin. A chest that isn't moving.

"Mom, wake up!" Arielle's fingers flutter to her mother's throat. Her knees go weak as she feels nothing. She presses harder, choking on tears that feel like broken glass. "Please, Mom."

When a faint pulse flickers over her fingertips, Arielle cries out. "She's alive!"

Reign rushes to her side, checking too. "Barely, but she's alive." He tries to slip his arm under her shoulder, only to frown. "She's stuck."

"What?" Arielle grips her mother's upper arms and tugs. Her body doesn't move. "No!" She yanks harder and her mother's body jerks, but doesn't lift from the stone table. Some sort of invisible ties have bound her to the sacrificial altar.

There are footsteps and Reign stands in front of Arielle and her mother, his gun poised. Gabby and Colt run in. Gabby gasps as she sees the seven women. Just like Arielle, she rushes from one to the next.

Except, after checking each one, she stops. Blinking, she does a slow revolution. "She's not here. My mom's not here."

Arielle does her own scan. Gabby's right. Aunt Shell isn't here.

"We need to get Sierra out of here, and then we can figure out what's going on," says Reign. "But we can't get her off the altar."

Colt points to the ceiling. "That's why."

Arielle leaps back when she sees what he's talking about. A red mist is trickling from each altar like blood, moving in small rivulets as it climbs up the walls. Each vein runs into the center of the room and disappears into a hole.

"They're draining their energy," Gabby gasps. She points to

the first woman Arielle checked. Her vein has dried up. Everyone turns to Arielle's mother.

The crimson thread winding from her altar is still visible. But barely.

Arielle's hand flies to her mouth. "We don't have much time."

"We need to find the source of the siphon to shut it off," Colt says. "And fast."

Panic clutches Arielle's chest, digging sharp fingers in as if it doesn't plan on letting go. The source is somewhere in the mansion.

And her mother is dying.

Reign takes her hand. "The sooner we start looking, the sooner we find it."

Clutching him, Arielle nods. "We have to save her."

She turns, ready to run like the wind, only to stop. Then take two steps back. The others quickly contract together as Kane enters.

He scans the room, something unholy lighting his eyes. "No one is going anywhere."

CHAPTER 39

REIGN

Reign makes sure his body is angled in front of Arielle's as a sick smile spreads across Kane's ugly mug. Reign's gaze flickers to the door behind him. It seems the cocky bastard came alone.

Kane rolls up his sleeves, the smile progressively inching higher. "You can't stop what's been started." He draws in a deep breath as if he's feeding off the essence of these women. "Not unless you kill me first."

Gabby's hands are fists by her sides. "That can be arranged."

As if by some silent agreement, she and Colt leap simultaneously. Kane must've been expecting it because he launches forward, too, his arms outstretched. They clash, and Gabby and Colt are launched backwards, slamming into the nearest altar. Kane continues to trudge forward as if he's just connected with his inner Terminator.

Colt leaps to his feet. "Find the siphon!" he shouts at Reign and Arielle.

Gabby is by his side as they run at Kane again. This time Colt leaps high while she slides low, her legs slicing toward

Kane's. Except Kane vaults into the air and spins. His fist connects with Colt's jaw. He powers his elbow across Gabby's. They both reel from the blows.

Reign clasps Arielle's hand as he glances at Mac. "We need to go. Now."

Kane is far more powerful than they thought. And stopping the draw of energy is the only way to save Sierra.

Mac is already running to the door. Arielle hesitates for the briefest of seconds, no doubt struggling to leave her mother, but then she's sprinting, too.

Kane sees them try to leave and he roars as he changes direction. It's all the distraction Colt and Gabby needed. They launch another attack, this time Gabby successfully sweeping out Kane's feet as Colt grabs him around the torso. Kane crumples as the two of them try to subdue him.

Reign, Arielle and Mac dash out the door. A last glance over Reign's shoulder shows Kane powering his feet, Colt and Gabby launching outward as if they were puppets.

If they don't find this siphon, then more than just Sierra will be drawing their last breath.

Back in the crypt, Reign doesn't stop. "We need to find the room right above where we just were."

Already breathing heavily, they bolt up the stairs. The library is still empty, and they race for the door. Reign takes the stairs to the second story two at a time. It means he's the first to see that there are several demons waiting for them, eyes glowing red with violence.

Reign doesn't slow his sprint. Demons mean they're getting close to the siphon.

He ploughs into the first one, using the demon as a battering ram to slam into the next one. The one he's holding lands several punches in his side, but Reign blocks out the pain. He can hurt later. There are people to save.

Two punches to the demon's jaw and he's out cold, blood trickling from his nose. The one beneath them hits his head on the wall on the way down, and he crumples, unconscious, too. Reign leaps to his feet, seeing Mac duck then uppercut another demon. Arielle is standing at the top of the stairs, looking determined and terrified.

The last demon launches at her and Reign leaps. If the demon reaches Arielle, all it will take is a push and she'll be tumbling back down the stairs. Unwanted images of Arielle lying at the bottom, limbs and neck at grotesque angles, has him pushing with all his might.

He sails through the air and collides with the demon, toppling him to the ground. Arielle darts out of the way a split second after the demon would've grabbed her. He roars as he hits the floor, twisting as his hands come up to grasp Reign's neck. Now on top, he grabs it and doesn't let go.

Reign struggles but the demon's hands are like a steel vice clamped around his throat. He flails his arms wildly, but the punches glance off the man's arms and face. He scratches, but the demon doesn't even flinch as red gashes open across his cheek.

Reign's lungs spasm in their desperation for air. His brain fights as hard as his body does, but they both lose strength as they're starved of oxygen.

"Die, human filth," growls the demon.

A second before there's the sound of something smashing and he crashes on top of Reign. Drawing in great gulps of air, Reign pushes him off. Arielle stands above them, shards of porcelain scattered around her.

Reign leaps to his feet, realizing oxygen never tasted so good. "Thanks," he pants.

She rolls her eyes. "I'm just repaying the favor."

Mac steps over the unconscious demon. "That was the

ugliest vase I've ever seen. You were doing the antique world a favor, too." She glances at the door they're beside. "My guess is that's the room above the altars."

It's why so many demons were outside guarding it.

Arielle yanks the door open, revealing an empty room. In the center, a scepter rises from the timber floor, a glowing red orb in the center.

"That's it," Arielle breathes, two emotions powering her voice.

Relief that they've found the siphon.

Worry that they're too late.

They enter the room and Reign's not sure how no one else can hear his heartbeat. Surely his pulse is registering on the Richter scale. Colt never said what to do with the siphon once they found it.

The scepter's been impaled into the center of the floor, the crimson, pulsing orb held by a golden claws.

Mac points at the sphere. "It's not completely full."

She's right. The last few millimeters at the top are empty.

"We got here just in time." Arielle goes to move but Reign shoots an arm out to stop her.

"I'll pull it out," he says, hoping to heck it's going to be as easy and straightforward as it sounds. "Then we bring it back to the altars."

Arielle frowns. She knows this could be dangerous. She opens her mouth, no doubt to object, when Mac strides forward.

"Let's save the arguing. I'll get it."

She's taken two steps when the door crashes open. A demon stands in the doorway, two jagged cuts down his cheek and blood trickling down his temple. It's the demon who tried to strangle Reign. The one he scratched. The one Arielle knocked out by smashing a vase over his head.

"Shit," Reign mutters, his stomach turning to stone. "They can heal."

And the demon's not alone. He enters the room, eyes as red as Hell as more step in, smiling as they spread around the room like the plague. They know they have Reign and the others trapped. There's no way out beyond a wall of demon.

The demons move in unison, becoming a tidal wave of evil trying to engulf them. Reign pulls his handgun out. He's pretty sure he hates these things more than Mac. He's lived on the streets long enough to have learned they're the embodiment of death. But right now, they're the only thing that will keep Reign, Arielle, and Mac alive.

He lines up the first demon, aiming for the chest, and pulls the trigger. His arms snap with the recoil and the demon drops, black mist coiling from his mouth. Reign swings his arms right and repeats the process. Aim. Shoot. Move onto the next murderous bastard.

He feels someone at his back, and he instantly knows it's not Mac. The shoulders are too high, the pressure more heightened. Arielle.

She's covering his back while Mac tries to get to the scepter.

Shutting down any chance of feeling guilt or regret or horror at what's happening, Reign hits replay. Aim. Shoot. Move onto the next murderous bastard.

"Mac!" Arielle shouts.

From the corner of his eye, Reign sees that a demon has hold of his best friend. The mammoth-sized man strikes her, then strikes her again, her body jolting with each blow. Except more demons are pouring through the doorway. Reign takes his sights off them, and they'll be overrun. But, Mac needs him...

Arielle's back jerks into his as she pulls her own trigger. The demon who was pummeling Mac drops like the sack of turds he is. Arielle draws in a sharp breath and Reign's heart constricts.

She just killed a demon so she could save Mac's life.

Mac sways for a few seconds then crumples, too. "Mac," Arielle shouts.

Mac falls onto all fours. Her head hangs down as if it's too heavy to hold up, blood dripping onto the demon Arielle killed. She looks up at Reign, her dark eyes filled with sorrow.

And as the one person who's always stood by Reign fails to find the strength to get back up, the new recruits who just arrived fan out, ready to repeat their own process—strike. Kick. Do whatever it takes to kill the humans.

"Get the scepter," Reign says to Arielle. "Now!"

Arielle vaults forward as Reign opens fire. He gets the first demon in the chest. The second in the arm. He steadies his aim, knowing he can't afford to lose his cool, and shoots again.

Click.

Nothing happens. His gun is out of demon-ending bullets.

His heart feels like it's turned to ice as Reign looks to Arielle. They have a few seconds at most before they're overrun by Hell spawn.

Arielle runs, her blonde hair a sail behind her as she leaps over the fallen bodies and reaches the scepter. Without looking up, she grabs it and yanks it out of the floor.

A ripple of energy blasts through the room like a tidal wave, rocking Reign hard enough that he braces himself, ready to run toward Arielle. But it's not them affected by the surge. It's the demons.

As the tide of energy explodes through them, they collapse. Their bodies convulse on the floor, backs arched and mouths gaping. Arielle and Reign freeze as black mist pours out like a silent scream. The columns of midnight vapor writhe and twist as they spew out, crawling and squirming along the walls and ceiling to the nearest exit. Every door and window and vent become clogged with escaping black souls.

"Reign," Arielle gasps.

He turns to see what she's looking at. Ice spears through his heart as he jolts into action.

"Mac!" Reign falls to his knees beside her. His best friend's eyes have rolled back in her head, the tendons of her neck standing out in sharp relief as her spine arches in a painful curve.

He doesn't understand what's going on.

She's convulsing like every other being in this room.

CHAPTER 40
ARIELLE

Arielle is frozen in place as Reign tries to take Mac in his arms, only for her to slip out over and over because her body is wracked with seizures. Around them, the demons have stopped convulsing, their bodies limp and lifeless.

Mac is still jerking in the same way the demons did, even though the others have stopped. There's also no black mist pouring from her mouth. What does that even mean?

Arielle takes a step toward them when her foot hits something solid. She leaps back, expecting to see another dead body, only to see it's not. It's a book. A large, leather tome. Two words are embossed across the front.

Infernal Damasicus.

She kneels down to pick it up, except the moment her fingers brush the aged leather, it flies open. Thick, aged pages flutter as if a breeze just blew in. As quickly as it started, the book stops, now open to a page somewhere in the middle.

Arielle's about to pick it up again when she sees the drawing on the right-hand side. An obelisk. Lying beside it is a woman, a dark line down her chest that can only be blood.

305

Cracks streak up the obelisk like lightning, wisps of black creeping up from it.

Although the image is in black and white, it's vivid and terrifying. It's like a sepia snapshot of her nightmares. Someone has painted what Arielle desperately hoped was impossible. What could never come true.

Her eyes flick to the second page. Three lines have been written in large, ornate print. The cursive would almost look beautiful if it wasn't for the ugly words they paint.

Seven Gates opened.

Seven Sins unleashed.

And the Lord of Hell will be free.

"Arielle," Reign says sharply, jolting her out of the strange hold the book had on her. "We need to get back to the altar room."

Arielle snaps the Infernal tome shut and tucks it under her arm. With the scepter in her other hand, she runs to Reign.

He's standing, an unconscious Mac in his arms. "Let's go."

Arielle nods. "Is she okay?"

"She will be," Reign states flatly. "Or I'll kick her butt."

They rush out of the room and down the stairs and Arielle ignores the bodies she has to navigate around. They've stopped the flow of energy.

There's a chance they could save her mother.

Arielle runs into the library, Reign still carrying Mac right behind her, and sprints to the trap door. They're almost there.

"You're not going anywhere."

Arielle spins around at the roared command. A demon is striding through the door, several more filing in behind him. They fan out along the circular wall, faces snarling and feral.

"In fact, you won't be leaving this library."

"You've got to be kidding me," mutters Reign. "There's more?"

"More what?" Mac murmurs groggily.

There's no time for Arielle to feel relief that Mac is coming to. The demons look like rabid dogs waiting for the command to attack.

Reign steps closer to Arielle, talking under his breath. "Give me your gun and get back to your mom."

She freezes, unsure she just heard him right. No...

"Now, Arielle!" he hisses.

Arielle does the first, slapping the handgun in the hand Reign is holding out. He's still cradling Mac, and he grips the gun with the arm supporting her head. Mac seems to instinctively understand that he needs help, because she wraps her own arms around his neck, freeing him to point the gun with greater accuracy.

But then Arielle hesitates. She can't be expected to do the second part of the order. "I can't leave you."

Not surrounded by demons. Not holding a barely conscious friend.

"Well, you're going to," Reign snaps.

Arielle shakes her head. Her chest feels like it's splintering. She can't leave Reign behind. Panic overwhelms her and she hovers on the balls of her feet. What is she supposed to do?

One of the demons launches at them, and Reign spins and shoots, Mac clinging to him. He doesn't look over his shoulder as he screams. "Go, Arielle! Do not make this all for nothing!"

So, she runs, even as she hates herself, even as she's not sure if she just made the right choice.

She dashes down the stairs, hoping she can live with what she just did.

CHAPTER 41
REIGN

The demons growl, their red eyes flaring, now that they're faced with a weapon that will snuff their lights out. Reign's pulse is everywhere and nowhere, like he's terrified of how this will end, and like he's kind of okay with it.

He did everything he could to save Arielle. To help Sierra. To protect Mac.

That's the best he could've hoped for in this wasted life that he led.

"You can put me down, Reign."

Reign startles at the sound of Mac's voice. He looks down and what he sees almost freezes his heart. His whole body short-circuits, and his arms fall to his side.

Mac lands gracefully in a crouch as if she wasn't just dropped. "Thanks."

Reign watches as she pushes herself upright, frowning. He's conscious he's not breathing, but he's lost the ability to do anything about that. Every cell in his body is consumed with trying to understand what he's seeing.

Mac blinks, her eyelids shuttering over the unholy glow that bathes her face.

What. The. Fuck.

Mac's eyes are the same Hellish red as the demons they're surrounded by.

"Mac..."

Except the demons have had enough of the intermission. "Attack as one," screams the first one who enters. Dammit. He's realized Reign can't shoot them all at once.

But that won't stop Reign from taking as many down as he can. Arielle and the others are going to need time to finish this, and the less douches to join the party downstairs, the better.

"You know what?" Mac says beside him. "I've had enough of these assholes."

Reign watches, astounded, as she leaps, and leaps high. The highest he's ever seen her jump. To a height that should be impossible for a human.

Just as she lands, two black wings explode from her back.

And then Mac is a blur of movement and power. She ploughs her fists into chests, she slams her feet through jaws. Even her wings become weapons, contracting then snapping out to strike. There is nowhere that is safe for the demons, no angle they can get the advantage on her. Something's been unleashed in Mac, and it's not the merciful type. The moment she has one down, she shoots it, making sure it won't be getting up again.

The demons tumble one by one. In fact, the last two are taken out simultaneously. As Mac shoots the first, Reign snaps into action and shoots the second. Mac looks up, her eyebrows high above her red eyes.

Reign shrugs. "This way you can't say I didn't help."

Mac blinks, her face puckering. The glow in her eyes slowly dies out, leaving behind the brown gaze that he's always known. She frowns and a second later, her wings contract and disappear.

Silence weaves its way through the bodies littered around them, tangled and taut. Reign's breathing heavily even though it's not him who just cleaned up an entire room full of soldiers of the devil.

"So," he says as casually as he can. "You're a demon, huh?"

She scratches her head. "Apparently so."

They stare at each other, and Reign can sense her hesitation. Mac's worried this is going to matter.

He raises a single eyebrow. "I'm still going to fight you for the good bedroom at the hangout," he states flatly.

Mac lets out a breath. "You're a douche," she says, her lips tipping up at the edges.

They both turn toward the trap door, a silent understanding that they'll have to discuss this later, when a scream echoes up the stone stairs.

A high-pitched, pain-filled scream.

Reign practically flies down the stairs, Mac close enough to be his shadow behind them. They burst into the altar room, seeing that Gabby's collapsed on the floor on the other side.

And Kane is stalking toward her like a predator.

A bloodied and bruised Colt runs at him, but Kane swipes him away like an insect. Although it was one sweep of Kane's arm, Colt flies through the air and slams into one of the altars. Stone explodes with the impact. Colt pushes himself up through the cloud of dust, his powerful body looking battered and broken. He's just got to his feet when his legs give out and he collapses among the shattered pieces of stone.

Kane looks away in disgust, clearly deciding Colt is no longer a threat. Two steps forward and he grips Gabby by the throat. He lifts her using that one point of contact until her feet are no longer touching the floor.

"One flick of my wrist and your neck will snap," he states coldly.

Gabby gargles as her head lolls.

Reign glances around frantically. Kane is showing super-human strength, even for a demon. He sees Arielle by her mother, sobbing as she holds her in arms. Sierra is no longer bound to the altar, but she's also not awake.

The scepter is on the ground beside them. Reign leaps toward it, knowing it's a long shot, but also knowing they have little else.

He picks up the gilt rod and swings it in a wide arc like a bat. The red orb smashes into the altar, shards of glass exploding with the impact. The pulsing red energy sinks, only to evaporate like it never existed.

"No!" screams Kane.

Gabby drops to the ground like she just became too heavy.

Kane spins around and pins his gaze on Reign. Behind him, Colt crawls to Gabby and they clasp each other.

Reign doesn't break Kane's glare as he says to Mac, "Protect Arielle and Sierra."

"But, I'm a—"

"You can back me up if I need it," he snaps. He and Kane have a score to settle.

"Fine," Mac huffs. "But you're gonna need it."

Kane adjusts his shoulders then stretches his neck as he steps into the center of the room. "Yes, you will," he snarls. "Even without the energy of the seven descendants, I'm a demon who trained with the Knights of Hell. I have thousands of years of fighting experience."

Reign clenches his fists. "The way I see it, that just makes you old."

Kane runs at him, the hunger for violence, for Reign's death, twisting his features. Reign propels forward, too. He tucks his head and prepares himself for pain.

Bring. It. On.

Kane swings the moment he's close enough and Reign ducks. He tries for an uppercut but Kane sidesteps it, following through with a volley of strikes. Reign blocks the first and the second, he leaps over a kick and ducks a furious swing at his head. With each movement, he realizes he's already on the defense. He needs to—

A fist that feels the size of a battering ram slams into his cheek, making his head snap to the side. Reign groans as agony tidal waves through his skull. It's as if Kane's hands are molded from cement.

Reign staggers left, expecting for the second blow to come in quick succession. When it doesn't arrive, he looks back, the room taking a second to catch up. Kane has taken a step backward, his face no longer warped with fury.

He looks...shocked.

Reign shoots out with his fist, trying to take advantage of the weird lapse. Kane's reflexes are instantaneous, and he catches Reign's clenched hand mid-strike. Reign tries to jerk it back, but the grip is vice-like. Kane's eyes flare with victory as he squeezes.

Pain rockets up Reign's arm as his hand is crushed. The agony amplifies as the pressure does. There's a hoarse cry and he wonders how it slipped past his gritted teeth. Then he realizes it wasn't his.

Kane practically throws Reign's hand back at him, his face tight with pain. "What is going on?"

Before Reign can answer, Kane strikes him again. He drives his cement-coated fist into Reign's gut. Reign doubles over, this groan most definitely his own.

Except the groan is echoed from the demon who just threw

the punch. Kane doubles over, too, as if it was him who just had his insides pulverized.

He staggers back, clutching his midriff. "What spell is this?"

Reign takes shallow breaths as he waits for the pain to subside. He has no idea what's going on. "I think it might be called karma."

Kane wipes his mouth. "I'll find out what magic you're wielding." He straightens as he takes several steps back. "Not that it matters."

"What are you talking about?" Reign demands. He doesn't like the smug look on the demon's face. Not when Kane just backed off.

"While you were here, play fighting, I instructed my man to kill the Innocent." Kane laughs as gasps echo off the stone walls. "It's only a matter of time before the first Gate of Hell is opened."

"You bastard!" Reign runs at Kane, figuring he'll use whatever this pain power is to his advantage. "Tell me where the Innocent is!"

Kane grins, his eyes flashing red a moment before he disappears. Reign stops in his tracks. The space that was occupied by the asshat is now empty, as if he was never there.

As if his terrible prediction wasn't said.

"Coward!" Reign shouts, breathing heavily.

Except the pain still crawling through Reign's gut and skull tells him Kane was most definitely here. And the demon's words feel like they were carved into the air.

I instructed my man to kill the Innocent.

It's only a matter of time before the first Gate of Hell is opened.

"Arielle?" asks a soft voice Reign's never heard before.

He turns to find Sierra sitting up on her altar. She lifts her arms, her face scrunched with the bittersweet joy only a mother can feel as she is reunited with her daughter.

CHAPTER 42
ARIELLE

Seeing her mother alive is the most beautiful thing Arielle has ever seen. It makes her knees go weak as she rushes into her arms, her steps wobbly and uncoordinated. "Mom..."

When her mother clasps her to her, though, it's the most heart clenching moment so far. Arielle wasn't sure she'd ever feel this sweet heaven again.

They made it in time. A part of her, a part that was steadily growing as it was fed by fear, was starting to believe she'd never feel her mother's warm touch again.

Her mother draws back, her gaze roaming over Arielle's face. "How did you find me?"

"That's a long story. I found the septagram in the board game and it kind of went from there." A fresh flood of tears tumbles down Arielle's cheeks. "We were almost too late."

Her mother brushes a strand of hair from Arielle's face, the motion so familiar it stings Arielle's eyes. "But you weren't." She frowns. "What do you know?"

Gabby steps forward with Colt, and Arielle's not sure who is holding up who. "We know about the obelisks and the Innocents and the Gates of Hell."

Colt nods. "And we know about Kane's plan to resurrect someone."

Arielle's mother's eyes widen. "Where is he?"

"The detective?" Arielle asks.

"That's the facade he uses. Kane is none other than Cain himself, the son of Adam and Eve." Her mother frowns. "The first murderer."

Shock has Arielle's breath dissolving. No wonder Cain was so confident he could fight. He's the oldest living being walking this earth.

Her mother slips off the altar, and Arielle quickly grabs her as her legs buckle. Her mom's face turns fierce as she grips the stone. "And this—" she glances around the altar room—"plan was secondary."

Arielle braces herself, not liking the weight that seems to have just settled on her mother's shoulders. She's pretty sure they've reached their quota of revelations for the day.

"I discovered who the Innocent is," she says heavily. "I was on my way to tell her when I was abducted."

Arielle gasps, the sound immediately echoed by Gabby. Reign blanches as he and Mac glance at each other. They've all realized who the Innocent is.

Arielle's aunt.

Gabby's mother.

Sierra pushes away from the altar. "Shell is the Innocent. And we need to find her."

"Where?" asks Arielle, desperation clogging her throat.

Her mother takes a tentative step forward, discovering that her legs are going to hold her weight. "The sacrifice of the Innocent must happen on seven sanctified grounds. The locations are unknown."

"No…" moans Gabby.

"But I deciphered the clues in the Infernal book. I know where she is." Arielle's mother glances around. "Where are we, by the way?"

"Beneath Sinclair Mansion," says Arielle. "In a secret room beyond a crypt."

Her mother draws in a sharp breath. "Then we might have time. The site for the ritual is the fountain. The one with the angel."

Reign breaks into a sprint, despite the injuries he sustained, Mac right behind him. Colt and Gabby limp after them, and Arielle notes that their cuts and bruises are already looking better. Arielle supports her mother as they rush up the stairs last.

It means Reign and Mac get to the fountain first. As Arielle approaches with her mother leaning heavily on her, she notices how still they're standing. Reign's outline looks like he's been carved from stone.

Colt and Gabby are next. The cry that pierces the air slices down Arielle's spine.

As she and her mother halt beside the others, Arielle sees why. Aunt Shell is lying on her back at the base of the fountain. She's unmoving. And her eyes are wide open in a silent scream.

Gabby rushes forward and crumples over her mother's body, sobbing. "Mom!"

But Aunt Shell won't be moving. She'll never blink or breathe or beam her beautiful smile again. Gabby draws back, running a trembling finger over the red line that runs down the center of her mother's chest.

Arielle's mother sags and Arielle quickly tightens her grip. "They stole her grace," she chokes out, clinging to Arielle.

Suddenly, Colt drops to his knees. Arielle assumes that he's going to comfort Gabby but he arches his back, body straining as ripples course through it. Mac follows suit, Reign catching her as she crumples. Her back curves, too, her face angling to the sky as she shudders.

"It's happening," Arielle's mother whispers. "They can feel it."

Arielle doesn't ask. In part because she doesn't want to. In part because she doesn't need to.

She looks to Reign and sees that he knows it, too. His face is pale, his jungle green eyes stark in his handsome face. The sky above him has turned an angry shade of fuchsia.

The first Gate of Hell has been opened.

Ready for the next installment in the Keepers of the Grail series? Check out GATES OF CHAOS!
http://mybook.to/GatesofChaos

GATES OF CHAOS

Reign and Arielle have discovered a hidden agenda neither of them could have fathomed.

One that will force Reign to accept the destiny he doesn't believe he's worthy of. One where Arielle will be asked to find an inner-strength she's not sure she has. One that will have them succumbing to their smoldering attraction, even as they question who or what is influencing their choices.

Because a battle for newfound power has begun, sparked by a drive for absolution that reaches as far back as the origins of man. A war that will wreak havoc in ways humanity has never seen before.

Finding the Grail is even more important. And finding the next Innocent isn't just about saving a life. This soul is the key to keeping the next Gate of Hell closed and the sin of Greed contained.

But who is the Innocent? And will they find the Grail in time to save them?

Fans of Richelle Mead and Jennifer L. Armentrout will devour the Keepers of the Grail series. Lose yourself in the breath taking paranormal romance, Gates of Chaos, today!

GRAB YOUR COPY HERE

THE KEEPERS-VERSE IS ALWAYS GROWING!

Exciting news! The Keeper Chronicles will continue to grow, with each new addition adding to its epicness. Each interlinked series will have you falling for unforgettable characters, being swept away by captivating romance and thrilling adventure, and re-visiting old friends (you'll discover all your favorites popping up when you least expect it!).

It's like your very own choose your own adventure! Where will you go next?

Keepers of the Chalice
A vampire. A huntress.
A cure that will change everything.
Check out Book 1, Vampire Unleashed, HERE.

Keepers of Excalibur
A fated love. A cursed wolf.
A supernatural war only they can stop.
Check out Book 1, Wolf Marked, HERE

Keepers of the Light

Angels and demons have battled for millennia. Their inevitable war has begun.

Check out Book 1, Hidden Angel, HERE.

http://mybook.to/HiddenAngel

HAVE YOU READ THE KEEPER CHRONICLES PREQUEL?

As an exclusive for my subscribers,
you can download it for free!!

When Sierra sneaks out, determined to escape her over-protective family, she stumbles across a young man covered in blood. His last words are a plea. *Find the Grail Keepers. Warn them.*

Ryder is the young cop who was last seen with the murdered victim. Sierra doesn't trust him, no matter how drawn she is to him. Except it turns out they're both looking for the same thing—the Holy Grail.

They're quickly drawn into a dangerous hunt involving cryptic clues, a mysterious stone, and a Grail that hasn't been seen for centuries. One that leads to more questions than answers. Can Sierra trust her impulsive emotions? Should she believe Ryder's words or the truth she sees in his eyes? And ultimately, should she follow her heart?

Especially when every decision will decide the fate of countless lives.

CLICK HERE TO DOWNLOAD FOR FREE!

Also by Tamar Sloan

A supernatural war only they can stop.

DESTINED DEMIGODS

Love that defies the gods.

Powers that define destiny.

ELEMENTAL GAMES

Elemental powers. Deadly Games.

No escape.

THE SOVEREIGN CODE

Humans saved bees from extinction...and created the deadliest threat we've seen yet.

THE THAW CHRONICLES

Only the chosen shall breed.

ZODIAC GUARDIANS

Twelve teens. One task.

Save the Universe.

About the Author

Tamar hasn't decided whether she's primarily a psychologist who loves writing, or a writer with a lifelong drive to make a difference. She must have been someone pretty awesome in a previous life (past life regression indicates a Care Bear), because she gets to do both. She divides her time between helping families and writing emotion driven YA stories set in amazing imaginary worlds that surprise even her.

The driving force for all of Tamar's writing is sharing and connecting. In truth, connecting with others is why she writes. She loves to hear from readers. Find her on all the usual social media channels or her website, www.tamarsloan.com where can download one of her books for free.

(Seriously, I LOVE hearing from you guys!)